ALPHA, BETA, GAMMA...DEAD

*Betty Rowlands titles available from
Severn House Large Print*

Party to Murder
Deadly Obsession
Dirty Work

ALPHA, BETA, GAMMA...DEAD

Betty Rowlands

Severn House Large Print
London & New York

SEVERN HOUSE PUBLISHERS of
9-15 High Street, Sutton, Surrey, SM1 1DF.
First world regular print edition published 2007 by
Severn House Publishers, London and New York.

British Library Cataloguing in Publication Data

Rowlands, Betty
  Alpha, beta, gamma - dead. - Large print ed. - (A Sukey
  Reynolds mystery)
  1. Reynolds, Sukey (Fictitious character) - Fiction
  2. Policewomen - Great Britain - Fiction 3. Christian
  antiquities - Fiction 4. Detective and mystery stories
  5. Large type books
  I. Title
  823.9'14[F]

  ISBN-13: 978-0-7278-7729-1

Printed and bound in Great Britain by
MPG Books Ltd, Bodmin, Cornwall.

One

A man strode through the swing door of the Mariners Hotel and up to the reception desk. Anyone observing him would have noticed a hint of impatience in the way he struck the bell with a closed fist. An olive-skinned, clean-shaven young man with smooth dark hair, who had just handed a key to a new arrival, moved across in response to the summons.

'May I help you, sir?' he said politely.

'Yes,' said the newcomer. He spoke a shade breathlessly, as if he had been hurrying. 'My name's Stephen Lamont and I've arranged to meet Doctor Whistler here. I understand he's a guest in this hotel?'

'Ah yes, Professor Lamont. Doctor Whistler expects you. Room 106 on first floor. Please be so kind as to go straight up. You find lift over there.' He gestured with a smooth, slightly feminine hand.

Lamont nodded. 'Thank you, I'll walk.'

On reaching room 106 he gave a double knock, lightly at first and then again, more

5

strongly, when there was no reply. He waited a few moments before knocking a third time, even harder. He put an ear close to the door and listened, then turned and dashed downstairs to the reception desk. It was momentarily deserted and he pounded on the bell. A young woman appeared; before she had a chance to speak he said urgently, 'I think Doctor Whistler in room 106 may have been taken ill. He's expecting me, but he's not answering my knock and I thought I heard a faint groan.'

'I'll ring his room.' She picked up the phone and keyed in the number. After a few moments she put it down and said, 'He's not answering; I'll get the manager.'

She vanished, reappearing a few seconds later accompanied by a man of about thirty-five, formally dressed in a dark suit.

'We'll go and check on him,' he said and led the way up to the first floor.

When they reached Whistler's room he knocked and waited a few seconds before opening the door with a master key.

The three of them took a few steps into the room before stopping short and gazing in mute horror at the crumpled figure lying on the floor in a pool of blood. Then the woman screamed, clapped a hand to her mouth and rushed into the bathroom, while Lamont moved forward and knelt beside the victim and the manager, his face the colour of clay,

6

stepped gingerly round him and picked up the bedside telephone.

In the canteen at the central police station, DC Vicky Armstrong led the way to a vacant table, sat down and raised her mug of coffee in salute. 'Congratulations on becoming a fully fledged member of the team!' she said.

'Thanks!' DC Sukey Reynolds raised her own mug and swallowed a couple of mouthfuls before adding, 'Particularly for your support and encouragement.'

'It's been a pleasure working with you.' Vicky's smile transformed her homely features. 'I must admit,' she went on, 'my heart sank when I heard we had another trainee joining the team and I'd drawn the short straw again. The last one was a dyed-in-the-wool sexist who found it hard to accept that a mere woman could teach him anything.'

'I know – experience counts for nothing when weighed against testosterone,' said Sukey. 'What happened to him, by the way?'

'Praise be, he was transferred to headquarters. Last I heard of him, he was putting people's backs up there like he did when he was based here. A pity about that,' Vicky added with a touch of regret, 'he's got the makings of a really good detective, but he does tend to rub people up the wrong way. That's why it came as a relief to know that you were female.'

'I felt the same about you,' Sukey admitted. 'I'd had more than enough of bossy men.'

'Women can be bossy too, and bitchy sometimes,' Vicky pointed out.

'True, and I have to admit Jim did change his tune after I told him I'd been accepted for fast-track into the CID.'

'Is Jim your partner?'

It was the first time Sukey had mentioned him, although she had volunteered a certain amount of information about her background, including the fact that she was a divorcee with a son at university. It was also the first time that Vicky had asked a direct question about her personal life. 'Not exactly,' she replied after a moment's hesitation. 'He's a DI I first met years ago, when we were both PCs on the beat. We had a kind of a thing going – and then I fell for someone else, got married and left the police to have Fergus. After the divorce I went back to work for them as a SOCO and found Jim had got married and divorced as well and was still based in Gloucester. So we got together again, but I haven't seen him for a couple of months. Not since I moved, in fact. He helped me get settled in the flat and did a few jobs for me, but—'

She lapsed into silence, recalling the sense of desolation she had felt as he drove away, leaving her alone for the first time in her new and still unfamiliar environment. For the past six months the intensive training involved in obtaining the necessary qualifications for a career in the CID had absorbed most of her time and energy, leaving little opportunity for a social life. Just the same, so long as she was still living in Gloucester, they had managed to spend the odd weekend together. During that period there had been the process of selling the house where she had lived with Fergus ever since his father walked out on them ten years ago, and finding somewhere to live in Bristol. She remembered with gratitude what a tower of strength he had been during that stressful time, but the move had not only marked a turning point in her career, it had had a similar affect on their relationship. Since then he had telephoned a couple of times to ask how she was getting on, but there had been no mention of any future meetings.

It was typical of Vicky that she asked no further questions, merely saying, 'Well, it's Friday tomorrow, thank goodness. You doing anything special at the weekend?'

'Gus is coming on Saturday and staying a couple of nights. I've been invited to some neighbours for supper this evening. How about you?'

'Chris said something about a movie on Saturday.' From odd comments Vicky had made during the six weeks they had been

9

working together, Sukey had formed the impression that she and Chris had a long-standing relationship with no firm commitment on either side. It was typical that she was as reticent about her own private life as she was incurious about that of other people.

Sukey finished her coffee and picked up her shoulder bag. 'Well, back to the grind,' she said.

'So what job have they put you on for your sins?' asked Vicky.

'Checking witness statements from the Bryony Close break-ins. Four in a single night, and in each case the residents were on holiday. The same package holiday,' she added.

Vicky gave a knowing grin. 'A mole in the travel agency?'

'That's one possibility we're working on, although there's another we have to consider.'

'Which is?'

'The bookings weren't made individually, but through a member of the group.'

'Well, that's not unusual.'

'No. Just the same, the organizer wasn't one of the victims.'

'Ah, well, keep digging!' Vicky said cheerfully.

It was a little after twelve and Sukey was beginning to think about lunch when DS Greg Rathbone tapped her on the shoulder.

'Drop that for now, we've got something a bit more interesting for you to bite on,' he said.

Sukey closed the file, pushed it into a drawer and stood up. 'What's that, Sarge?'

'GBH at the Mariners Hotel. Gentleman attacked in his room, apparently while waiting for a visitor.'

'Well, there's something to brighten a dull morning,' she said. 'Is he badly hurt?'

'Sounds like it. He was found unconscious and bleeding heavily but we don't know yet what his injuries are. The manager called an ambulance and they carted him off to the hospital before uniformed arrived. They're protecting the scene, but there's bound to have been some contamination before they took charge.'

'We know the victim has to be the first consideration, but it can be a headache for the CSIs,' Sukey remarked as they hurried down to the yard where the cars were parked. 'Where is this hotel, by the way?'

'On the A38, not far from the airport. That's our car; you drive.' He tossed a key at her and settled into the passenger seat of a silver-grey Astra.

'Right, Sarge.' She got in and started the engine while Greg settled down beside her and closed his eyes. Sukey gave him a sideways glance as she pulled out of the yard. She had taken to him on their first meeting;

11

he gave the impression of being what her late mother would have described as 'a nice dependable sort', with his clean-cut features, keen blue-grey eyes and firm handclasp. In the short time she had been at the station she had learned that he had a reputation – which she suspected had been carefully cultivated – for never missing an opportunity to relax. During the fifteen-minute drive he remained silent, apparently asleep, but the minute she slowed down and signalled before turning into the hotel car park he opened his eyes and sat upright.

'Park round the back,' he ordered. 'The manager has asked us to be as inconspicuous as possible to avoid unnecessary upset to the guests.'

'That's understandable,' Sukey said as she pulled in alongside the police cars discreetly parked out of sight of the road. 'This kind of thing can't be very good for business.'

'Not much fun for the victim either,' he remarked dryly.

Two white vans belonging to Crime Scene Investigators were already there and Sukey experienced a sudden buzz of anticipation. This time last year her remit would, like theirs, have been the collection of evidence for passing on to the investigating officer. There had of course been other cases during the past few weeks in which she had played an active role, but always under Vicky's tutelage. Now she was a fully fledged member of the team.

A woman constable was standing guard outside a door labelled 'Staff Only'. As they approached she punched a code into the keypad on the wall and held it open for them. 'The manager's waiting for you in his office, Sarge. The name's Maurice Ashford. Go along that passage, turn right and it's the second door on the left.'

The manager had thick brown hair that looked to Sukey as if agitated fingers had recently passed through it and the hand he offered felt cold and clammy.

'This is a dreadful business,' he said nervously. 'Nothing like it has ever happened in this hotel before – in any hotels in the group, come to that.' He made a sweeping gesture that encompassed the entire room, with its heavy, slightly old-fashioned furniture, crimson velvet curtains and dark green, deep-piled carpet, before coming briefly to rest on a pier table on which stood a handsome silver trophy. 'That's the annual award for the Hotel of the Year,' he informed them. 'We've won it two years running.'

'Well, congratulations to you and your staff,' said Rathbone. 'Now perhaps you'd be kind enough to tell us how you came to find the injured gentleman, whose name, I understand is – ' he glanced at his notebook – 'Doctor Whistler?'

13

'That's right: Doctor Edwin Whistler. An archaeologist, I understand. The gentleman who actually found him – at least, who alerted me that something was amiss – is a Professor Stephen Lamont. I have a master key in my desk and we immediately went up to Room 106 to investigate.'

'Just the two of you?'

'No. Erika, my assistant, came with us. They're both waiting for you in her office. I imagine you'll want to see them as well?'

'Thank you, all in good time. Do I take it Professor Lamont came to your office to tell you of his concern?'

'No, he told Erika. She happened to be at the reception desk, and she came running in to tell me.'

'I see. Right, sir, before we go any further, DC Reynolds and I would like to have a look at the room where this unfortunate incident took place. If you would be so kind—?'

'Certainly,' said Ashford. 'Your people are up there already, of course. I'll get a porter to...' He reached for the telephone on his desk, but Rathbone leaned forward and put a hand on the instrument.

'If you could spare the time to take us there yourself, sir?' he said quietly.

Two

The uniformed officer guarding room 106 stood aside and pushed open the door to admit Ashford and the detectives. Inside were two CSIs in white overalls; one was checking for fingerprints on the safe, which was set in the wall behind a desk on the far side of the room, and the other was down on one knee focusing his camera on the ugly stain on the carpet. He looked up as the newcomers entered and put up a hand.

'Just wait there a moment, Sarge,' he said and the three obediently halted in the doorway while he clicked away for a few seconds. Then he stood up and nodded.

'You can come in now. We've checked that side of the room, so if you wouldn't mind waiting there for a bit while we finish this side.'

'I see you've dusted the door for prints,' Rathbone remarked. 'Was that there when you arrived?' He indicated a 'Do Not Disturb' sign hanging from a small hook below the room number.

'Yes, Sarge.'

'You noticed it too, sir?' Rathbone turned to Ashford, who was staring in fascinated horror at the patch of blood. He jumped as the detective addressed him.

'Oh, er, yes, Sergeant,' he said. 'Yes, I'm sure it was there.'

'Right. Now, sir, I'd like you to go over your exact movements after you entered the room. As you had the key, I imagine you were the first to go in?'

'Yes, I suppose I must have been.' With an apparent effort, Ashford switched his gaze to the detective. He closed his eyes and said, his voice unsteady, 'The minute I saw him I stopped and ... I think for a split second I just stared ... it was like a nightmare, I couldn't believe it ... and then Erika screamed and made a dash for the bathroom and I heard her gagging ... I felt sick myself, but I knew I had to get help so I went to the phone—'

'Which is on the table on the other side of the bed,' Rathbone interrupted. 'Did you walk round, or reach across the bed?'

'I walked round the body ... I mean the man on the floor ... I kept as far away from him as I could—' Ashford put a hand over his eyes and swallowed. 'There was all that blood ... I'd never seen so much blood.'

'I appreciate that this is difficult for you, Mr Ashford,' said Rathbone patiently, 'but I'll ask you to try and picture the scene and tell me exactly how the man was lying and

16

where the blood was coming from.'

Ashford swallowed and put a handkerchief over his mouth.

'Try taking a few deep breaths,' said Sukey, recalling that this was how she had learned long ago to deal with similar situations. Ashford flashed her a weak but grateful smile and inhaled deeply several times.

'That's better,' said Rathbone. 'Just take your time.'

'Thank you.' Ashford put away the handkerchief. 'He was lying face down near the end of the bed, at a bit of an angle,' he said slowly. 'I couldn't see where the blood was coming from ... but I'm afraid I didn't look very closely.'

'You couldn't see any wound?'

Ashford shuddered. 'No.'

'"Near the end of the bed" is a bit vague. Can you be more exact? For example, could you see his entire body, or was it partly behind the bed?'

Ashford swallowed hard. 'I think – yes, you could see all of him except the lower part of his legs and his feet.'

'Good.' Rathbone gave a nod of approval. 'Did he make any sound or movement while you were there?'

'I don't think so. No, I'm sure he didn't.'

'So you rang reception and told them to send for an ambulance. Did you also tell them to call the police?'

'No, not straight away, not until after the paramedics had taken the man to the hospital.'

'I see. And did all three of you wait in here for the ambulance?'

'No, I sent Erika downstairs to look out for it and direct the driver to the staff entrance. I wanted to avoid alarming any of the other guests ... and in any case, that was the shortest route to this room.'

'And what did you do while you were waiting?'

'I stayed by the phone.'

'And Professor Lamont?'

'He ... I think he bent down beside Doctor Whistler ... and then he came and stood beside me.'

'Did he say anything?'

'I think he said something like, "I think he's still alive, but only just" – I can't remember his exact words.'

'Perhaps he felt for a pulse?'

'I suppose he might have done. I'm afraid I wasn't looking, I—'

'So the two of you just waited by the phone until the paramedics arrived?'

'I went to the window after a few minutes to look out for the ambulance. When I saw it arrive I went over to the door to be ready to let them in.'

'And Professor Lamont? What did he do?'

'I suppose he stayed where he was. I don't

know. I was in such a state of shock—'

'Yes, quite.' Rathbone's jaw tightened and Sukey had the impression that he was becoming a little irritated by the man's repeated reference to his sensitivity, but he kept his voice level as he continued. 'Did you touch anything else, other than the phone?'

'No.'

'You're sure about that?'

Ashford nodded. 'Oh, yes, quite sure.'

'And the safe was open, like it is now?'

'I suppose so ... I didn't notice.'

One of the CSIs looked up from his task and said, 'That's how it was when we arrived, Sarge. It's empty,' he added.

'Thanks, Joe.'

Rathbone glanced at Sukey and raised an eyebrow, inviting her to join in the questioning. She gave a slight nod and said, 'Mr Ashford, had Doctor Whistler stayed in this hotel before?'

The manager appeared taken aback by the question, although he answered readily enough. 'I don't know; he may have done. I can't remember every guest who stays here.'

'So to your knowledge, you had never met him before today?'

'That's right, but I don't see—'

'But you did know he was an archaeologist,' Sukey persisted.

This time Ashford was clearly disconcerted by the question. He nibbled his lower lip and

19

frowned. 'I think ... yes, I'm sure Professor Lamont mentioned it. He said something about him working on a dig somewhere in Greece, I think.'

'This was while you were waiting for the ambulance?'

'Yes, I suppose so.'

'Did he say anything else about him?'

'I don't think so.'

Sukey glanced back at Rathbone, who said briskly, 'Right, I think that's all we can do here at the moment. Let us have your results ASAP, boys.' He turned and led the way out of the room.

Back in Ashford's office he said, 'Thank you, sir, you've been a great help. We'll prepare a statement for you to sign later on, if you'd be so kind. One more thing: please instruct your staff not to speak to the press. It's important that Doctor Whistler's name is withheld until we've traced his next of kin.'

Ashford nodded. 'I'll get Erika to deal with that right away.' He pressed a button on his telephone and gave the instruction.

'And now perhaps we should have a word with Professor Lamont,' said Rathbone.

'Yes, of course.' Ashford appeared to relax, as if relieved that the interview was over. 'You can see him in here, if you like. I'll go and—'

'We'll need to question some of your staff as well, so it would be helpful if you could

20

put a separate room at our disposal,' Rathbone broke in.

'Oh ... yes, that won't be a problem. I'll check what's available, if you'll bear with me a moment.' He consulted his computer and said, 'You can have 107 for the time being; that's directly opposite 106. I'll get the key; I won't be a moment.'

As the door closed behind him, Rathbone turned to Sukey and said, 'What do you make of him?'

'On the face of it, he wouldn't appear to have any motive for attacking Whistler. He denies ever having met the man before, although he knew he was an archaeologist and he seemed a bit thrown by the question. And he referred to the victim the first time as "the body" and then corrected himself.'

'Yes, I noticed that. Anything else?'

She hesitated. 'He did make a great thing about not being able to stand the sight of blood. I suppose it was genuine – he certainly looked pale and he was obviously badly shaken.'

He nodded. 'Yes, I thought it was a bit OTT, but—' He broke off as Ashford returned, accompanied by a tall man with aquiline features and a mop of grey curly hair.

'Professor Lamont, these officers are conducting the enquiry into the attack on Doctor Whistler – Detective Sergeant Rathbone and Detective Constable Reynolds.' Ashford

21

rattled off the introductions as if he was in a hurry to be rid of them. 'Here's the key to room 107,' he went on. 'I've ordered some coffee to be sent up for you.'

'That's very thoughtful of you, sir. Thank you,' said Rathbone. 'I don't suppose you could manage a sandwich as well? DC Reynolds and I haven't had time for lunch.'

'Certainly. I'll send up a selection. Perhaps you would also care for something to eat, Professor?' he added with an ingratiating smile.

Lamont nodded, but did not return the smile. 'Thank you,' he said curtly.

The manager vanished once again and the detectives and Lamont made their way in silence up to room 107. The moment the door closed behind them Lamont crossed the room, sank into a chair, adjusted the lapels of his safari jacket and stretched out a pair of long legs clad in immaculately creased linen trousers.

'How on earth does a wimp like that get to run a hotel?' he exclaimed. 'His PA showed a bit more backbone – once she'd got over the initial shock she more or less took charge.'

'I gather the sight of blood doesn't affect you in quite the same way then?' said Rathbone. He settled in the second chair in the room, leaving Sukey to perch on the edge of the bed.

'It wasn't exactly a pretty sight, but I did feel his reaction was a bit excessive,' agreed Lamont. 'You want an account of my movements, I take it?'

'If you'd be so kind, sir.'

'Well, I had an appointment to meet Doctor Whistler here at twelve o'clock. I was late – by nearly fifteen minutes, I think, on account of some heavy traffic. I gave my name to the chap on the desk and he sent me up to Whistler's room. I knocked several times, but got no answer. At first I thought he must have given me up and gone out, but then I thought that was unlikely so I knocked again and put an ear to the door and I thought I heard a sound like a sigh or a faint moan. It occurred to me that he might have been taken ill, so I hurried downstairs and got the manager. He and his assistant came up with a key and we found Doctor Whistler lying on the floor in a pool of blood.'

'Can you remember what position he was in?'

'Face down with his head diagonally towards the door.'

'Could you see any wound?'

'No. The blood seemed to be coming from beneath his body, but I was afraid to move him in case I did any further damage. I knelt down beside him and spoke to him; I could tell he was alive because he seemed to be trying to say something although I couldn't catch the words, so I told Ashford to get an ambulance and say it was an emergency. He called reception and gave the instruction, and then spent the next I don't know how long telling me how sick he got at the sight of blood.'

'And what about Erika – his assistant?'

'I think she threw up in the bathroom, but she very soon pulled herself together and went downstairs saying she'd direct the ambulance to the staff entrance and Ashford said, "Good idea."'

'You're certain that was her initiative – to bring the ambulance to the staff entrance?'

'Oh, yes. As soon as he'd made the call, Ashford collapsed on the edge of the bed like a lump of jelly.' Lamont's cultured, slightly high-pitched voice, registered undisguised contempt. ' "As a sick girl," as Cassius said when speaking of Caesar. That's a quotation from—'

'Yes, sir, I am familiar with the play,' said Rathbone evenly. 'While you were waiting for the ambulance, did the two of you speak to each other?'

'He kept wittering on about how awful it was and how he'd never been able to stand the sight of blood. I couldn't be bothered to answer and after a while he shut up and went over to the window. When the ambulance arrived he mumbled something about letting them in and sort of tiptoed past Whistler with his face averted to open the door. Like a woman drawing aside her skirts,' he added with a sneer.

Once again, Rathbone gave Sukey a sign that she was to take over the questioning. 'What happened after the paramedics had taken Doctor Whistler to the hospital?' she asked.

As if mildly affronted at being addressed by an inferior officer, Lamont raised an eyebrow before saying, 'We just stood there and after a minute or two the girl came back and said we should inform the police and we weren't to touch anything. Ashford told her to go ahead and we all waited until some officers arrived and took charge.'

'And did you notice any signs of disturbance in the room?'

Lamont closed his eyes for a moment as if trying to recall the scene. Then he said, 'The only thing I remember is the empty safe with the door open.'

'No suitcase with its contents spilling out, or other signs that the room had been searched?'

'No.'

Rathbone took up the questioning again. 'Professor Lamont, will you please tell us the purpose of your proposed meeting with Doctor Whistler?'

'Yes, of course. He'd been working on a dig on Rhodes – that's a Greek island in the

Mediterranean – at a place called Lindos, and he'd come across an ancient document buried on the site of an early Christian basilica that he believed to be a letter from Saint Paul. He wrote to Professor Thornton, the Head of the Faculty of Hellenic Studies at the university here, inviting him to visit the site and examine the document. Archie Thornton wrote back and said he'd be happy to look at it, but was unable to travel to Rhodes in the foreseeable future and suggested Whistler bring it to England, which he eventually agreed to do.' Lamont broke off to drink some of the coffee that a waiter had brought to the room and then reached for a sandwich, which he examined minutely before biting into it.

'And Professor Thornton asked you to meet him to collect this document on his behalf?' Rathbone prompted.

'He asked me to handle the whole matter. It so happens I'm currently preparing a paper on the subject of the letters of Saint Paul and I also have a specialized knowledge of classical Greek – which happens to be the language in which the apostle wrote his letters,' he added with an air that struck Sukey as unashamedly condescending.

'You would seem to be the ideal person to entrust with the mission,' Rathbone observed.

'Precisely.' Lamont showed no sign of

having recognized the dry note in the detective's voice.

'So when Professor Thornton handed the enquiry over to you,' Sukey began, in response to the by now familiar nod from Rathbone, 'presumably you contacted Doctor Whistler to arrange this meeting?'

'That's right,' Lamont said stiffly.

'Would you mind telling us how the meeting was set up?'

'It was done mostly by an exchange of emails, although we did have one or two telephone conversations.'

'How many people besides yourself and Professor Thornton knew about it?'

Lamont made an impatient sound at what he appeared to consider an irrelevant question. 'One or two people in the department, I suppose. Archie's secretary, of course, and someone may have seen the messages on my desk – for example, while I was out of my office, but if you're suggesting that anyone there—'

His colour had risen and he showed signs of becoming aggressive. Rathbone quickly stepped in and said quietly, 'No one is suggesting anything at this stage, Professor Lamont. DC Reynolds and I are simply trying to build up a complete picture of the events leading up to this attack. Would you kindly let us have a note of the people who have access to your office?'

'Very well,' Lamont said grumpily.

'Meanwhile, we'll prepare a statement for you to sign. And one other thing,' Rathbone continued without waiting for a response, 'I imagine that if this document is genuine it will be of considerable value to scholars?'

'Yes, of course.'

'So did Doctor Whistler at any time give you the impression that he feared having it stolen?'

Lamont shot Rathbone a keen look from his steel-blue eyes and hesitated for a moment before replying. 'Not exactly, but the last time I spoke to him he said something like, "I hope you haven't mentioned this to too many people" and then he said rather hastily, "I have to go. I'll see you at twelve", and hung up.'

'And that conversation took place this morning?'

'Yes, at about nine thirty. I called him from my office to check that he had reached the hotel and to confirm our arrangement.'

'I see. Thank you, Professor Lamont, you have been very helpful.'

Three

The minute the door closed behind Lamont, Rathbone exploded. 'Of all the self-important, pompous prats, that one leaves the rest of the field standing! Giving us lessons in geography and Shakespeare as if we were fourth formers! Now if someone clobbered *him* you'd feel like applauding.'

Sukey grinned. 'You deserve a medal for being civil to him,' she said. 'Ashford was a bit pathetic, but by the time the learned Prof had finished sneering I began to feel sorry for him. I'm a bit bothered about the timing,' she went on. 'Did the attacker know that Whistler was expecting Lamont at midday and make a point of arriving well before then? And how did he know which room to go to without asking at reception?'

'You've got a point there,' said Rathbone. 'If someone had called earlier claiming to be Professor Lamont, the receptionist would hardly have sent the real one up a short time later.'

'Unless he spoke to a different receptionist,' Sukey pointed out.

'Unlikely, but you'd better make a note to check. By the way, I thought it was interesting how their two accounts differed.'

'You mean Ashford making out he'd taken charge of the situation and Lamont giving the credit to "the girl", as he so patronisingly called her?'

'Exactly. What do you reckon?'

'My guess is that Lamont's version is the more accurate, although he might have exaggerated a little. Ashford was probably feeling pretty embarrassed at his performance and was trying to save face.'

'That's how I read it too.' Rathbone finished his coffee and swallowed the remains of the last sandwich. 'Before we see anyone else, let's try and figure out the chain of events. We know Whistler was all right at nine thirty when Lamont called from his office, although he expressed concern about the number of people who might know about the business and then hung up rather hastily. I wonder why?'

'Someone at the door?' Sukey suggested.

'Could be. Of course, at that time in the morning it would probably have been the chambermaid.'

'She wouldn't have knocked if the Do Not Disturb sign was on the door.'

'So perhaps he told her to come back later and then put the sign up.'

'That's probably what happened – but if

30

the bed hadn't been made, we'd have noticed.'

'Just the same, you'd better go and check.'

Sukey crossed the corridor, examined the bed in room 106 and returned to report that the bedding had been roughly pulled together and the cover drawn over, and that the bathroom hadn't been tidied. 'Which means the chambermaid never went in,' she said.

'Suggesting he was so jumpy that he didn't want anyone in there until Lamont had been and gone,' said Rathbone.

'So between nine thirty and around twelve o'clock, someone, who presumably persuaded Whistler that he was Lamont, entered the room, attacked him and made off with the document leaving him lying bleeding on the floor.'

'But Whistler wasn't expecting Lamont until midday, so if the attacker arrived much before then he'd surely have been suspicious,' Rathbone pointed out. 'Well, there's no point in speculating any further for the moment. Incidentally, we still don't know the nature of his injuries, but my guess is he was knifed. PC Hackett is at the hospital; I'll give him a call.' Rathbone took out his mobile and keyed in a number. After a brief exchange with the officer at the other end he switched off and said, 'He's been taken to the theatre but Hackett doesn't have any

31

details. OK, we'll see Erika next and listen to her version.'

Erika Henderson was a tall, slim brunette of about thirty. She was conventionally dressed in a well-cut navy blue skirt and jacket over a plain white shirt, with gold stud earrings and a gold choker. She showed no sign of her earlier distress, although her smile as she acknowledged Rathbone's greeting failed to mask the anxiety in her eyes. She sat down in the chair vacated by Lamont with her hands in her lap and her ankles neatly crossed.

'I won't keep you for long, Ms Henderson,' Rathbone began. 'We just want to check a few details. You must have found all this very upsetting.'

'Yes, very,' she replied gravely. 'I've experienced a few crises in my time, but never anything as bad as this. Tell me, Sergeant, what news is there of Doctor Whistler? I asked Mr Ashford, but he hasn't heard anything.'

'We understand he's undergoing emergency surgery; we have an officer at the hospital waiting for news and we're trying to locate his next of kin. That's all I can tell you at the moment, but you will of course be kept informed.'

'Thank you.'

'Now, perhaps you wouldn't mind answering a few questions. How did you first learn that something was wrong with Doctor Whistler?'

'Professor Lamont came to reception to tell us of his concern and I happened to be there at the time. I'd been with Mr Ashford in his office and I'd popped out to check something. I ran back and alerted him straight away and we all went up to Doctor Whistler's room together.'

'I see. How long had you been with Mr Ashford in his office?'

'I suppose ... for about an hour or so. We were working on our Christmas and New Year programme.'

'You say you "popped out" at one point to check something – how long were you out of the office?'

'Only a few seconds. Professor Lamont was already at the desk.'

'Was anyone else on the desk at the time?'

She frowned and thought for a moment. 'Now you come to mention it, I don't think there was, but Boris – the member of staff who was on duty at the time – was there when I returned with Mr Ashford a minute or so later.'

'You and Mr Ashford had no other interruptions?' She shook her head. 'And neither of you left the room until this happened?'

'No, of course not.' Her expression became wary, as if she suspected some ulterior motive behind the question.

'That would be about what time?'

'About a quarter past twelve ... or maybe a little after. I can't say exactly.'

'Thank you. Please tell us what happened next.'

Listening to her while making notes, Sukey had the impression that she had used the time spent waiting to be questioned to organize her thoughts. Her account, which agreed in all essentials with that of Lamont, was given in a brisk, businesslike voice with a trace of a West Country accent.

At the end of his questions, Rathbone said, 'Thank you very much, Ms Henderson, I think you've covered pretty well everything we wanted to know.' He glanced at Sukey and she shook her head. 'Right, that's all for now – oh, yes, there is one other thing. The member of staff who directed Professor Lamont to Doctor Whistler's room – I think you said his name was Boris – is he still on duty?'

'Boris Gasspar – yes, he's on until five.'

'How long has he worked here?'

'He came to us about six months ago. I take it you'll want to see him?'

'If you would kindly ask him to come up here in five minutes?'

'Certainly.' She stood up and impulsively put a hand on Rathbone's arm. 'I do so hope you find whoever was responsible for this horrible attack,' she said. 'It's been very

34

upsetting for us all.'

'We'll do our best,' Rathbone promised and she thanked him and left, closing the door quietly behind her.

'Well, that would seem to put Ashford in the clear, although I never seriously thought of him as a suspect,' said Rathbone.

'Neither did I,' Sukey agreed. 'It's nice that someone showed concern for the victim, isn't it?' she added. She was tempted to stress the fact that the concerned party was a woman, as she would have done had it been DI Jim Castle sitting opposite her, but resisted. She liked what she had seen of Greg Rathbone so far, but she had yet to get his measure.

'Anyway, it seems Lamont's account was the more accurate, although it doesn't really—' Rathbone broke off as his mobile phone rang. He answered, gave his name, said, 'Yes, Den. What news?' and then listened in silence for a minute. Sukey watched him closely, but his face gave nothing away. Then he said, 'Right, thanks. Report back to the station and tell them to inform the coroner. There'll have to be a PM, of course. And find out whether we've been able to locate the next of kin.' He switched off and said, 'I take it you got that?'

She nodded. 'Whistler's dead and we've got a murder on our hands.'

'Right.' He got up and went over to the

window. 'It seems that document was worth a great deal to someone. What did Lamont say about it?'

'He said Whistler thought it might be a letter from Saint Paul.'

'I thought all the saint's correspondence was already in the public domain, as the saying goes,' said Rathbone with an attempt at levity.

'Researchers are always coming across ancient documents relating to various religions,' Sukey pointed out. 'I imagine that to scholars they can be as valuable as a work of art. Remember the Dead Sea Scrolls?'

'That's true. Well, we'd better have another word with Lamont and see if he can give us some idea of—' He broke off as someone knocked on the door. 'That'll be Boris. We'll talk about this later. And not a word about Whistler's death,' he warned before calling, 'Come in!'

A slightly built young man with dark hair smoothed back from his forehead entered, closed the door behind him and took a couple of tentative steps into the room. 'You want see me, sir?' he said.

'You're Boris Gasspar?' The man nodded. 'Come and sit down.' Rathbone indicated the chair vacated by Lamont and after a moment's hesitation he complied, perched on the edge of the seat and waited.

It seemed to Sukey that Rathbone made a

point of consulting his notebook for several seconds before saying, 'Your full name is Boris Gasspar, I believe?' The man nodded again. 'How do you spell that, please?'

'G-a-s-s-p-a-r,' he replied.

'Where are you from, Boris?'

The man licked his lips. 'I am from Vlora. That spell V-l-o-r-a,' he added.

Rathbone glanced at Sukey, who gave him a blank look and shook her head. He turned back to Boris. 'Where exactly is Vlora?' he asked.

'In Albania. I have passport, work permit, everything in order.' There was a look of apprehension in the man's coal-black eyes and his hands were shaking.

'That's all right, we aren't checking up on your status,' said Rathbone reassuringly. 'As you've no doubt heard, a guest at this hotel – a Doctor Whistler – has been attacked and seriously hurt in his room. My colleague and I are police officers and we're trying to find out who did it.'

'I know nothing. I hurt no one,' said Boris. He shot a desperate glance at Sukey as if pleading for help.

'Boris, no one's saying it was you who attacked Doctor Whistler,' she said gently, 'but we think you may be able to help us find the person who did. We just want to ask you a few questions.'

Boris moistened his lips a second time. 'I

try,' he said.

'Good man,' said Rathbone. 'Now, we understand that Professor Lamont came to the desk at about a quarter past twelve and asked for Doctor Whistler. Was it you he spoke to?'

'Of course. I am on duty.'

'And you directed him to Doctor Whistler's room?'

'Yes. Doctor Whistler say me he expect Professor Lamont and I have to send him to room.'

'What time did he say he expected Professor Lamont?' Sukey asked.

Boris glanced down at his hands for a moment before replying, 'He say twelve o'clock.'

'So he was fifteen minutes late?'

'Yes. That is, no. He come earlier, but not to desk. I see him when he go out to car park by back door. In great hurry, and carry bag,' he added as an afterthought.

'You mean the staff entrance?' Boris nodded. 'How did you come to see him use that door if you were on duty at the desk?'

'Please?'

'The staff entrance is invisible ... that is, you can't see it from the desk,' Sukey explained patiently. 'Where were you when you saw Professor Lamont the first time?'

Boris shifted uneasily, avoiding her eyes. 'Outside door. I go for smoke.'

'Leaving the desk unattended?' He gazed blankly back at her and she tried again. 'Was there another person on the desk?'

'Oh yes. Millie from office stay there for me.'

'And while you were having your smoke just outside the staff entrance,' Sukey went on, 'you saw Professor Lamont go out into the car park.'

'That right, but I not know then that it was the professor.'

'But you're sure it was the same man?'

'Oh, yes, quite sure.'

'In a hurry and carrying a bag?'

Boris nodded and passed his tongue over his lips before saying, 'Yes.'

'What sort of bag?'

'Small bag, with handles. Dark colour.'

'Let's get this straight,' said Rathbone, speaking slowly and deliberately, 'Doctor Whistler told you he was expecting Professor Lamont at twelve o'clock and said you were to send him straight to his room. Why did you leave the desk around the time he was expected?'

Boris fidgeted with his hands and his eyes darted to and fro between the detectives. 'I need smoke, and I tell Millie the message in case he come early. When I go back just after twelve, she say Professor not come yet. Please–' the man's eyes were wide with fear – 'you not tell Mr Ashford? I not allowed smoke while on duty. I lose job, my family need money—'

'Boris, what you have told us may be very important,' Rathbone said gravely. 'I can't promise to keep it from Mr Ashford, but if he has to know I'll be sure to put in a word for you ... tell him what a help you have been to us. I'm sure it won't mean losing your job.'

Boris appeared far from reassured, but he gave a faint, hesitant smile. 'Please, I go back to my work?'

'Yes, Boris,' said Rathbone, 'that will be all for now.'

The man fairly scuttled out of the room as if fearing that a moment's delay might lead to more questions.

As the door closed behind him, Rathbone said, 'Well, that alters the picture more than somewhat. We must have another chat with Lamont. I'll set that up for tomorrow; meanwhile I'd like you to check with any hotel staff and guests who might have been around at the crucial time and ask them if they saw anyone near Whistler's room. And track down the paramedics who collected Whistler and find out whether they found him in the position described by Ashford and Lamont. And do statements for everyone we've seen so far, OK?'

'Right, Sarge.' Sukey made a note of the instructions. She forbore to ask Rathbone what action he proposed to take, apart from setting up the interview with Lamont. 'Just one thing,' she added, 'should we perhaps have a word with Millie to see if she can add anything useful?'

'Good point.' He called reception to make the request. 'She's gone to lunch,' he said as he put the phone down. 'You can see her when you come back after dropping me off at the station.'

'Well, thanks a bunch,' Sukey muttered under her breath as she followed him downstairs and out of the hotel.

Four

By the time Sukey returned to the station it was gone four o'clock. She went straight to her desk in the CID office and began work on statements for signature by Ashford, Lamont, Gasspar and Erika Henderson. The shorthand she had learned years ago while working on her degree in media studies made the task fairly straightforward. It was with a sigh of relief that she finished the last one and began on the results of her afternoon's work.

With any luck, she thought, she could get

41

away by five thirty and be home in time to wind down and have a shower before getting ready for what was described in the invitation as an informal supper. It was the first time she had been invited to a social event in a neighbour's home, although she already knew several of them by sight through encounters in the street or in one of the local shops. One in particular, who introduced herself the day after Sukey moved into her new home just off Whiteladies Road as Priscilla Gadden, had gone out of her way to offer information and advice on local amenities and services, and it was from Priscilla and her architect husband Tom, who lived in what the residents in Sherman Lane referred to as 'the big house', that Sukey had received this evening's invitation.

At five o'clock Greg Rathbone entered the office, rested his posterior on the edge of her desk, picked up the completed statements and glanced at them briefly before saying, 'I've had a preliminary chat with Doc Hanley, the forensic pathologist. He says Whistler was stopped in his tracks by a single stab wound from a thin-bladed knife that penetrated the heart. It didn't do enough damage to cause immediate death so it carried on pumping out blood. So much had leaked into the chest cavity that by the time they got him to the theatre it was too late to save him.'

Sukey shuddered and swallowed hard. 'Poor man, how awful,' she said.

'Did you get a word with the paramedics, by the way?'

'Yes, I managed to catch them and they confirmed the position they found Whistler in. They also said that when they got him into the ambulance he seemed to regain partial consciousness for a few moments and was trying to say something, but the only words they could make out sounded like "No" or "not" and then "Greek".'

'Presumably he was talking about the document,' said Rathbone, 'because Lamont implied that it's written in Greek, but on its own it doesn't help us much. The CSIs found traces of blood on the side of the bed away from the door, suggesting that the wound was delivered there and Whistler staggered forward a few steps before he fell.' He tossed the statements aside. 'Anything else to report? I suppose it's too much to hope for that you happened to find someone who saw a tall man with a bag near Whistler's room at the relevant time?'

Sukey shook her head. 'Most of the rooms on that floor were occupied by business people who went out soon after breakfast. The ones I did catch weren't much help and the chambermaids had all gone home so I'll have to speak to them tomorrow. But I did have a word with Millie, the girl who stood in for Boris while he went outside for his smoke. She confirms the time he went out, but she didn't actually see him come back because she was busy with a hotel guest at the time. All she can say is that when she turned round after finishing with the guest, Boris was there. She told him Lamont hadn't yet arrived and went back into the office.'

'It's a busy hotel,' Rathbone remarked. 'I'm surprised they have only one person on reception.'

'I asked about that,' Sukey said. 'Normally there are two, but the second one who should have been there this morning was off sick.'

'You'd think that in the circumstances Boris could have done without his smoke,' Rathbone observed.

'That occurred to me; in fact, I asked Millie if he was a heavy smoker and she didn't know, but I suppose there's no reason why she should. She spends most of her time in the admin office, which leads off the reception.'

'So I suppose she didn't actually see Lamont arrive?'

'She did, as it happens. The door was ajar and she confirms the time as just before twelve fifteen. She added that he seemed breathless and a little agitated, but he didn't wait for the lift; he ran up the stairs in a great hurry.'

'*Did* he?' said Rathbone with meaningful emphasis.

'And Boris mentioned that he seemed in a great hurry when he went out through the staff entrance,' Sukey pointed out.

'So he did.'

'I wonder—' she began, then broke off, afraid he might think she was trying to be clever at his expense.

'Yes?' prompted Rathbone.

'If Lamont did stab Whistler,' she said hesitantly, 'you'd expect him to have blood on his clothes.'

'Well done for spotting that.' Rathbone gave a nod of approval. 'I thought the same, but Doc Hanley said blood doesn't spurt from that type of wound the way it does when a vein or artery is cut. It was only because Whistler fell on his face that there was all that blood on the carpet. It'll be interesting to have Lamont's reaction to the latest developments. He's coming in at nine thirty tomorrow and I want you there.'

'Very good, Sarge. I'll just finish writing up the notes about my chat with Millie and then if it's all right with you I'll go home.'

At seven thirty that evening Sukey, freshly showered, put on a flowered skirt with a loose white top, brushed her short chocolate-brown curls into their most becoming shape and paused briefly to study her reflection in the full-length mirror in her bedroom. The image that stared back at her was bright-eyed, the cheeks slightly flushed under a light make-up, the expression eager and full of anticipation. Today, she decided, would go down as having a double significance: for the first time as a fully fledged detective constable she had been at the sharp end of a murder enquiry and she was about to fulfil her first social engagement since moving to Bristol. With a nod of satisfaction she slipped on a pair of sandals and a loose cotton jacket, picked up a handbag and the bunch of roses purchased on her way home, and set off.

A couple of centuries ago, the estate agent had informed her, the area surrounding Sherman Lane had formed part of a gentleman's estate, and relics of those far-off days remained in the nostalgic names given to the conversions of the out-buildings into modern dwellings, such as the Coach House and the Lodge. As her own flat abutted on to the Stables, the home of a retired army major called Matthews, Sukey had been tempted to commission a sign reading the Hayloft to hang above her own front door, but when she tentatively mentioned it to Matthews he showed little enthusiasm for the suggestion. 'He seemed to think it suggested naughty goings-on between the stable lads and the housemaids and so lower the tone of the neighbourhood,' she told Fergus, who had guffawed and called the man a silly old fart, but advised her not to do anything to antagonize him.

Sherman House, which stood behind wrought-iron gates at the end of the cul-de-sac, was a Georgian building with a plain but elegant and well-proportioned facade of Bath stone that reflected the warm glow of the setting sun. When Sukey pressed the button on the keypad set into the gatepost, the voice of Priscilla Gadden greeted her by name; then a buzzer sounded and the personal gate swung open. A short gravelled drive led to the house; as she approached she spotted a CCTV camera and several discreetly positioned lights. Before she had time to press the brass bell push, the heavy oak front door was opened by a slim girl with spiky blond hair clad in a body-hugging black top and a magenta frill – hardly long enough to be described as a skirt – above sheer black tights and enormous platform shoes. Her pale face and her voice were equally expressionless as she beckoned Sukey into the hall with a hand tipped with fingernails that matched her skirt and said, 'Come in. We're in the drawing room.' She led the way across a flagged stone floor and up a stone staircase with a wooden handrail, both of which looked as old as the house. There was a window on the half-landing with a deep sill on which stood a huge bowl of roses, making Sukey conscious of the modesty of her own offering. The window frame was obviously new; what was also obvious was that it had been custom-made to be an exact copy of the original.

They reached the first floor; a door on the right stood open and a buzz of conversation and laughter flowed out on to the landing. As her young guide led her into the room Sukey caught her breath at the scale and beauty and at the same time the sheer opulence of it all: the waxed wooden floor under a scattering of richly coloured oriental rugs: the high ceiling with its ornamental plaster moulding: the Adam fireplace with its marble surround: the sparkling chandelier: the huge windows that gave a panoramic view over the city. 'What a superb room!' she exclaimed almost reverently and the girl shrugged and said, 'If you say so. Mum's over there,' before melting away.

A little diffidently, Sukey made her way towards the far corner where Priscilla Gadden, clad in a loose-fitting aquamarine jacket over a calf-length matching skirt with diamonds at her throat and ears, was talking animatedly to a stout, balding man in shirtsleeves. She held a glass of champagne in one hand and with the other, also bedecked with jewels that flashed in the light of the chandelier, she pointed in various directions while the man swivelled his gaze this way and that and gave appreciative nods between taking sips from his own glass.

Watching them, Sukey had a disconcerting sensation of being a visitor to a National Trust property rather than an invited guest, but at that moment Priscilla caught sight of her, said something to her companion and came forward with her right hand outstretched.

'Sukey, how lovely to see you! I'm so glad you could come!' she exclaimed, and the illusion of a moment ago was immediately dispelled by the warmth and sincerity of the welcome and the obvious pleasure with which she accepted the bouquet Sukey offered. 'Patsy!' she called, glancing round the room, and the girl detached herself from a small group of young people by the window and wandered towards them. 'Ah, there you are. Aren't these lovely – put them in water for me, there's a love.' As the girl took the flowers without a word and walked away, her young shoulders seemed to register a simmering resentment. Her mother turned to Sukey and sighed. 'I do so wish today's young wouldn't turn themselves into freaks – but I suppose she'll grow out of it. And she hardly ever smiles at me or her father these days, although she seems happy enough with that lot over there. Do you have this problem with your Fergus?'

'He does wear some pretty way-out gear,' Sukey admitted, 'and he gels his hair into some weird shapes – but at least he's quite amenable most of the time – and he showers regularly as well, which is more than you can say for some of them.'

'Indeed. Ah, Tom,' Priscilla turned to her husband who had materialized at her side, 'will you get Sukey a drink? I simply must go and talk to the Shearers.' She glided across the room to greet a couple who had just entered while Tom Gadden, whom Sukey had met only briefly before, brought her a glass of champagne.

'Your house is beautiful!' Sukey exclaimed and his normally grave face lit up with pleasure. 'It must have been a real labour of love – restoring it, I mean.'

'When it wasn't giving us nightmares,' he replied. 'It's a listed building, of course, so making it comfortable by twenty-first century standards while preserving all the original features was something of a juggling act. Heating was a major headache – double-glazing was out of the question of course, but I think we managed to get it right in the end. Oh, I think I hear the phone – would you excuse me a moment?'

'Of course.' He hurried away, leaving her sipping her champagne and admiring the view. He reappeared a few moments later with a phone, which he handed to his wife with a few murmured words before returning to Sukey's side.

Priscilla took the phone out of the room; when she returned she came over to her husband and said, 'Hester was practically hysterical – she kept saying a friend of Stephen's has been attacked and robbed. Then Stephen took the phone from her and explained that she's upset because a man he was supposed to meet has been mugged and taken to hospital. It seems a rather important document has been stolen. Anyway, he says they won't be coming.' She turned to Sukey looking slightly apologetic and said, 'Some friends of ours who live the other side of the Downs have had a rather distressing experience. He's very clever, he lectures in Greek and biblical studies at the university, but she's, well, she's had rather a lot of illness and gets upset easily.'

'She's a raving neurotic,' said Tom. 'Leads poor old Stephen a hell of a dance.'

'Tom, that's unkind,' his wife scolded gently. 'She's been loads better lately. I wonder if that's the document she was prattling on about when I met her in the library the other day,' she added.

'Oh – what document was that?' said Tom.

'An archaeologist has found what he thinks might be a letter from Saint Paul. Hester was very excited because Stephen has been asked to say if he thinks it's genuine or not. She seemed to think it was a feather in his cap to be chosen for the honour.'

Tom shrugged. 'Well, we all know she thinks he's the greatest genius in the world since Einstein,' he said with a wry smile.

'That's true,' she agreed. 'Tom, please introduce Sukey to some of our other guests and show her where the food is. I must circulate.'

As she disappeared among the chattering crowd Tom remarked, 'Shouldn't say this I know, but when he gets on to one of his hobby horses that chap could bore for England. Hester's his sister, by the way. She won't accept any invitations without him and Pris feels sorry for her because she doesn't have much social life so we have to invite the pair of them.'

Adrenalin had been pumping through Sukey's veins for the past couple of minutes but she managed to keep her voice casual as she enquired, 'What are his hobby horses?'

'Biblical texts, especially the epistles, and ancient Greek,' said Tom. 'I can't say either of them turns me on, but some people seem to find them fascinating. Come to think of it...' His tone altered and he looked at Sukey with a sudden show of interest. 'I was forgetting – you're in the police, aren't you? I suppose your people will be involved if the chap's badly hurt. Or maybe they're involved already?'

He fixed her with an enquiring expression as if hoping for inside information, but at that moment Major Matthews bore down on them, glass in hand. 'Ah, Gadden, I've been looking forward to the chance of a word!' he barked. 'Please excuse us if we talk a bit of shop,' he said to Sukey. 'Local politics and all that. I'm afraid you'd find it rather boring stuff really but—' He treated Sukey to a patronizing smile as if a mere woman could not be expected to take an intelligent interest in such matters. Relieved rather than offended, she smiled politely, took the hint and headed for the buffet table on the other side of the room.

Five

By eleven o'clock the guests began to leave. Only a few had come by car; the majority lived in Sherman Lane and headed for home in a cheerful, chattering group, exchanging remarks about the mildness of the September night and making admiring comments on the spectacle of the brilliantly lit city spread out beneath them under a clear moonlit sky. One by one they called out

53

'Good night' and went into their respective homes until only Sukey and Major Matthews were left. With exaggerated gallantry he insisted on accompanying her right up to her front door, solemnly taking her key, opening it for her and waiting until she had stepped inside before handing back her key, giving a smart salute and saying a hearty 'Splendid evening, what! Cheerio!' before marching back to the Stables.

Sukey went straight to her study and made notes of the information she had gleaned about the absent guests, Hester and Stephen. Although the name of Lamont had not been mentioned there was no doubt in her mind that Stephen was the man whose appointment with Doctor Whistler had in some way led to that unfortunate man's violent death and whom she and DS Rathbone had interviewed that day. She had earlier been relieved to find, on reading the evening edition of the local paper, that the front page had been devoted to a story about a local teacher claiming compensation for alleged sexual harassment in the staff room, while the report on the incident in the hotel had been reduced to a short paragraph on an inside page. News of Doctor Whistler's death had not of course as yet been released and to her relief the few references to local news she had heard at the party were mostly concerned with the former story; no one referred to the latter. If it hadn't been for that telephone call, she reflected as she got ready for bed, no one would have been any the wiser, although fortunately it had not occurred to anyone apart from Tom Gadden that she might have some inside information, and Major Matthews had inadvertently rescued her from the necessity of responding to his question.

The following morning she set off early to avoid the rush hour traffic and had been at her desk for fifteen minutes when Rathbone strolled over with a mug of coffee in one hand and a folder in the other.

'Ashford has given us a room in his conference suite to use as an incident room,' he announced, adding with a mischievous grin, 'You should have seen his look of horror when I suggested bringing one of our vans into the hotel car park! By the way, I've booked an interview room here for our chat with Lamont for nine thirty. He thinks it's mainly a matter of checking and signing his statement, by the way; I didn't tell him what Gasspar has been saying and he doesn't know Whistler's dead.' His eye fell on her notebook; it was open at her jottings of the previous evening and she had been in the act of adding a further comment as he entered. 'Any new ideas?' he asked between swigs of coffee.

'As it happens, yes,' she said. 'Something

rather interesting happened at the party yesterday.'

She relayed the scraps of information she had picked up at the Gaddens' and his slightly languid expression became alert. 'You didn't reveal your involvement?' he said sharply.

'No, and I didn't let on that Whistler had died. To be honest, I think they were more concerned about the neurotic sister than either the mugging or the theft of the document.'

'Just as well Lamont didn't show at the party or I'd have had to take you off the case, which would have been unfortunate – just as I'm getting used to having you around.' He looked at her as if he was expecting some expression of gratification at what he evidently considered a compliment, but she merely stared blandly back at him. 'So whatever you do,' he went on, 'make sure you don't have any contact with him outside the investigation.'

'Right, Sarge.'

'Let's run over the evidence – or lack of it – and discuss the line we're going to take. I've asked him to bring in the clothes he was wearing, by the way. He didn't sound too happy about that, which might or might not be significant.'

At a little before half past nine, Stephen

Lamont sat in the reception area in New Bridewell Police Station, trying to appear relaxed. The call from DS Rathbone asking him to visit the station to sign his statement and 'help to clear up one or two other points' had been disturbing enough; Hester's uncontrollable distress on learning that his story about Whistler having been taken ill and was having to postpone their appointment was untrue had been the last straw and made it impossible for the two of them to turn up at the Gaddens' party as if nothing had happened. If only he hadn't been out of the room when the police rang; if only Hester hadn't taken the call; if only she hadn't called the Gaddens and blurted out the story before he had a chance to stop her. He just hoped it wouldn't go any further; he'd warned her not to go spreading it around, but she was inclined to be unpredictable and to act on impulse without considering the possible consequences. Which, had he but known it, was what was happening at that very moment.

A bespectacled young woman with a dark ponytail arrived to escort him to the interview. Stephen entered with his head held high; he was damned if he was going to be intimidated by this smooth-talking policeman or his sharp-featured female sidekick. He acknowledged Rathbone's polite greeting with a curt nod, sat down at the table in the

57

drab, featureless room and stared defiantly back at his two interlocutors.

'I hope this isn't going to take long,' he said. 'I have a meeting at eleven.'

In response, Rathbone handed him a sheet of A4 paper and said, 'This is a record of the statement you made to DC Reynolds and myself yesterday. If you agree that it's correct, perhaps you would kindly sign it.'

Nothing would have given Stephen Lamont greater pleasure than to find a glaring mistake in the brief printed account, but on reading it through and finding it scrupulously accurate he merely grunted, pulled out a fountain pen, signed it and handed it back without a word.

'Thank you, sir.' Rathbone slipped it into a folder and sat back in his chair. 'I want to make it clear that you are here voluntarily and are free to leave at any time, you are not under caution and this interview is not being tape-recorded, although DC Reynolds may make a few notes. Is that clear?'

Lamont permitted himself a slightly disdainful smile. 'Perfectly,' he said.

'Good. Now, as I mentioned on the telephone, it is possible that when you bent over Doctor Whistler as he lay on the floor you picked up certain evidence on your clothing. I believe I asked you to be good enough to bring it in for examination.'

'You did, but I'm afraid you were too late.

My sister looks after my clothes and it transpired that she had already put them all in the washing machine.'

The woman detective looked up from her notebook. 'Just the same we'd like to examine them,' she said briskly. 'By the way, what about the shoes you were wearing?' she added.

'You wanted those as well? I'm afraid I haven't brought them either.'

'That's no problem, sir. We can send an officer to pick them up, with the clothes, from your home.' He had a feeling as she spoke that she expected him to protest, but he maintained a dignified silence.

'Now, sir,' said Rathbone. 'I have to inform you that since you made your statement yesterday we have found a witness who claims to have seen you leave the hotel by the rear entrance almost half an hour before you came to the front desk and informed the clerk on duty that you were there to keep your appointment with Doctor Whistler. Have you any comment about that?'

Lamont managed to meet the detective's searching gaze without flinching. 'There must be some mistake,' he said. 'I arrived a few minutes late, parked my car, entered the hotel by the main door and went straight to the desk.'

'I see.' Rathbone looked down at his notes before saying, 'The witness also states that

Doctor Whistler had told him to expect you at twelve, but that it was nearly twelve fifteen when you arrived. He also states,' he said before Lamont had a chance to say anything, 'that when he saw you leave by the side door you appeared to be in a great hurry and you were carrying a small, dark-coloured bag such as a holdall.'

'How many times do I have to tell you, I didn't arrive early and I didn't go out by the side way. The man obviously confused me with someone else.'

'All right, we'll leave that for the moment. But you admit you were late for your appointment. Why was that?'

'I was a few minutes late leaving my Greek class, and then I was delayed by traffic.' He saw the detective's eyebrows go up and added hastily, 'I teach classical Greek in an extra-mural class three mornings a week.'

'No doubt your students will confirm this.'

'Unfortunately not as they had all left a few minutes earlier.'

'So what was the reason for your delay?'

'I was sorting through some exercises they had handed in.'

'Couldn't that have waited, considering you had an appointment at midday?'

'I suppose I ... well, I must have forgotten the time for the moment. I do have a lot of other things on my mind.'

'Ah, yes,' said Rathbone, 'the paper about

the letters of Saint Paul. I'm surprised that in view of your other commitments you find time to take on additional teaching at such an elementary level.' His tone was casual, but his gaze was keen. Lamont stiffened. Archie Thornton, his head of faculty, had also expressed some surprise on learning that he had applied for the part-time post and he had been forced to admit that he needed the money because of having to meet the cost of his sister's treatment. But he was damned if he was going to reveal his personal problems to this blighter. So he maintained a dignified silence and awaited the next question.

'Well, sir, as you insist that the witness I mentioned earlier made a mistake, no doubt you'll be willing to take part in an identity parade so that we can eliminate you from our enquiries?'

The suggestion took Lamont completely by surprise. He felt his face burn and it flashed across his mind that perhaps he should have brought his solicitor.

While he was desperately thinking how to respond, Rathbone said, 'I should make it clear that you are entitled to refuse.'

'Then I do refuse. I find the suggestion extremely distasteful.'

'We understand your feelings and there is an alternative, sir.' It was the woman speaking again. 'One of our photographers can take a shot of you and we can insert it into a picture of a group of people of about your age and build. We can then show the montage to our witness and ask if he can identify you as the man he saw. If he fails to do so, then of course—'

Lamont pushed his chair back and leapt to his feet. 'I'm not staying here a moment longer!' he said furiously. 'I'm a highly qualified academic of impeccable character and I find this line of questioning extremely insulting!' He marched to the door and wrenched it open. 'Good day to you!'

'Before you leave,' said Rathbone, 'there is something you should know.'

'And that is?'

'Doctor Whistler has died from his injuries. That means we are conducting a murder enquiry.'

Lamont was halfway through the door, but he immediately stopped short and rounded on the detectives. 'Why the hell didn't you say so at the outset?' he demanded. He found himself back in his chair without being quite sure how he got there.

'We've been waiting for you to enquire about his condition,' said Rathbone in the smooth, bland voice that made Lamont feel uncomfortable. 'And there is also the question of the missing document—'

'I ... yes ... of course I should have ... it's terrible news about poor Whistler. I imagine that when you find the villain who attacked him you'll recover the document as well.'

'Naturally that is what we're hoping for. This document – can you give us a rough idea of what it might be worth?'

Lamont made a vague gesture with his hands. 'In cash terms, I've really no idea. If it's genuine, then it should be entrusted to a museum or other collection of rare biblical writings for safe keeping.'

'What about a private collector?'

'In that case, its value would depend on what he is willing to pay for it.'

'Or what lengths he would go to in order to get his hands on it?' suggested Rathbone. The sub-text of the question was unmistakable and for the second time Lamont sought refuge in a dignified silence. 'Do you happen to know of such a person?' the detective persisted.

There was something disconcerting at the unwavering gaze of the two detectives, but Lamont did his best not to appear intimidated. 'Certainly not!' he declared. 'What kind of people do you think I associate with?'

Rathbone ignored the question. 'Perhaps in the circumstances you might like to reconsider your refusal to co-operate over the matter of identification,' he suggested.

Something in his manner indicated that a change of heart was a foregone conclusion. Making a mental note to contact his solicitor at the earliest opportunity, Lamont replied with as much dignity as he could muster, 'I see no reason to.'

'In that case it is my duty to inform you that we are free to take any legal means available to us to obtain whatever evidence we consider essential to our investigation,' Rathbone said.

Lamont was conscious of only one thing and that was a desperate need to get out of the place and seek advice. 'Do what you damned well please!' he said.

'Your response is noted,' said Rathbone. 'That's all for now, thank you, sir. We'll keep you informed ... we'll send an officer to your home to pick up the clothes and shoes.'

Lamont muttered something inaudible under his breath and left the room. The moment the door closed behind him, Rathbone and Sukey exchanged glances. 'Well, that cut him down to size,' she remarked. 'And that outburst – outraged dignity or guilty conscience?'

'My guess is the latter,' Rathbone replied. 'He looked distinctly jumpy when he first came in, as I'm sure you noticed. We'll have to get a covert shot of the bugger; get the techies on to it, will you?'

'Sure.' Sukey made a note before saying, 'So, you reckon he's our man?'

'Who's most likely to be interested in a

letter supposed to be from Saint Paul than someone who's currently working on a paper on that very subject? My guess is that from the moment he heard about it he's been slavering at the thought of getting his hands on it.'

'But Whistler was planning to pass it over to him anyway,' Sukey pointed out, 'so why on earth should he go to such desperate lengths to steal it? And besides, Whistler did give the impression when he spoke to Lamont that morning that he thought someone else might be after it.'

'We only have Lamont's word for that,' Rathbone reminded her. 'Besides, he implied that it's valuable and we know he's had to shell out a small fortune for his sister's treatment.'

'That's true,' she agreed. 'It'll be interesting to see whether Boris picks him out when we show him the mock-up. Incidentally, I thought he seemed a bit jumpy as well; would it be a good idea to run a check on him to make sure he's not an illegal?'

'Some people are often uncomfortable with the police, even when they have no reason to be,' said Rathbone. 'He was very anxious to impress on us that his papers were in order and I imagine the hotel would have made sure before taking him on, but you're right, it wouldn't do any harm to check. I'll leave that with you. Meanwhile, I'll update DCI Leach and ask him what he wants us to tell the press.'

Six

'DCI Leach and I will be meeting the press at midday,' Rathbone informed Sukey half an hour later. 'We're not planning to add much to what they already know – just tell them that the man who was attacked at the Mariners Hotel was the victim of a stabbing, that he died later of his injuries and that we're still looking for the weapon. We haven't traced Whistler's next of kin yet so we can't release his name. We'll say we're following one or two leads and end with the usual appeal for members of the public to report anything suspicious.'

'What about the theft of the ancient document he's supposed to have brought with him?' she enquired.

'We're not saying a word about that or the jackals will sniff out his identity in no time and that will lead them straight to Lamont, or at least to his department. Incidentally, I had a word with Lamont's head of faculty – Professor Thorne – and asked him not to talk to the press either. If he is our man, any publicity at this stage could kybosh our case before it got to court.'

'I take it I shan't be appearing?' said Sukey in a sudden panic. 'I've never had to face the press.'

'Don't worry – it'll just be the two of us plus DS Bob Douglas who's in charge of the incident room. In any case, we want you to keep out of the limelight. We know that your hostess and the sister are buddies and we also know the sister is inclined to be unstable. If she found out that one of the officers on the case was a guest at the party she might take it into her head to try and contact you "off the record", so to speak. We don't want her rushing off to her friend and trying to worm your address out of her, do we?'

'Perish the thought,' Sukey said fervently. 'I hope Priscilla would have the sense not to give it to her. Perhaps I should have a word to make sure she doesn't?'

'Definitely not. That would inevitably mean letting her know that you're involved in the investigation. Say nothing and keep your head down. Have you spoken to the hotel about Boris, by the way?'

'Yes, I've just been having a word with Erika Henderson and she assured me that he was thoroughly vetted before they took him on. She did say that he was in a bit of a state after we'd interviewed him and she'd had to reassure him that he wasn't under suspicion.'

'Well, anyone who's grown up under a communist regime is likely to be wary of the police,' Rathbone observed. 'We must remember to treat him gently next time we talk to him. When are you going back to interview the chambermaids?'

'This morning, if that's OK with you; I arranged it with Erika at the same time. The two who service the first floor rooms are on duty again this morning and she says I can use the linen room to interview them. I gather they're both foreign so language might be a problem.'

'I'm sure you'll cope,' said Rathbone confidently. 'If by any chance they did see anyone at the crucial time we can show the mugshot of Lamont to them as well as Boris.'

'That's in hand, Sarge. The techies know it's a murder case so they'll give it priority.'

'Good. Well, you might as well go to the hotel now and talk to the chambermaids. Be sure and let Bob Douglas know the result – and ask Ashford to repeat the instruction to his staff not under any circumstances to talk to the press. They'll get on to it eventually,' he added resignedly, 'but we'll make it as difficult for the buggers as we can.'

'Will do, Sarge.'

* * *

Verena was a thin, pale girl with mousy hair tied in a ponytail. When Erika Henderson accompanied Sukey to the first floor they found her in the linen room, loading her trolley with clean sheets and towels together with the usual assortment of minuscule tablets of soap, sachets of shampoo, body lotion and other luxuries with which hotels the world over provide their guests. Erika had forewarned her of the reason for the visit and although she had raised no objection to being questioned she was evidently ill at ease and maintained a defensive position behind her trolley throughout the brief interview. Her English, however, was reasonable and she appeared to have no difficulty in understanding the questions although her replies consisted as far as possible of monosyllables. Yes, she was responsible for servicing seven of the fourteen rooms on this floor; yes, she was on duty the previous day; yes, she remembered tapping on the door of room 106 and being asked to come back later; no, she couldn't be sure of the time but yes, it might have been around half past nine; yes, the gentleman put the 'Do Not Disturb' notice on the door at the same time; yes, several people had passed along the corridor while she was doing the rooms; no, she hadn't noticed anyone in particular.

In complete contrast, Nina was plump, rosy-faced and cheerful with a mop of bushy black hair. She was much more forthcoming than her colleague, who had made it clear as much by her wooden expression as by the brevity of her answers that she considered her responsibility was to service the rooms and not to concern herself with their occupants. Before Sukey could stop her, Nina offered several titbits about the guests for whose rooms she was responsible: the lady in number 109 was American and left a generous tip every morning; the gentleman in number 110 had slipped – rather furtively, judging from Nina's antics as she attempted to mime his movements – out of number 112 a little before eight o'clock; the couple in number 115 had left the 'Do Not disturb' notice on the door until lunchtime and 'seem very happy' – this information confided in a stage whisper with much eye-rolling and little puffs of laughter.

It was only after several minutes of this performance that Sukey managed to get a word in. In response to her patient probing Nina finally produced an item of significance: a tall gentleman with 'much grey hair' had come up the stairs while she was in the corridor. 'He look first here, then there. Then he go that way,' she explained, energetically waving her chubby arms. 'No, I not see what room he go. No, I not notice time.'

'Was he carrying anything? A bag, for example.'

'I not notice,' the girl repeated. 'I talk to Manuel. He porter,' she added, anticipating the next question.

'Did this gentleman speak to you or Manuel?'

'No.'

'Did you see him again?'

'No.' Nina gave an impatient shake of her bushy head. 'That all? You finish questions?'

'Yes, thank you, Nina. You've been very helpful.' Sukey saw the girl's large brown eyes travel hopefully towards her shoulder bag and she hastily rummaged for some loose change and handed it over. She retraced her steps along the corridor with the intention of giving Verena a similar reward, but there was no sign of her so she began making her way downstairs. Halfway down she met a swarthy young man in hotel livery coming up; on an impulse she stopped him and said, 'Excuse me, is your name Manuel?'

'Yes, madam,' he said. She showed him her warrant card and he nodded. 'You are here about the attack on the gentleman in room 106?' he said, speaking impeccable English but with a strong Spanish accent.

'That's right. You heard about it?'

'Of course. Everyone has heard. It was a terrible thing to happen in this hotel, was it not? How is the gentleman?'

'I'm afraid I don't have that information,' said Sukey and he gave a sad shake of the head. 'But I would like to ask you one or two questions if you'd be kind enough to spare me a few minutes,' she added.

Manuel's face lit up and she guessed that from the moment she showed him her warrant card he had been itching to be asked. He proved to be a useful witness; he told Sukey that while he was talking to Nina some time before twelve o'clock the previous morning a gentleman matching Stephen Lamont's general description had passed them in the corridor. Questioned a little further he confirmed that the man had come up the stairs rather than using the lift and he had appeared to be in a hurry. He apologized at length for being unable to state the exact time but he thought soon after eleven forty-five and certainly well before midday. He also expressed sorrow that, unfortunately, a bend in the corridor had made it impossible to see where the man went. With one hand placed theatrically somewhere in the region of his heart, he swore in language to match the gesture that had he realized the significance of the occurrence, he would have taken steps to obtain this information, but alas...

Sukey thanked him, assured him that he had been very helpful and headed for the incident room. Bob Douglas greeted her with a friendly nod and said, 'Get anything interesting?'

'Could be.' She gave him a brief summary of the three conversations before saying, 'If I can use one of the computers I'll bash out a report right away.'

'No problem. Have that one; Anna's taking an early lunch so she can hold the fort while I'm meeting the press.' He indicated an unoccupied workstation and she sat down and began setting up a new document on the screen. 'Want a coffee?' he added.

'Thanks. White no sugar, please.'

When she had finished she saved her work before printing off a couple of copies and giving one to him. He glanced through it before pinning it up on the board, but made no comment. 'I don't suppose the weapon's turned up?' she said.

'Not a smell so far. The search party's been told to look for a knife with a thin blade, maybe about six inches long. I doubt if they'll find it; my feeling is it's more than likely the killer took it with him. If it was a professional job he's probably keeping it for the next contract.'

Sukey looked at him in surprise. 'Professional? Whatever gave you that idea?'

'Just that academics don't normally carry knives. Just the same, it's pretty obvious that Lamont is Greg Rathbone's prime suspect and no doubt he has his reasons. But why commit murder to get the document when Whistler was going to hand it over?'

'On the face of it, he had a pretty strong motive for making it appear the document had been stolen,' Sukey pointed out. 'We suspect he's got money problems and on his own admission it could be worth a lot in the right quarters.'

Douglas shrugged. 'If you say so. You're the ones who've met the guy. Ah, here's Anna.'

A woman in civilian clothes entered the room and went over to the workstation Sukey had just vacated. 'Anna, this is DC Sukey Reynolds. She's working on the case with DS Rathbone; she's been interviewing some of the staff and I've pinned up her report.'

'Fine,' said Anna. The two women nodded and exchanged smiles. Douglas glanced at his watch. 'It's twenty to – I'd better be going.'

Sukey stayed for a few minutes chatting to Anna, who had worked for the police for several years and been involved in some major crimes. 'So far, there's precious little to go on and Bob and I have been able to cope on our own,' she explained as she ran through the procedure for handling reports and pieces of evidence as they came in. 'Of course, if things start hotting up we may need some extra help.'

'Right, thanks for showing me round,' said Sukey. 'I'll just have a quick word with Ms Henderson and then I'll be on my way.' She went to the reception desk, where Boris Gasspar had just handed a key to a new arrival. As soon as he saw her he stiffened and his eyes narrowed.

'Can I help you?' he said.

His voice was not quite steady but she affected not to notice. 'Good morning, Boris,' she said with a friendly smile. 'I just wanted another word with Ms Henderson; is she in her office?'

He relaxed visibly as he replied, 'Sorry, she has gone to city. You want speak Mr Ashford?'

'Yes, perhaps I should. Will you tell him I'm here?'

'One moment please.' He spoke briefly on the telephone before turning back to Sukey and saying, 'Please go to office.'

Maurice Ashford practically leapt to his feet as Sukey entered. If anything, she remarked later to Greg Rathbone, he seemed almost as jumpy as Boris, although for different reasons.

'How much longer are they going to be here?' he demanded, pointing through the window at the group of uniformed police officers meticulously checking a taped-off section of the car park. On the perimeter of the restricted area a handful of reporters, cameras at the ready, were waiting in groups, doubtless hoping for a chance to record a successful outcome of the search. 'It's most inconvenient, having to direct our guests to park first here and then there,' Ashford continued peevishly. 'It's true most of them have been reasonably co-operative,' he went on without giving her a chance to speak, 'but one or two have made it clear in no uncertain terms that they'll think twice about staying here again. And two families have checked out because their children have been upset. What are they looking for anyway?'

'The weapon used to attack Doctor Whistler or any other piece of evidence that could lead us to his assailant,' she explained patiently.

'What kind of weapon? That other detective who came with you promised you'd keep us informed, but we've heard nothing. We don't even know how the man is. Is he still in hospital? People keep enquiring and we can't give them any satisfactory answers.'

'That information hasn't been officially released yet,' said Sukey, 'but as the Senior Investigating Officer will be making a statement to the press at – ' she glanced at her watch, which stood at two minutes to twelve, and decided to take a chance – 'in fact, within the next couple of minutes. I think I can reveal that Doctor Whistler suffered a fatal stab wound. They're looking for a knife or something similar and it's possible that the attacker discarded it before driving away.'

'You mean he's dead? Stabbed? Oh, how awful! How absolutely shocking!' Ashford shuddered and covered his eyes as if he was reliving the moment when he came on the scene. Remembering the fuss he had made about all the blood, Sukey had a sudden mischievous impulse – hastily repressed – to regale him with the graphic details of Doctor Hanley's provisional findings. 'Now I suppose the press will be pestering us again,' he said gloomily.

'I'm afraid there's nothing we can do to prevent that, but please don't repeat what I have just told you until the news has been officially released – and remind your staff not to give any interviews.'

Ashford nodded. 'Yes, I'll do that right away.'

'Thank you.' She went to the door. 'I'll go now. I just popped in to thank Erika for arranging for me to speak to some of your staff. She's out of the office at the moment so I asked for you. By the way, the people I spoke to were all very helpful,' she added as he made no reply.

'Oh, er, good. Thank you,' said Ashford distractedly.

As she drove slowly towards the exit to the car park the reporters, who moments ago had been hanging listlessly around looking bored, suddenly became a herd that went charging towards the hotel entrance with cameras and microphones at the ready. Evidently the news had reached them via their respective networks, which meant that she no longer needed to feel uneasy about having given it to Maurice Ashford. She drove back to the station in an optimistic mood, little suspecting that before long she would find herself in a potentially far trickier situation.

Seven

Back at the station, Sukey found the occupants of the CID office clustered round a TV screen. Rathbone beckoned her to join them.

'What's going on?' she asked.

'We're just about to run a recording of our meeting with the press,' he said. 'Locals for the most part; the nationals haven't shown much interest so far, but no doubt they will now they know it's a murder hunt.'

The meeting had been brief; DCI Leach revealed that the victim of the attack had died in hospital from massive internal bleeding as the result of a stab wound to the chest.

It was suspected that robbery was the motive, but so far it had not been possible to establish what, if anything, had been taken. The identity of the victim would not be released until the next of kin had been informed. The police were following one or two lines of enquiry but no arrest had so far been made and they were still searching for the weapon. One member of the audience claimed to know that the victim had arranged to meet someone at the hotel that morning. This provoked a barrage of questions: was this true and did the police know who that person was? Did he or she arrive to keep the appointment and was he or she a suspect? These and similar questions were politely but firmly stonewalled, the meeting was declared closed and the reporters hurried away to file their stories.

'So how did you get on?' asked Rathbone as the monitor was switched off and people returned to their desks.

'One possible sighting.' Sukey handed him a copy of her report.

He studied it briefly and then grunted. 'Well, it's something to put to Lamont, I suppose, but it's hardly enough evidence for us to pull him in for a formal interview. We'll show the mugshot to Manuel when we get it, of course. Anything else?'

'Erika Henderson wasn't there, but I had a word with Ashford and reminded him about telling the staff not to talk to the press. In the nick of time, judging from the way the reporters hanging around outside the hotel suddenly came to life and made a beeline for the front entrance.'

Rathbone nodded. 'They probably got texts from their mates at the briefing. I daresay some underlings will step out of line just to get their picture in the paper, but the important thing is to avoid identification of anyone connected with the case. The last thing we want is for Lamont's name to be publicized before we have enough to charge him.'

'You're absolutely sure he's our man?' said Sukey.

'Ninety per cent,' said Rathbone in a matter of fact tone. 'Aren't you?'

She hesitated a moment before saying, 'I still don't understand why, no matter how badly he wanted that document for himself, he had to attack Whistler to get it. I thought the whole point of the meeting was so that he could take it away and study it to see if it was genuine.'

'He must have figured that if he'd collected it as arranged he'd have been obliged to go straight back and show it to his head of faculty, who might even have kept it under lock and key in his own office when Lamont wasn't actually working on it.'

'You're suggesting he set out early with the

deliberate intention of sticking a knife into Whistler, making off with the document and then returning at the appointed time to find his body in the presence of witnesses?'

'Something like that. It wouldn't surprise me if we discover he's a closet collector of ancient documents and artefacts that by rights should be in museums, as he so virtuously pointed out.' Rathbone gave a harsh chuckle. 'It must have been a shaker for him to realize when he and the others went back to Whistler's room that the guy was still alive and might be able to give a description of his attacker.'

'But he knew he was still alive – he heard him groaning and that's why he raised the alarm.'

'So he says. No one else heard it.'

'That's true,' Sukey admitted. 'Just the same, you'd have thought he could have dreamed up something a bit less risky,' she said doubtfully. 'It seems a pretty foolhardy thing for a clever man like Lamont to do.'

Rathbone treated her to a condescending smile that was like a pat on the head.

'My dear girl, when you've been in this job as long as I have you'll know that even hardened villains are capable of doing the most stupid and apparently pointless things. Lamont might be clever at deciphering musty old documents, but I don't think he falls into that category, do you?' He spoke patiently, as if he were speaking to a raw recruit. 'Any more bits of advice to give me?'

Sukey felt her cheeks grow hot under the put-down. She had been about to mention Boris's apparent unease on seeing her that morning, but held her tongue.

After a moment she said, 'What do you want me to do now?'

'It's occurred to me that we've only got Lamont's word for it that the document was the only thing of any value unearthed on Whistler's dig. There might have been other equally valuable stuff that he conveniently forgot to mention. Whistler's luggage has been thoroughly checked, but apart from what appeared to be the latest e-mail from Lamont confirming their appointment we found no reference to anything like that. His wallet with cash and credit cards was in his jacket pocket, together with his passport and airline ticket, but we found nothing else in the way of correspondence. So I've arranged for us to go and see Professor Thorne this afternoon to see if he can recall anything that might be significant.'

The Hellenic Studies Department of the university was located in a leafy square a short distance from the main campus. It occupied two former private houses knocked into one, each doubtless once owned by wealthy merchants who had over several centuries contributed to the city's importance both as a port and a centre of trade and industry.

A sign on a door in the entrance hall read Enquiries; DS Rathbone marched in without knocking and informed the middle-aged blonde behind the desk that he and DC Reynolds had an appointment with Professor Thorne. Her expression was almost disdainful as she scrutinized their warrant cards before picking up a telephone and announcing their arrival in a deferential voice. She put the phone down and said, with another noticeable change of tone, 'Professor Thorne will see you now. His office is on the first floor at the end of the corridor.'

'Quite the little ray of sunshine,' Rathbone remarked to Sukey as they climbed the stone staircase. On reaching the landing he cast an appraising glance around and commented, 'I can't think why they use these old buildings; they must be hellishly inconvenient to work in – and cost a fortune to heat in winter,' he added a trifle waspishly. Sukey made no comment; she sensed that it was frustration at the lack of progress in the enquiry that was making him irritable. Meanwhile, she paused for a few seconds at the top of the stairs, mentally contrasting the sickly green walls lined with notice boards, the cold neon lighting and the grubby, uncurtained windows with the unashamed opulence of the

Gaddens' house. Both buildings dated from approximately the same period, but they might almost belong to different worlds.

'Come on, let's not hang around,' Rathbone said impatiently. He led the way along the corridor towards a door on which was painted in gold lettering, Professor Archibald Thorne, Head of Department. This time he knocked, but opened the door and entered without waiting for a response.

The man who rose from behind the desk to receive them presented a striking contrast to Stephen Lamont, being short, on the portly side and almost completely bald. Everything about him seemed colourless, from his grey flannel suit to his pallid features and pale eyes behind the rimless glasses that were perched precariously on his small sharp nose. But his voice when he greeted them was surprisingly resonant, and his manner as he waved them to the chairs placed conveniently in front of his desk was brisk and authoritative.

'This is a terrible, terrible business,' he said after the formalities had been exchanged. 'Everyone in the department was greatly concerned to hear of the attack on Doctor Whistler – and then we heard on the midday news that he has died.' He assumed a mournful expression and gave a sorrowful shake of the head. 'It's difficult to believe that these things can happen in a civilized country. Have you any idea at all who did it, Sergeant?'

'It's early days yet, but we're following one or two leads,' said Rathbone. 'When we find the weapon it will take us a big step forward.'

'Quite so.' Thorne cleared his throat. 'I must say, Lamont was particularly distressed at being interviewed a second time,' he continued with an air of mild reproach. 'I'm sure you find it necessary to question everyone very closely, but after the shock of finding Whistler it was a considerable ordeal for him. And before we go any further,' he said before either Rathbone or Sukey had a chance to speak, 'I have known him for many years and in my opinion he is the last person who would commit an act of violence.'

'Thank you, sir, we'll bear that in mind,' said Rathbone.

'Needless to say,' Thorne added, 'you can rely on my complete co-operation, and that of my staff, in your efforts to bring the perpetrator of this monstrous crime to justice.'

'Thank you, sir, that's much appreciated. If you don't mind, I'd like to run over the details of this case from the beginning.'

Thorne nodded. 'Yes, of course, although I fear I can add little to what Stephen Lamont has already told you.'

'Just checking that nothing significant has been overlooked, sir. I understand that Doctor Whistler's initial approach was to you

85

personally. Were you and he already acquainted?'

'No, not at all.'

'Have you any idea why he should have approached you?'

It seemed to Sukey that a hint of self-importance crept into Thorne's manner as he replied, 'Presumably because he knew me by reputation.'

'But I understand you asked Professor Lamont to handle it rather than deal with it yourself.'

Thorne nodded. 'It seemed the obvious thing to do, given the nature of the enquiry. In addition to his specialized knowledge of classical Greek, Lamont has a particular interest in the apocryphal epistles of Saint Paul – that is, letters attributed to him by scholars but for various reasons never included with his other writings in the New Testament. In addition, it is generally believed that others exist but have been lying undiscovered for centuries. In his letter, Doctor Whistler stated that he believed he had found one such document and wanted it subjected to expert examination.'

'Did you reply to the letter yourself, or did you hand the whole matter over to Professor Lamont and ask him to deal with it?'

'I acknowledged the letter and informed Doctor Whistler of the action I had taken.'

'And you then handed the letter over to

Professor Lamont?'

'I gave him a photocopy, together with a copy of my reply.' Thorne picked up a folder lying on his desk and offered it to Rathbone. 'The originals are here if you would like to see them. Naturally, I asked to be kept fully informed so you will also find in here copies of all the emails and notes of telephone conversations that were exchanged between Lamont and Whistler.'

'Thank you.' Rathbone took the folder but made no attempt to open it. 'Apart from yourself, and presumably your secretary, who else might have seen this correspondence?'

Thorne frowned. 'It's difficult to say. I'm out of my office quite a lot and if any messages arrive in my absence my secretary puts them on my desk.'

'What about callers – for example, colleagues or people from other departments?' Sukey asked. 'Presumably they leave their queries and so on with her if you're not here.'

'Sometimes, but my door is never locked during the day and it's not unusual, for example in the case of a minor or non-urgent query, for a note to be left in my in-tray.'

'So any one of a number of people might have seen some or any of the correspondence relating to Doctor Whistler's visit?'

Thorne shrugged. 'I suppose so, but I can't see...'

'It would be helpful if you could ask your secretary to make a list of everyone who has access to this office during the day and fax it through to us,' said Rathbone. 'And if you have no objection we should like to take this – ' he indicated with the folder – 'back to the station so that we can study the contents in detail. We will of course give you a receipt.'

Thorne frowned. 'I am reluctant to allow a file to leave the department,' he said.

'Perhaps your secretary could provide us with photocopies?' Sukey suggested.

'Good idea,' said Rathbone. He handed the folder to Sukey and tilted his head in the direction of a door to the left of Thorne's desk. 'Is that her office?'

Looking slightly displeased at having the initiative taken from him, Thorne said, 'Oh, very well. I'll just—' He pushed back his chair, at the same time holding out his hand to take back the folder.

'No need to disturb yourself, sir,' said Rathbone quietly.

Sukey, who had read his thoughts, was already on her feet. She quickly crossed the room, tapped on the door and opened it. A slim, attractive woman with dark hair falling in glossy waves on either side of her face was standing at an open filing cabinet. On the desk behind her a telephone handset lay beside its cradle; evidently she was in the act of dealing with a query.

She turned as Sukey entered and said, 'Yes? What is it?' in a voice suggesting she resented the intrusion.

'DC Reynolds, Bristol CID.' Sukey held up her warrant card.

The woman picked up the handset and said, 'I'll call you back,' before replacing it. She turned back to Sukey and said sharply, 'What do you want?'

'Detective Sergeant Rathbone and I are enquiring into the murder of Doctor Edwin Whistler,' Sukey explained. 'Professor Thorne has very kindly agreed to our having copies of all the relevant correspondence that passed through this department. Would you be kind enough...?' She held out the folder.

The woman's attitude appeared to soften. 'Oh ... yes, of course, I'll do them as soon as I've finished dealing with this query. It'll only take a minute. Leave it on my desk and I'll bring them in when they're ready.'

'That's all right, I'll wait,' said Sukey. The woman hesitated, then shrugged, went over to the machine and in a resentful silence ran off a copy of each document as Sukey passed it to her. When she had finished she put them in an envelope and handed it over before returning to the filing cabinet, ignoring Sukey's polite expression of thanks.

As the detectives returned to their car after taking their leave of Thorne, Rathbone said casually, 'I've no reason to suppose he'd have held back anything in that file before getting the copies made, but well done for beating him to the draw.'

'Thanks.' Sukey clipped on her seatbelt and turned on the ignition. 'Do you think we'll find anything interesting?'

'I doubt it, but we have to show that we've covered every possibility. Go through that lot with a toothcomb and make a detailed record of every item. If anything particular strikes you, let me know. And when that fax comes through, have a word with everyone who's on it. Which reminds me, Lamont was supposed to let me have a similar list. I'll give him a nudge when we get back.' With that, he settled back in his seat, closed his eyes and said nothing more until they arrived at the station.

It was with a vague feeling of disappointment that Sukey returned home that evening. Her search through Thorne's file had yielded nothing of any apparent significance, the weapon used to kill Whistler had still not been found and it would be some time before the results of forensic tests on Lamont's clothing became available. The initial excitement of being for the first time at the cutting edge of a murder enquiry had begun to wear off and she recalled a comment Jim Castle had once made about the periods of boredom and frustration that characterized detective work. A little wearily, she pushed open her front door, gathered up the day's post and carried it into the kitchen with the shopping she had done on the way home. She cheered herself up with the thought that it was Saturday tomorrow and Fergus would be arriving in the morning for a two-night stay.

She put the kettle on for a cup of tea, stowed the food items away and sorted through the letters. Among them was a brief handwritten note reading, 'Would you give me a call when you get home? Please treat as urgent. Priscilla.' The last words were underlined in red.

With a sense of apprehension, Sukey tapped out the number scribbled beneath the signature. Her call was answered immediately.

'Oh Sukey, I'm so thankful you're back,' Priscilla almost gasped. 'Can you possibly come round right away? I've got Hester Lamont here, in a terrible state. She keeps saying her brother killed that man in the hotel and it's all her fault.'

Eight

The Gaddens' daughter Patsy opened the door. In contrast to her somewhat bizarre appearance of the previous evening she wore little make-up and wore well-fitting jeans and a T-shirt that flattered her young figure. Instead of greeting Sukey in her earlier off-hand, almost hostile manner she smiled a welcome.

'Mum will be so relieved you're here,' she said. 'She's in the television room with Hester. She's completely batty, of course – Hester, I mean,' she added in a breathy whisper. 'My dad reckons she must cost her brother a fortune in visits to the funny farm. They're in here.' She opened a door leading off the hall and ushered Sukey into a cosy room furnished with little more than a few comfortable chairs arranged in a semi-circle in front of a large modern television set. 'Would you like some tea?'

'Thank you.'

'I've made one lot but it'll be stewed by now. I'll make a fresh pot.'

On a low table in the centre of the room

was a tray of used tea-things. Patsy picked it up and went out, closing the door softly behind her.

Priscilla was sitting on a low stool in front of one of the chairs, holding the hand of a small figure with bowed shoulders and straight, mouse-brown hair hanging limply on either side of pale, nondescript features. As Sukey approached she gave the hand a gentle tug and said quietly, 'Hester, I want you to meet my neighbour, the one I've been telling you about. I think she may be able to help you.'

'No one can help me,' Hester replied without raising her head. She spoke in a monotone, like someone in a trance. 'I'm wicked. I'm the one who should have died.'

Sukey crouched down beside Priscilla and said quietly, 'Why do you say you're wicked? What have you done?'

There was a long silence. Sukey was about to repeat her question when Hester straightened up and looked directly at her.

'Are you the police?' she said fearfully.

Instinctively, Sukey prevaricated. 'Do you want to talk to the police?'

'Pris said you could help me.'

'I'll try. What's the problem?'

'I know I ought to go to the police, but I daren't. Stephen would never forgive me. He's in enough trouble with them as it is and it's all my fault.'

'Stephen?'

'My brother. He's looked after me since...' Her voice broke and a few slow tears trickled down her colourless cheeks.

'Would you like to tell me about it?'

'I'll try.'

'Just take your time.'

At this point Patsy appeared with a tray. She set it down on the table and began pouring out tea. She served first Sukey, then her mother, and finally offered a cup to Hester, who accepted it with shaking hands and a whispered word of thanks.

Patsy quietly left the room and for a while the three women sipped their tea in silence. There came into Sukey's mind a piece of advice that DC Vicky Armstrong had given her during her probationary period: "Be patient with a genuinely nervous witness; avoid pressurising; build up confidence gradually." So she drank her tea slowly, never taking her gaze from Hester's face and giving a nod and a smile of encouragement every time their eyes met. She was struck by the contrast between brother and sister – the former well-built, handsome, confident to the point of arrogance, the latter frail, timid and pathetic looking. The hackneyed phrase 'scared of her own shadow' might have been coined with Hester Lamont in mind.

After what seemed an eternity, Hester finished her tea, placed her empty cup on the tray and spoke again in the same expressionless voice.

'Stephen would never have taken that knife if it wasn't for me. He would never have needed all that money and he wouldn't have killed that man if I hadn't caused him so much trouble.' She hid her face in her hands and began to cry in a series of jerky, heart-rending sobs that threatened to rip her slight body apart. Priscilla stood up and put an arm round her shoulders and Sukey took hold of both her hands, while between them they soothed and persuaded and reassured until at last the paroxysm ceased and she sat quietly weeping into the handkerchief that Priscilla gave her. Eventually she turned to Sukey and said in a small, quavering voice, 'Please tell me, what should I do?'

'Why don't you tell me exactly what happened?' said Sukey.

Hester bit her lip, hesitated for a moment, then slowly and deliberately undid the cuff of her long-sleeved shirt and pushed it up, exposing her arm from wrist to elbow. It bore the scars of several wounds, one clumsily bandaged and still oozing blood. 'This,' she said simply.

Priscilla gave a horrified gasp. 'You mean Ste—' she began, but just in time she caught Sukey's urgent gesture and bit back the words.

'You made those cuts yourself, didn't you?'

95

said Sukey quietly. Hester nodded. 'Because you feel badly about something you've done?' Another nod. 'When did it start?' Silence. 'Just lately?' A shake of the head. 'A long time ago?' Another nod. 'And Stephen caught you with the knife and took it away from you?' This time the only reaction was a gaze of stark misery. 'Do you want to tell us about it?'

It was several seconds before she got a response. Then Hester whispered, 'You won't tell Stephen I told you?'

'Not if you don't want us to.'

It was a sadly familiar tale of a young and impressionable woman carried away by the persuasive charm of a dashing, romantic lover who, despite swearing eternal devotion, had abandoned her on learning that she was to bear his child. Torn between the need to confess her predicament to her brother – her sole relative after the death of their parents in an air disaster some years previously – and having a secret abortion, she had chosen the latter course. Racked with grief and guilt, she had suffered a nervous breakdown and ever since had been in the care of counsellors and psychiatrists.

'Stephen never liked Wayne and all he could say when he left me was that I was better off without him,' she said miserably when the pitiful saga came to an end. 'He had no idea about the baby; he just thought

96

I was being feeble and sorry for myself and he got impatient with me until the doctor convinced him that I was ill and needed help. Poor Stephen; I've been a millstone round his neck for such a long time. All that money he's had to find for treatment ... and he lost the woman he wanted to marry because he couldn't leave me and she wouldn't have me to live with them. I should have made the cuts deeper ... maybe then I'd have died and been no more trouble to him.' More tears threatened to engulf her.

Sukey took one of her small, fragile hands in both hers. 'You mustn't think like that,' she said urgently. 'It wouldn't have solved anything. You have more important things to think of now. Tell me, what made you say your brother killed that man?'

'It was when the police came for his clothes.' A noticeable change came over Hester; obviously, speaking of recent, tangible events came more easily than reliving the tragedy of her past. 'I'd already washed them because of the stain on the safari jacket he was wearing that day, but it didn't wash out so it must have been blood.'

'Where do you think the blood came from?'

'From the knife, of course – the one he used to kill the man.'

'Why do you suppose he killed him?'

'For the valuable things he'd brought with

him, of course.'

'What valuable things?'

'Holy things like an ancient document and relics from an old church in Rhodes. Stephen's very clever,' Hester continued proudly. 'He knows Classical Greek and he's a famous biblical scholar. He tried to teach me Greek once but I'm too stupid – I could never remember anything after Alpha, Beta, Gamma, Delta.' She gave a shy, nervous giggle. 'Isn't it funny how a brother and sister can be so different?'

'Tell us more about the valuable things,' Sukey said patiently.

'Stephen didn't tell me much except he thought they must be worth a lot of money. At the time he didn't seem all that interested in the ancient relics, although he was very excited about the document. Afterwards he must have decided to steal them so he could sell them to pay for my treatment. I suppose the man caught him in the act and that's why he killed him.' She sat back with an air of weary resignation.

'That knife,' Sukey said gently. 'Are you saying Stephen took it to the meeting with this man with the deliberate intention of killing him?'

Hester shook her head in evident bewilderment. 'All I know is that he put it in his pocket when he took it away from me. Perhaps that's what gave him the idea. He'll go

98

to prison and it's all my fault.' Once again, grief and guilt threatened to overwhelm her and it was some minutes before she was calm enough to speak again.

When at last the storm subsided she said in a pathetic whisper, 'Now you know everything but please, please don't tell him I've told you.'

'Of course we won't,' Priscilla said gently, 'but I expect he'll be worried about you and wondering where you've gone. You look cold. Let me put this round you.' She took a rug from one of the empty chairs and draped it round Hester's shoulders and across her lap. 'Just rest quietly for a little while and then I'll take you home.' She made a sign to Sukey and they both went out of the room. Moving away from the door, she said in a low voice, 'What are you going to do?'

Sukey shrugged. 'I've got no choice. I have to report this.'

'You surely don't believe her brother killed this man?'

'Whether I believe it or not has nothing to do with it. What Hester has told us could be important evidence.'

'But she's unbalanced ... she obviously has a history of mental instability.'

'That doesn't mean she was making everything up.'

'No, I suppose not, but what if she has to be interviewed? It wouldn't take much to tip her over the edge. Do you know the detectives who are conducting the enquiry?'

Once again Sukey avoided giving a direct answer. 'Don't worry, I'll make sure they understand she'll need very careful handling.'

'What about the abortion and everything? Do they have to know that?'

Sukey hesitated. 'I'll have to mention the self-harm because of the knife. Maybe not the reason for it, for the time being at any rate.'

'I suppose that's something,' said Priscilla. She gave a despairing sigh. 'Oh, dear, I'm beginning to wish I hadn't asked you to come. Nothing personal,' she added hastily, putting an apologetic hand on Sukey's arm, 'and thank you very much anyway. I was at my wits' end wondering what to do with her. First she was going to the police, then said she daren't because her brother would be furious ... I just thought you—'

'You did the right thing.'

'Do you think they'll want to question me?' said Priscilla.

'I'm afraid so, and if you find out anything else after I've left, will you please be sure to tell them?'

Priscilla sighed. 'All right. What do you think I should say to her brother when I take her home?'

'I suggest you say she was so distressed at

the thought he might be a suspect that she turned to you for comfort. And please be sure to keep my name out of it.'

'If you say so.'

'It's important.' Sukey edged towards the front door. 'Look, I must go now,' she said. 'I have to make a note of everything Hester told us. You do realize, don't you, that I won't be able to answer any questions about the investigation from now on?'

The bus from Cheltenham arrived on time the following morning. Fergus flung his bulging holdall into the boot of Sukey's car, settled into the passenger seat, gave his mother a peck on the cheek and said, 'Hi Mum, how's the murder hunt going?'

'What murder hunt?' she asked cautiously.

'The stabbing in the hotel. It was in the late edition of the *Gloucester Gazette* yesterday. Are you involved in it?'

'I am, as it happens, but I'm not sure I ought to tell you about it.'

'Oh, come on, Mum, you know you can trust me. I might even be able to give you some tips on solving it,' he added. 'We had our first lecture on criminal psychology on Thursday.'

'Oh, well, the case is as good as solved,' she said dryly. 'If anything breaks over the weekend I'll refer the SIO to you.'

'Seriously though, you will give me the

gory details, won't you?'

She gave a resigned sigh. 'Knowing you, you'll give me no peace until I do.'

When they were back at her flat she prepared coffee and croissants while outlining the details of the case that had not so far been released to the press and the events of the previous evening.

'So far as I know we haven't been able to contact Whistler's next of kin, which is why his name hasn't been released,' she said. 'And Hester Lamont's reference to other treasures confirms what Greg Rathbone already suspects, that he was carrying items of considerably greater value than the Pauline epistle.'

'So you reckon you've got your killer?'

'It certainly looks like it, although there's no evidence so far that would stand up in court.'

'All purely circumstantial, and Hester would hardly make a reliable witness,' Fergus pointed out. 'The thing is, do *you* think he's guilty?'

'I see no reason to doubt it, but—'

'You've got one of your famous hunches?' her son suggested slyly.

'Not exactly, but I can't help thinking it all looks a bit too obvious.'

'I suppose you were hoping to come up with a sensational new lead, solve the crime single-handed and get a commendation from the Chief Constable,' he teased her.

She laughed. 'Hardly. Anyway, I'm sure Greg Rathbone will be delighted when he sees my report. He's been sure from the word go that Lamont's our man.'

'Never mind, Mum.' He gave her a consoling pat on the arm. 'Your chance will come.'

Nine

Having emailed over to the incident room her report on her encounter with Hester Lamont, Sukey was half expecting to receive a call from Greg Rathbone, if for no other reason than to express his triumph at the apparent confirmation of his suspicion that, in addition to the Pauline epistle, Whistler had been carrying items of possibly far greater value. But Saturday ended and Sunday came and went without any word from him.

As Fergus got out of the car at the bus station where she dropped him on Monday morning en route for work, he said, 'So long, Mum, thanks for a great weekend and I hope you get brownie points for having turned up valuable evidence.'

'It would be nice to think so, but what

Hester told me is only hearsay – it would never be admitted in court,' she said. 'Still, it could be a useful opening. It'll be interesting to see how Greg Rathbone handles it.' She leaned across the empty passenger seat and they exchanged a brief parting kiss before he shut the door. 'Take care, Gus; see you soon.'

On arrival at the police station she was met at the door by Rathbone who tossed her the keys to one of the pool cars and said, 'We're going straight to the incident room at the hotel. A few interesting bits of information from the public came in over the weekend.'

He did not speak again until they were in the car and heading out of the city centre. Then he said, with obvious satisfaction, 'Told you there'd be more stuff than one grotty old bit of parchment, didn't I?'

'You did indeed, Sarge.'

'And you'll be pleased to know that the team has turned up another nugget, this time from one Mrs Potter, a very chatty widow who lives round the corner from Lamont and acts as a sort of part-time cook-housekeeper for him and his sister. She happened to answer the door when PC Lucy Jennings called to pick up the clothes and while she was making out a receipt Mrs P made some interesting comments about how upset the sister was at what had happened and how worried he was about the effect on her mental state. Her actual words were, "what she might do to herself", which ties in with what you found out.'

'I take it Hester herself didn't appear?'

'No, and unfortunately at that moment a man turned up to fix the boiler, which meant end of conversation. Anyway, tell me more about your friend – the one who asked you round to talk to Lamont's sister.'

'Her name's Priscilla Gadden. She's not exactly a friend – I mean, I don't know her all that well. She lives just up the road from me and she invited me to the party she and her husband gave last Thursday.'

'Does she know you're a police officer?'

'Oh, yes. I imagine everyone in Sherman Close knew before I moved in. It's the kind of neighbourhood when things get around; I happened to mention it to the woman who sold me the flat and no doubt she passed it on.'

'Did you tell her you're working on the case?'

'No, and I've managed so far to avoid letting anyone else know, but before I left after talking to Hester I made it clear I'd have to report everything that passed between us. Incidentally, Priscilla was concerned that she might be questioned and I told her it couldn't be ruled out. And before you ask, I made a particular point of asking her not to mention my name in connection with the case.'

'You reckon she'll take any notice?'

Sukey shrugged. 'I hope so. She doesn't strike me as a gossip, but I expect she'll tell her husband, and the daughter knows I was there although she wasn't in the room while we were talking.'

'What about Hester Lamont? Does she know you're a copper?'

'Definitely not. At first she thought I might be and hastened to tell me she knew she should talk to the police but was afraid to. It seems she went rushing round to Priscilla in a state of hysteria saying her brother had committed the Mariners Hotel murder. Priscilla couldn't think what to do so she turned to me for advice. She introduced me to Hester as "someone who might be able to help her", that's all.'

'I see.' Rathbone, as was his habit, closed his eyes and remained silent until they were turning into the hotel car park. Then he said, 'I'd like to keep you on the case if possible, but we'll have to tread carefully. I'll show your report to DCI Leach and see what he thinks. D'you reckon Hester will tell her brother about meeting you?'

'I should think it's the last thing she'd do. She begged us not to let him know she'd told us her story. I got the impression she's scared of him.'

Rathbone grunted. 'We already know he's

an arrogant bastard,' he commented as he got out of the car and slammed the door, 'and he's quite likely a bully as well. The fact that his sister didn't dare tell him about her pregnancy says a lot.'

'He obviously cares about her, judging by what she says about the trouble he's taken to get treatment for her,' Sukey pointed out.

'Think of the expense he's incurred along the way,' he reminded her. 'The proceeds of a few valuable artefacts could pay for quite a lot of visits to a shrink.'

They were admitted through the staff entrance by the officer on duty and went straight to the incident room, where they found DS Douglas studying the notice board while Anna sat working at her computer.

'Anything fresh?' asked Rathbone.

'Apart from the bits I've already mentioned, nothing significant,' said Douglas. He handed some computer printouts to Rathbone, who studied them for a few minutes without speaking before passing them to Sukey. Three members of the public had reported possible sightings of Stephen Lamont: one a Mr Busbridge who had noticed someone answering to his description hurrying across the car park and getting into a car at around the time Boris claimed to have seen him leave, and two women who had been waiting in reception for a taxi at the crucial time and who believed him to be a man they had seen arrive, go to the desk and then 'go haring up the stairs' as one of them described it. They also saw him come rushing down again a few minutes later, but at that moment their taxi arrived and they left.

'And that's it?' said Rathbone.

'More or less.' Douglas showed him a list. 'These are from people who "thought they saw someone acting suspiciously", but when questioned were obviously so wide of the mark they were hardly worth logging. Oh, and the manager's PA came in a few minutes ago to say that when she went out to her car on Saturday, young Boris what's-his-name was outside the staff entrance having what sounded like a furious argument with someone on his mobile.'

'Any idea what it was about?'

Douglas grinned. 'Not a clue. She said he was talking in a foreign language, which I presume was Albanian.'

Rathbone shrugged. 'It was probably nothing. These types get so excited ... They were probably talking about a match between their rival football clubs.' He glanced at Sukey. 'Want to raise anything about those statements?' he asked.

What she really wanted to do was challenge him about what he meant by 'these types', but instead she said, 'There's nothing in Mr Busbridge's statement about the kind of car the man he saw was driving. I take it that's because he didn't give any details?'

'I took the call,' said Anna, 'and naturally I asked that question, but he'd just pulled into a space and was getting his stuff out of the boot when the guy appeared. First he thought it might have been dark coloured, then he changed his mind and asked me to scrub that out because he wasn't sure. And he had no idea of the make or the registration number. And he didn't notice whether the man drove off straight away either.'

'Well, it's another presumed sighting, I suppose,' Rathbone commented, a trifle grudgingly, 'but it doesn't take us very far forward.'

'The timing's right,' Douglas said. 'I checked on the desk and Busbridge filled in his registration form a few minutes after Boris saw Lamont leave. We managed to trace the taxi driver and the time he arrived to pick the women up tallies with the time Erika Henderson says Lamont came to the desk to say he thought Whistler was ill.'

'That's good.' Rathbone appeared marginally less gloomy at this piece of information. He took the printouts from Sukey and gave them another cursory glance before handing them back to Douglas. 'Well, we'd better get back to the station. I've sent someone to pick up Lamont and bring him in for another interview. We'll have this one on tape.'

109

★ ★ ★

Stephen Lamont had brought his solicitor, John Goodacre, to the interview. Sukey guessed his age at about forty; he had sleek brown hair, smooth, unlined pink cheeks and a perfect set of white, even teeth, all of which contributed to a slightly ingenuous appearance that was belied by his crisp, businesslike manner and the shrewd expression in his light brown eyes.

As soon as the formalities were over and the tape was running, he said, 'I should like to begin by making it clear that my client categorically denies any involvement in the death of Doctor Edwin Whistler, he has told you all he knows about the case and he is at a total loss to understand why he should have been brought here for further questioning.'

'You have made your client's position perfectly clear,' said Rathbone. He switched his gaze to Lamont, who was lolling back in his chair with his legs crossed and his hands clasped round one knee. 'So, Professor Lamont,' he continued, 'we are to conclude that after careful reflection there is nothing you wish to add to your earlier statements?'

'Are you asking me to repeat what Mr Goodacre has just said?' asked Lamont, with more than a hint of insolence.

'Just answer my question please, sir,' said Rathbone.

'All right, you may conclude that I have nothing I wish to add.'

'So you had no idea that in addition to the ancient document Doctor Whistler wanted you to authenticate he was carrying some valuable artefacts also recovered from the dig on Rhodes?'

Rathbone spoke slowly and deliberately, never taking his eyes from Lamont's face. Sukey watched in fascination as the expression of lofty disdain on the classical features gave way to a blend of consternation and disbelief. She saw Goodacre's head turn sharply and saw his mouth open as if he was about to request a word in private with his client, but if that had been his intention he had no chance to say so. Lamont banged a fist on the table and almost shouted, 'Where did you get that idea? Who have you been talking to?'

'Please answer the question, sir,' Rathbone said again.

This time Goodacre intervened before Lamont answered. His request for a brief suspension of the interview was granted and the pair were escorted from the room.

The minute they were gone Rathbone rubbed his hands together in glee. 'That knocked the toffee-nosed bugger off his high horse, didn't it?' he gloated.

'Are you going to tell him it was his sister who told on him, Sarge?' Sukey asked uncomfortably.

'Only if I have to – but it's more than likely he'll guess. Serve him right for boasting about what a clever boy he is.'

'Do you suppose he mentioned these artefacts to Thorne?'

'Shouldn't think so, or Thorne would have said.' A barely detectable hesitation before Rathbone answered made Sukey suspect that it was a point that had not occurred to him, but if that were the case he was not going to admit it. 'I take it you didn't find anything in the file to make you think information was being withheld?' he added.

'Absolutely nothing. Not that there was any reason to think there might be, although I hadn't had that meeting with Hester at the time.'

'It wouldn't do any harm to have another look through it. Ah, here they come.'

It was a somewhat chastened Lamont who took his seat and listened passively as Goodacre said, 'My client has agreed to answer your questions in full, while reaffirming his total lack of responsibility for Doctor Whistler's murder.'

'Thank you.' Rathbone leaned forward and propped his chin on one hand. 'So Doctor Whistler did tell you about these additional valuable items I referred to earlier?'

'He did mention them, yes,' Lamont said tonelessly.

'Did he say what they were?'

'There was a gold crucifix, some ornaments and a small jewelled casket that he thought might be a reliquary. It seems there's a local legend that after the saint's death some fragments of his bones were taken back to Rhodes.'

'I don't know a great deal about antiquities,' said Rathbone, 'but as the site of this dig is on Greek territory, wouldn't the correct procedure have been, in the case of such apparently valuable items, to hand them over to the Greek authorities?'

'I suppose it might. The document was the only item that directly concerned me and Whistler assured me he had permission to bring it to England for examination.'

'So why do you suppose he brought the other items?'

Lamont shook his head. 'I've no idea – unless it was to have them valued.'

'Right.' Rathbone sat back in his chair and waited for a few moments before saying, 'Why didn't you tell us all this at the outset?' in a tone that reminded Sukey of a kindly schoolmaster encouraging a pupil to own up to some minor misdemeanour.

Lamont looked uncomfortable, almost embarrassed. He glanced at the solicitor, who nodded. 'The fact is, I have had some financial problems lately. I was afraid that if you knew Whistler was carrying a lot of valuable stuff you'd start prying into my affairs and find out—' He broke off and for the first time showed signs of emotional stress. 'Do I have to tell you everything?' he said. 'You have my word that it's got nothing to do with the case and there's nothing shady or underhanded about it. It's just ... very personal.'

'Unfortunately, when a serious crime has been committed it's not always possible to respect personal feelings.' In a sudden change of manner, Rathbone sat upright and spoke in a hard, measured tone, emphasizing each point by jabbing with a forefinger on the table. 'Professor Lamont, you have informed us that you arrived late for your appointment with Doctor Whistler whereas we have witnesses who saw you leaving the hotel by a side entrance a good fifteen minutes earlier; you attributed your later arrival first to heavy traffic and then to a delayed departure from the college; you declined to take part in an identity parade; you disclaimed knowledge of the items of value that Whistler was carrying whereas we now know that was a lie, and you admit that you are in need of money. You knew those items would be worth a small fortune to a collector and I suggest you saw them as a way out of your financial difficulties. Perhaps you hoped to persuade Whistler to let you take charge of them for valuation purposes and later fake a robbery and sell them to an unscrupulous dealer. So, far from arriving late for your appointment you arrived early, but you didn't go to the desk because you already knew Whistler's room number from your latest conversation with him. No doubt he was ready to hand over the document that started this whole thing going, but not the other items. Maybe he'd already made arrangements to entrust them to someone else – unfortunately he is not in a position to tell us. But you were determined to have them; you were desperate; you happened to have a knife in your pocket and when he refused to hand them over you lashed out with it and fatally stabbed him before grabbing them and making off. You didn't dare leave by the front entrance so you slipped out through the staff door and returned shortly afterwards, announced your arrival to the desk clerk, went up to Whistler's room and came dashing down a few minutes later with that cock and bull story about him being taken ill.'

Throughout this recital Lamont had been sitting with a dazed expression on his face, slowly shaking his head from side to side. When Rathbone mentioned the knife his mouth fell open and he cast a despairing glance at Goodacre, who appeared for the moment equally nonplussed. It was, however, the latter who recovered first.

'This is quite preposterous, Sergeant!' he exclaimed. 'Why on earth would my client "happen" to have a knife in his pocket?'

'It was the knife he'd taken from his sister,' said Rathbone. He turned back to Lamont. 'That's right, isn't it, sir?'

Before Lamont had a chance to speak, Goodacre put a hand on his arm.

'My client has nothing further to say at this stage,' he said.

Ten

'We'll let him stew for a while,' said Rathbone as he and Sukey returned to the CID office, leaving a glum Stephen Lamont closeted with his solicitor. 'We haven't got enough to charge him yet, of course, but he's obviously badly rattled and I don't reckon he'll enjoy his lunch.'

'It seems to me,' said Sukey, 'that one of the weaknesses in our case is that no one's come forward to say they saw him arrive at the hotel the first time.'

Rathbone, who was obviously in an optimistic mood, brushed the objection aside with a gesture. 'My guess is that someone will before long. It's early days yet – you have to learn to be patient in this job,' he added with the now familiar touch of condescension that Sukey was beginning to find irksome. 'What's more significant is that he hasn't been able to produce anyone to confirm his story about leaving late after his Greek class on the morning of the murder. The woman in charge of the office found the register in his pigeonhole but she had no idea what time he put it there.'

'It's a bit like that in colleges,' Sukey commented. 'People are coming and going all the time and no one takes much notice of them. By the way, will the bloodstains on the clothing be any help, do you think?'

'We'll have to wait for the report from forensics.'

'What I mean is, will they yield DNA after washing?'

For the second time that morning, Rathbone took a fraction of a second before replying, 'It probably depends on what temperature the sister washed them at – but he's not to know that, is he?'

'No, I suppose not. When do you suppose we'll get the mugshots?'

'They shouldn't take too long. Ah, what have we here?' He stopped speaking as a uniformed officer entered and handed him an envelope.

'The montage you asked for, Sarge.'

Rathbone opened the envelope and scanned the contents. 'Great, you managed to get him from several angles. I see they've lined up a load of prize villains to slot him in with,' he added, grinning.

The officer grinned back. 'Cream of the county force, Sarge.'

Rathbone handed the photos and the envelope to Sukey. 'There's your next job. Take these out to the hotel, show them to DS Douglas, and then go with him to see if Boris and the other guy who thought he'd spotted Lamont can pick him out.' He glanced at his watch. 'I'm giving our friend until two; that means you've got comfortable time to get there and back before we see him again. If you get a positive ID out of them we'll be well on the way to getting the case sewn up. Meanwhile, I'm going to have another word with Professor Thorne to see if he's remembered anything else that might be important.'

'Right, Sarge,' said Sukey.

You mean you're going to quiz him on the point you didn't think to raise until I mentioned it, she thought to herself with a little inward glow of satisfaction.

'By the way,' she added, 'is someone taking care of Hester? I notice Lamont hasn't expressed any concern about her, which seems a bit odd.'

'We left a Family Liaison Officer with her

118

when we went to pick him up and he seemed reasonably satisfied with the arrangement. She'll stay until he gets home – unless of course we're in a position to detain him today. In that case we'll have to consult her doctor about arrangements for her welfare, but so far the FLO reports that she seems almost unnaturally calm, even resigned to the fact that her brother's going to be charged with murder. We've stressed the importance of making sure there aren't any knives lying around and explained that if they want anything to eat the helpful Mrs Potter has promised to see to it. OK? On your way, then.'

After checking with Erika Henderson that Boris and Manuel were both on duty, Sukey set out for the Mariners Hotel. It was a bright early autumn day and as she left the city behind her she was struck afresh by the abundance of open country that lay on its doorstep and the patches of richly coloured foliage along the way. After living for so many years with views of the Cotswolds from her back garden, she had had reservations about living in an urban environment; to find so much natural beauty within easy reach had gone some way to make up for what she had left behind.

The car park was less full than on her earlier visit with Rathbone and she was able to park fairly close to the staff entrance. The police guard had been removed, but like all the officers working on the case she had been issued with the key code and was able to go straight in. She went first to the incident room, where DS Douglas and his civilian assistant were seated at their respective computers.

'Back already?' he said. 'How did the interview with Lamont go?'

'It's been suspended until this afternoon. DS Rathbone is convinced we're wearing him down, but he hasn't cracked yet. He was pretty shaken when he realized how much we'd uncovered, though.'

'Greg has a good track record for getting his man,' Douglas remarked. 'So what brings you here this time?'

'We've just received the mock-ups from the techies,' she explained, holding up the envelope. 'I've checked with Ashford's PA and the two potential witnesses are available.'

'Good, we'll see them together. You can hold the fort for a few minutes can't you, Anna?' he added over his shoulder and the woman looked up from her screen and nodded.

'Has any more info come in during the morning?' Sukey asked as they walked along the corridor leading to Erika Henderson's office.

'Two separate sightings of cars, one leaving in a hurry and the other arriving in a hurry, but not enough detail to establish whether it was the same one. The timings are about right, though.'

'You're thinking in terms of Lamont carrying out the attack, making off, driving a short distance and then turning round to come back as if for the first time?'

'Something of the sort,' he said.

'That would have given him an opportunity to get rid of the knife, wouldn't it?'

He nodded. 'Exactly, and that may have been part of the plan. The search has been widened for a mile in either direction.'

'Plan?' Sukey said in surprise. 'My impression, from what Hester told me, is that the reason he had a knife with him was that he had taken it away from her and that it was only by chance that he had it in his pocket.'

'You're saying you don't think it was premeditated then?' said Douglas.

'Frankly, no,' she said candidly.

'There's no proof that the knife he took from his sister was the same one that killed Whistler,' he pointed out.

'No, I suppose not,' she admitted. 'I wonder what he did with the loot, by the way?'

'The boys have been turning the place over all morning, but they haven't found anything so far. He had plenty of time to stash it somewhere safe – or he may have had a buyer waiting. We've taken the seal off room 106, by the way, which made the manager a fraction happier. He makes no secret of the fact he'll be glad to see the back of us,' he added with a grin.

'He's probably seeing the Hotel of the Year Award slipping away from him,' she commented, grinning back.

'Could be.'

'Boris is not a happy bunny,' Erika Henderson confided while they waited for him to respond to her summons. 'The other staff have noticed it as well, but he insists when asked that there's nothing wrong.'

She waited with the two detectives until the receptionist appeared and then discreetly withdrew. He was obviously nervous; there were small beads of sweat on his forehead and his hands were trembling. Sukey took the photographs from the envelope and spread them out on a table by the window.

'Come over here please, Boris, and look at these pictures,' she said, beckoning him as he appeared reluctant to come forward. 'We want you to look very carefully at them and tell us if there is a person in any of them that you recognize. There's no hurry, just take your time.'

So far from taking his time, Boris seemed anxious to be finished with the task as quickly as possible. There were three separate photographs; in each of them a shot of Stephen Lamont had been placed in a different position and among different people, but in all three Boris identified him with little or no hesitation as the man he had seen leaving the hotel by the staff entrance and a short time later asking at the desk for Doctor Whistler.

'Well, that seems pretty conclusive,' Douglas remarked as Boris withdrew and they waited for their next witness to appear.

'He certainly seemed in no doubt that it was Lamont he had seen,' Sukey agreed. 'It would be interesting to know what's on his mind to make him so jumpy, though.'

'A lot of immigrant workers are uneasy with the police, even when they've nothing to fear from us,' Douglas replied.

'That's what DS Rathbone said,' she acknowledged, 'but we aren't here all the time, are we?'

'He knew we'd be turning up sooner or later and he's probably been on edge wondering if he'll be able to pick Lamont out,' said Douglas. There was a tap on the door and the porter entered. 'Ah, here's Manuel.'

'Good morning, officers,' said the porter, beaming. It was clear that, so far from being reluctant, he was positively eager to co-operate. 'Ms Henderson says you want my help.'

'Yes, please, Manuel,' said Sukey. 'Do you remember telling me about a gentleman you saw come up the stairs to the first floor while you were talking to Nina, one of the chambermaids?'

He nodded eagerly. 'Yes, yes, of course I

remember. It was Thursday of last week, was it not?' His eyes travelled to the pictures. 'You want me to point him out to you?'

'We want you to study these very carefully and tell us if any of the men in them is the one you saw,' said Douglas.

'Yes, yes, I understand.' He studied each photograph in turn with an air of great confidence that, to the increasing disappointment of the watching detectives, gradually gave way to doubt and perplexity. A carefully manicured forefinger hovered over first one face and then another; the detectives held their breath as it appeared on the point of descending on Lamont's image in one of the shots before moving on.

Eventually, he gave a despondent shake of the head. 'I am sorry, I cannot be sure,' he sighed. 'It might have been him – ' he indicated a grey-haired man who, Douglas later informed Sukey, was a sergeant based at a station some miles outside the city – 'or him.' This time the finger rested briefly on Lamont before moving to the other two pictures, where the performance was repeated without Lamont featuring in either case. 'No, I cannot be sure,' he admitted. His demeanour left them in no doubt that he was as disappointed as they were.

'He probably had dreams of being feted as the hero who played a vital role in nailing a desperate criminal,' Douglas remarked dryly

124

as they returned to the incident room. 'Ah, well, you can't win 'em all and at least Boris had no difficulty at all picking out Lamont. Of course, he'd had more than one chance to get a look at him; Manuel saw him only once and he quite likely had one eye on Nina at the time.'

On her way back to the car with the latest piece of the jigsaw, Sukey found her thoughts turning once again to Boris. She could not help wondering whether there was more to account for the unease that his colleagues had reportedly noticed during the past few days, not only towards the police but in his general demeanour. On an impulse she returned to the hotel; Boris was dealing with a guest, but he caught sight of her over the man's shoulder and his eyes widened with alarm. When he was free she took from a stand on the counter a leaflet about local attractions, unfolded it, approached him with a smile and said, 'Can you tell me about some of these places?'

It was clear that he was not deceived by her subterfuge, for he responded by saying in a frantic whisper, glancing round fearfully as he spoke, 'I tell you all I know. Please, make no trouble for me.'

'I have a feeling you're in trouble already,' she said, lowering her own voice to avoid being overheard, 'and, if so, I may be able to help you.' She put her bag on the counter and used it as a shield while sliding one of her cards towards him. 'You'll find my mobile number on this and you can call me any time if there's anything you want to tell me.' He stared at the card as if it were poisonous, but made no move to take it. 'Believe me, Boris, you have nothing to fear from us if you have done nothing wrong,' she assured him. 'Go on, take it. I'm not going to leave until you do,' she added as he still made no move. At last, he picked it up and put it in his pocket. 'Well done,' she whispered. She refolded the leaflet, put it in her bag and said in her normal voice, 'Thank you so much, that's really helpful.'

'I don't need to tell you that you're in a pretty sticky situation.' Goodacre looked across the table at his client, who sat with his head bowed and his breath coming in ragged gasps.

Lamont made an effort to steady himself. He raised his head and gazed back at his solicitor. 'I can see that,' he said despairingly, 'and I'm sure you don't need me to tell you it wasn't I who killed that man.'

'I'd like to believe that, of course, but—'

'John! What are you saying? You don't seriously think I'm capable of murder?' He felt as if all hope of establishing his innocence was being torn from him. 'For God's sake, man, you've known me for years.

Surely you—'

'In a professional capacity, yes,' Goodacre agreed, 'and I've never had any reason to doubt your integrity until now. But we have to be realistic; the evidence against you isn't conclusive, but it is beginning to stack up and—'

'But it's all circumstantial,' Lamont pleaded.

'So far, yes, but you have withheld vital information and you haven't been able to find anyone to support your account of your movements before you left the college to meet Doctor Whistler. Supposing these witnesses at the hotel do identify you, how will you explain that?'

'What can I say except that they're mistaken? Anyway, I don't see how they can because I declined to take part in an identity parade or to allow my picture to be taken.'

'As you had every right to do,' Goodacre said, 'and in the light of your refusal they in turn had every right to obtain your picture by other means.'

'What other means?'

'Covertly, of course. Weren't you told that?'

Lamont put a hand to his forehead and closed his eyes, trying to recall the moment when he refused for the second time to co-operate in the matter of identity.

'Something was said about "other legal means",' he said after moment's thought. 'I assumed they'd use a photo from the university prospectus or something like that. What do you mean by "covertly"?'

'Someone tracks you with a hidden camera.'

'Good heavens, I had no idea!' He felt the net closing ever more tightly, but to his surprise Goodacre allowed himself a fleeting smile of satisfaction.

'That could be useful,' he said, making a note. 'Right, let's run over one or two other points that are likely to prove tricky. For example, I do happen to know that you've been a little, shall we say, pushed for money these past few months.'

'All right, so I had to raise a loan to meet Hester's expenses,' Lamont admitted. 'The drugs she's on at the moment are costing me more than I bargained for.' He put his hands up to his temples and groaned. 'It's so ironic, isn't it? She's been much better these past few months and now this ... even she believes I killed Whistler ... and you've as good as said you've got serious doubts. I don't think I can bear much more.'

'I'd like to believe you Stephen, believe me I would,' Goodacre said quietly, 'but we have to face facts. If these witnesses do identify you, and forensics find Whistler's blood on your clothes, it's more than likely you'll be charged. There's no guarantee the CPS will allow the case to come to court, but we have to prepare for the worst. All I can promise at this stage is to consider who best to brief in your defence.'

Eleven

'It's a pity Manuel didn't come up with the goods, but at least Boris didn't let us down,' Rathbone commented. He put the photographs, together with Sukey's report, into his case file before saying, 'There's been a very interesting development. DCI Leach has been in touch with the man in charge of the dig Whistler was working on, a Doctor Makris of the Greek Ministry of Culture. He confirms that in addition to the document, Whistler was carrying certain items that would not normally have been allowed out of the country. He was granted a special dispensation in this case because he wanted them examined by a senior fellow of the University of Athens, who is in London for medical treatment and unable to travel.'

'Did Doctor Makris have any reason to believe Whistler might be targeted by criminals?' Sukey asked.

'On the contrary, according to Leach he's absolutely astounded that such a thing could happen. He's been given the usual assurances that we're doing everything in our power to find Whistler's killer and recover the stolen property, but apparently he sounded pretty miffed. He didn't go so far as to accuse the police of negligence, but apparently he had some rude things to say about security at the hotel.'

'That was a bit unfair,' said Sukey. 'What does he expect – guards and sniffer dogs all over the place?'

'I suspect he realizes he's dropped a clanger by allowing valuable antiquities out of the country so he's trying to shift the blame for their disappearance on to someone else.'

'Doesn't this rather suggest that Lamont might be telling the truth when he said he thought Whistler sounded jumpy?' Sukey said tentatively. 'He might have felt uncomfortable at being entrusted with such precious items.'

Rathbone shrugged. 'It's possible, I suppose, but it doesn't count for much in the overall picture.'

'What about Whistler's next of kin? Is there any news of them?'

'That's another point Makris was able to help with. According to him, Whistler was a bachelor who lived alone and never mentioned his family. The Greek police found an Australian address in his personal effects of someone called Whistler, presumably a relative, but it turned out the person died some years ago. DCI Leach will be fending off demands for more details at tomorrow's briefing,' he added, 'but to be on the safe side I've warned Professor Thorne that if the media get wind of Whistler's reasons for being in Bristol he and members of his department are likely to be targeted by the paparazzi.'

'Which would mean Lamont might be identified as the person he was at the hotel to meet?'

Rathbone nodded morosely. 'I've asked Thorne to avoid naming names and to ask his staff to do the same, but there's no guarantee someone won't slip up. It certainly wouldn't do our case any good.'

Especially as it's not all that strong anyway, was Sukey's instinctive reaction, but she kept the thought to herself. Instead she asked, making the question sound as casual as she could, 'Did Professor Thorne know about the other things Whistler was supposed to be carrying?'

'He had absolutely no idea, and he sounded pretty shocked when I told him. He admitted he'd been puzzled to think that anyone would commit murder for a document of interest only to scholars, but could see the existence of the other items puts an entirely different slant on the case. I explained that we'd deliberately kept that information under wraps and asked him not to mention them to anyone until it was officially released; for his part he assured me that had he known about them he would have spoken up right away.' Rathbone glanced at the clock. 'Well, we've given our man time to consider his position,' he said. 'Let's hear what he's got to say in response to Boris's testimony. Yes, Fleming, what have you got there?' he added as a uniformed constable entered carrying a green metal box.

'We found this stashed behind some books in a cupboard in the suspect's study, Sarge,' said the officer. 'We haven't been able to open it; we've tried all the keys in the desk but none of them will fit. There's something more in it than papers, by the sound of it.' By way of demonstration he shook the box, causing a metallic rattle.

'Careful!' said Rathbone. 'If this contains what I'm hoping, we have some very precious items in here.' He stood up and took the box from Fleming's hands. 'Come on Sukey, let's see what our friend has to say about this.'

Lamont could almost feel the blood draining from his face as he saw what Rathbone was carrying. The detective placed it on the table, checked the time, switched on the tape, ran through the brief formalities and said, 'Right, Professor Lamont, perhaps we can clear up a few points. I see you recognize this box?'

Lamont attempted to moisten his lips with a tongue that seemed to have turned to cardboard in his mouth. 'I have a box at home that looks very like that one,' he muttered.

'This was found in a cupboard in your study and we have reason to believe it contains items relevant to the present enquiry. It's locked, as I'm sure you're aware, but no doubt you have the key with you so perhaps you'll be kind enough to unlock it.' Rathbone slid the box across the table. In silence, after receiving a nod from his stony-faced solicitor, Lamont took a bunch of keys from his pocket, selected one, unlocked the box and lifted the lid.

'Thank you,' said Rathbone. He drew the box towards him and peered inside 'Well, what do we have here?' His tone was almost jocular as he peered inside. 'Quite a little armoury!' Without touching any of the items, he began a recital of the contents. 'One Swiss army knife, assorted cook's knives, very sharp by the looks of them, one very pretty paper knife with a jewelled handle that looks as if it could do some damage. Tell me, Professor Lamont, which one of these did you take to the meeting with Doctor Whistler?'

He was vaguely aware of Goodacre's warning hand on his arm, but he ignored it. 'The paper knife,' he said in a voice that he barely recognized as his own. 'I think you already know the truth, Sergeant. My sister has a history of self-harming. These are knives I've taken away from her. I keep them locked up for obvious reasons.'

'So when did you catch her using this one?'

'It was the morning I had the appointment with Whistler. I found her with it in her hand … one of my students brought it back from a recent trip to Syria and gave it to me, but I never showed it to her because … well, you can guess the reason. I kept it in the desk in my study … I thought it would be safe as she never has reason to go in there, but for some reason she must have. She cut herself with it that morning – not seriously, it never is. I took it away from her; I should have locked it up with the others immediately, but I was in a hurry so I put it into my pocket and—'

'And used it later to threaten Whistler and then stab him when he refused to hand over the valuables from the dig?' said Rathbone.

'No!' Lamont shouted, thumping the table. 'I didn't kill him – I could never kill anybody! You must believe me!' he implored, but he saw no mercy in the implacable gaze of the detective or that of his woman colleague, who sat there watching and listening, as keen-eyed as a blackbird waiting to pounce on a worm.

'All right, Professor. Let's go over it once

more, shall we? Do you still maintain that the first and only time you arrived at the Mariners Hotel last Thursday was at approximately twelve fifteen?'

Temporarily thrown, first by the discovery of the knife and then by the sudden change of tactic, Lamont took a few moments to recover before replying, with a desperate show of defiance, 'Of course I do, because it's the truth.'

'And what if I were to tell you that the hotel employee who directed you to Doctor Whistler's room has now positively identified you as the man he saw leaving by the back door some fifteen minutes previously?'

In an attempt to elicit an admission that the evidence had been obtained covertly, Lamont – briefed by Goodacre – said, 'I fail to see how he could do that without my co-operation.'

'So you persist in your denial?'

'Of course I do. He's completely mistaken. The first man he saw must have been someone who looks like me, that's all I can suggest.'

'Let's leave that for the moment,' said Rathbone, 'and consider the explanation you gave for your supposed late arrival. Or rather, explanations, because you gave two.' Lamont experienced a further sinking sensation as Rathbone remorselessly drove his points home. 'According to reports from our traffic division, there were no unusual delays either in the city centre or on the A38 at the crucial time, which would seem to put paid to the first excuse you offered. As to your second version, we have not been able to find any witnesses to support it. Unless you've managed to find one, I'm afraid we can draw only one conclusion, namely that your story is exactly that – a story. Or, to be more accurate, a string of deliberate lies.'

Lamont glanced at Goodacre, who gave an almost imperceptible shake of the head. 'No comment,' he said sullenly.

'There remains the possibility of blood-stains on your jacket, Professor.' Now the woman took up the questioning. 'In the event that we find any, how would you account for them?'

'But I thought—' he began, but this time Goodacre came to his rescue.

'My client has already admitted that he took a knife from his sister and put it in his pocket,' he said. 'It is of course likely that her blood is on the knife and no doubt you will be subjecting that to tests as well. It is un-fortunate that the jacket was washed before being submitted for examination, but my client could hardly have anticipated coming under these totally unjustified suspicions.'

'The fact that the garment in question was washed is not crucial,' said Rathbone and the flicker of hope that Lamont felt at his solicitor's words died away as the detective continued silkily, 'you'd be amazed, Professor, at the sophisticated techniques available to forensic scientists nowadays.' He paused for a moment as if allowing time for the information to sink in before saying, 'Think for a moment. Supposing there is blood from another source than the wound your sister inflicted on herself?' The detective leaned forward wearing the accusatory expression Lamont had come to dread. 'Doctor Whistler's blood, for example? How will you explain that?'

Once again, Goodacre intervened. 'That is a purely hypothetical question, Sergeant, and I advise my client not to answer it,' he said firmly.

'Very well. We'll leave it at that for now. Interview terminated at three fifteen p.m.' Rathbone reached forward and switched off the tape recorder.

'You mean I'm free to go?' said Lamont in bewilderment.

'For the time being, yes.' Rathbone closed the folder that had lain open on his desk throughout the interview and stood up. 'Kindly remain at your present address until we contact you again.' He left the room, followed by the woman, leaving Lamont feeling utterly bemused. He remained seated for several seconds until his solicitor took him by the arm and half-pulled him to his feet. Escorted by a uniformed officer, the two of them went downstairs and out of the building in silence; it was not until they were driving back through the city centre that Goodacre said quietly, 'Stephen, are they likely to find traces of Whistler's blood on any of your clothing.'

'Yes, John,' he said miserably, 'I'm afraid they are.'

Back in the office, Rathbone rubbed his hands together and said, 'Well, we've really got him rattled now. Even his brief doesn't believe him.'

Sukey looked at him in surprise. 'You reckon?'

'Couldn't you tell from the body language? That professional mask conceals a very worried man,' he said confidently. 'It wasn't very bright of Lamont to keep the knife, but it's a very distinctive item and I suppose he figured that if he chucked it away it'd be found sooner or later and traced back to him. I expect you're wondering why I let him go,' he added as if anticipating a question she had not thought of asking. 'Think about it. He's hardly likely to do a runner with his sister in such a precarious mental state, and the longer he sits at home chewing his nails the more likely he is to crack.'

'So what's our next move, Sarge?'

'We wait till we've got all the reports from

forensics. I know what Hanley said about bleeding,' he went on, again anticipating her question, 'but there must have been traces of Whistler's blood on the knife after the killing and some of it's sure to have found its way on to Lamont's clothes. The boffins don't need much – even a tiny drop can make a usable sample.' He gave a prodigious yawn and said, 'Anyway, now we have the weapon we're on much stronger ground.'

To her surprise, Fergus rang that evening. 'Hi, Mum, how's it going?' he asked. Then, before she had time to do more than return his greeting, he added, 'No, I didn't leave anything behind this time – I just thought you'd be interested to know we had another lecture in criminal psychology this afternoon, this time from a woman who talked about professional hit men.'

'I'm sure that was fascinating,' said Sukey. 'Tell me about it while I drink my evening snifter.'

'Mum, you shouldn't drink on your own,' he said, a sudden note of anxiety in his young voice. 'It's well known that—'

'I know, lonely women who sit at home and tipple are on the slippery slope into alcoholism,' she interrupted flippantly. 'For goodness' sake, Gus, you know I always relax with a glass of wine when I get home – it gives me an appetite for my dinner.'

'I know, but you're on your own much more these days and—'

Touched by his genuine concern, and guessing what lay behind it, she said gently, 'I know what you're thinking and yes, there are times when I miss having Jim around, but I promise you don't have to worry. Listen, are you going to tell me how to spot a professional hit man? Not that I can see our learned professor falling into that category.'

'No, well, you never know when this might come in handy. We were told that they're not always independent of the people who use them; some of them have had military training and they've learned to regard the victim as an object rather than a person with a life and a family and so on. It's important to get into their minds, try and figure out how they see themselves, which more often than not is simply as a criminal ... and proud of it.'

'Did the lecturer give you any tips for getting into the criminal mind?'

'Er, not exactly; I guess that's for a later lecture. One thing we were told by another tutor was that the police use the acronym MOPS, which stands for a series of key-words—'

'Motive, Opportunity, Preparatory Action and Subsequent Action,' Sukey chipped in. 'Yes, I learned that during my probationary period.'

'Ah, I thought you might have. This lecturer said motive isn't always a useful line of investigation. Were you taught that?'

'I don't remember hearing that one. What reason did he or she give?'

'Something like there could be any number of possible motives and it wasn't important at the start of an enquiry.'

'It's a point of view, I suppose. There doesn't seem to be much doubt about the motive in this case.'

'Has there been an arrest yet?'

'No, but there have been some important developments – and before you ask, I'm not going to tell you.'

'All right, be mysterious. By the way, I forgot to ask how you're enjoying working with DS Rathbone on this case?'

'No serious problems, although now and again I sense that he misses something that could be important and I have to be very tactful in drawing it to his attention. I think he still looks on me as a rookie and doesn't consider my SOCO experience counts for very much.'

'What about your early years as a beat copper – before you married Dad, I mean?'

'That was too long ago to be worth much – at least, not in his eyes. He pointed out to me during my first week that we don't rely on whistles and truncheons any more.'

'Cheek! I'll bet you're hoping to spot a

vital clue that he's missed and so cover yourself with glory?'

'It doesn't look very likely, but I live in hope,' she said with a chuckle. She hesitated for a moment before saying casually, 'Seen Jim around lately?'

'As it happens, I bumped into him an hour or so ago. He said something about giving you a call to see if you were free at the weekend. I take it he hasn't been in touch?'

'Not yet. Did he say anything else?'

'Only that his promotion to DCI has come through at last.'

'Only? But that's great news. I'm so pleased for him.'

'I thought you would be. Shall I mention I've told you if I see him again?'

'Why not? Say I look forward to hearing from him.'

'OK. Talk again soon,' he said and hung up.

Sukey finished her wine, switched on the radio and set about preparing her evening meal. It crossed her mind to call Jim and congratulate him on his promotion, but she decided to wait until he called her. As she peeled vegetables to accompany her supermarket chicken joint and took a dessert from the freezer, she found herself mulling over two of the points Fergus had made about hit men: their need for preparatory action and a contingency plan for subsequent action. A

142

sudden thought made her stop in the middle of slicing a carrot while she allowed it to take shape in her mind. 'Just supposing,' she heard herself say aloud, and then, 'no, don't be daft, forget it.' But despite the apparently damaging nature of the day's discovery, the possibility that the whole thrust of the current investigation was heading in the wrong direction refused to go away. She spent the rest of the evening trying to decide whether, at the risk of being told to leave theorizing to the more experienced, to share her thoughts with DS Rathbone.

Twelve

'So, who d'you reckon did it, then? Boris the Albanian Avenger? Professor Thorne, the Hellenic Hijacker?'

Even before he spoke, Sukey knew from the patronizing smile that spread over his features that DS Rathbone was going to react to her theory in the way she had anticipated. Nevertheless, she stood her ground and replied calmly, 'I haven't anyone particular in mind, Sarge. All I can say is I have a gut feeling about Lamont – I know every piece of evidence we've got so far points to him, but somehow I just don't see him as a killer.'

'I do realize your experience of murderers is limited,' he said indulgently, 'but believe me, they come in all shapes and sizes. Take that case a few years ago of a respected family doctor, with an unblemished reputation, topping God knows how many of his trusting patients before someone started asking questions.'

'Yes, I remember the case, but the man was a psychopath who killed because it made him feel godlike,' Sukey countered. 'Surely you aren't suggesting Stephen Lamont—'

'I'm not suggesting he's a potential serial killer, if that's what you mean,' Rathbone interrupted, 'but it's obvious he's been under a lot of stress over a long period and in those circumstances the most unlikely people act out of character. I'm pretty sure traces of Whistler's blood will be found on that knife, which should be conclusive even if forensics can't recover DNA from Lamont's clothing.'

'I think it's more than likely,' Sukey agreed, 'but there could still be an innocent explanation.'

'Such as what?' She could tell by his tone that he was beginning to lose patience with her.

'Supposing his story is true and the first time he saw Whistler was when he went up to Room 106 with the manager. He told us he knelt down beside him and we know there was a lot of blood about; supposing he got some on his hands and clothing without realizing it and then put his hand in his pocket and transferred some on to the knife?'

'Supposing, supposing!' he jeered. 'Remember, Whistler was still alive when he was found, and I can assure you a professional hit man would have done a thorough job so the victim would never have an opportunity to identify him. And did you notice any blood on Lamont's hands when we interviewed him shortly after the killing?'

'No,' she admitted, 'but if it was only a smear we could easily have missed it, or he could have wiped it off with a handkerchief. And I know neither you nor DS Douglas think it's significant, but I still think it would be interesting to know why—'

'Sorry, your next bit of theorizing will have to wait,' he interrupted with a glance at the clock on the canteen wall. 'DCI Leach wants to see me in five minutes and he doesn't like being kept waiting.' He gulped down the remainder of his tea and was gone, leaving her fuming.

'OK if I sit here?' DC Vicky Armstrong appeared from behind her with a mug of tea in one hand and a plate containing two buttered scones in the other.

'Please do. You'll be better company than

DS Rathbone,' Sukey said with feeling.

'I thought you were looking a bit miffed,' Vicky said, grinning. 'Has he been telling you how much you have yet to learn about the noble art of detection?'

'That's what it amounted to,' Sukey said ruefully. 'I should have known better, I suppose, but I just have a hunch that our chief suspect – no, our only suspect – is either the victim of an unfortunate chain of coincidences or there's something very sinister going on in the background.'

'Something nasty in the woodshed, eh?' Vicky took a bite from one of her scones and followed it with a mouthful of tea. 'Do you often suffer from hunches?'

'Yes, now and again – and sometimes they turn out to be right.'

'I take it we're talking about the Whistler killing?'

'That's the one.'

'Want to tell me about it?'

'As long as you keep it to yourself. I don't want Rathbone to know I've been talking behind his back.'

'My lips are sealed,' Vicky said solemnly. She swallowed the last morsel of her first scone and started on the second. 'Get on with it then.'

When Sukey had finished she sat deep in thought while gathering the remaining crumbs on her plate with a moistened finger.

At last she said, 'You reckon someone at the dig knew there were goodies to be picked up and passed the information to someone over here, and that person wanted them badly enough to commit murder to get hold of them?'

'Why not? There could easily be more than one villain involved, maybe even a gang trading in stolen antiquities. One possibility that occurred to me is that the killer tried to con Whistler into believing he was Lamont so that he'd hand over the stuff without quibbling. He only used the knife when Whistler didn't fall for it.'

Vicky pursed her lips and frowned. 'I know you won't want to hear this,' she said, 'but it seems to me that Lamont has a very strong motive. He's admitted being strapped for cash; couldn't he have been the one who tried to con Whistler into handing over the valuable bits as well as the scroll or whatever the epistle was written on and stabbed him when he refused?'

'In that case, you'd expect him to have shown some signs of stress when making his statement after the crime had been discovered,' Sukey pointed out. 'In fact, he was just the opposite – very composed and sure of himself and quite sniffy about the manager who almost keeled over at the sight of blood. It was only later, when he realized how the evidence was stacking up against him and how much we'd found out about his personal circumstances, that he started to lose his cool.'

'Do you think Boris is part of the plot? From what you say, he had no hesitation in picking Lamont out – how do you reckon your master crook managed to organize that?'

'I have to admit that's one thing I haven't been able to figure out, but I'm convinced there's an explanation for it.'

'Well, even if you are on to something, there doesn't seem to be much you can do about it,' said Vicky. 'If you can't convince Greg Rathbone you can hardly go off and start your own line of enquiry.'

'No, I suppose not,' Sukey sighed. 'Thanks for listening anyway.'

'No problem. You doing anything special tonight?'

'Not that I know of. How about you?'

'It's Chris's birthday so I'm taking him out to dinner.'

'That's nice. Where are you going?'

'Oddly enough, to the Mariners Hotel. The head chef is Chris's best mate and he's planned a special treat for him.'

'The Mariners?' Sukey had a sudden flash of inspiration. 'Could you do something for me while you're there?'

'What's that?'

'Find out what time Boris Gasspar finishes

his shift.'

Vicky looked at her in astonishment. 'What on earth for?'

'I'd like to know where he lives and what sort of people he mixes with.'

'I'm not even on the case,' Vicky objected. 'What reason do I give for asking that sort of question?'

'Not you, make some excuse to ask Chris to do it. His mate works there, he could find out, surely.'

Vicky looked dubious. 'I'm not sure I want to get involved,' she said.

'You don't have to. Please, Vicky, I've a feeling it's really important.'

'One of your famous hunches?'

'If you put it like that – yes. I'm sure he's got something on his mind and it's not just that he's uncomfortable talking to the police. The staff at the hotel have noticed it even when we're not around, and at least once he's been heard arguing with someone on his mobile. I'm convinced he's under some kind of pressure.'

'Mmm, I think I see what you're driving at,' said Vicky. 'We know criminals from abroad are running scams over here; in fact the Super has set up a special task force to deal with that very problem.'

'Well there you are then. Boris insists his papers are in order and the hotel confirms it, but they could be forged and he could still be an illegal. In that case it would be easy to coerce him into making a false statement.'

'I take it you've raised this with DS Rathbone?'

'Yes, and he simply brushed it aside, put the nerves down to a mistrust of the police after living in former communist states, and DS Douglas said much the same thing.'

'It seems to me they've got a point.'

'I'd still like to know more about Boris.'

'So that you can do some unofficial surveillance?'

'I suppose you could call it that – but only when I'm off duty. I gave him my mobile number and said he could call me if he had a problem, by the way.'

'*Did* you?' Vicky raised an eyebrow. 'I'm not sure that was wise.'

'I don't see what harm it can do. Anyway, will you do it?'

'I suppose so,' Vicky sighed, 'but please keep me out of it.'

According to Chris's friend the head chef at the Mariners Hotel, receptionists on duty during the day normally finished at six o'clock, but it was Friday before Sukey was able to get away from the station in time to take up a position in the hotel car park that enabled her to keep an eye on the staff entrance. When Boris emerged she had just enough time to recognize him before he put on a helmet, mounted a rather noisy moped and set off in the direction of the city centre followed by a trail of exhaust fumes. She kept him in sight without difficulty; when they reached Bishopston he turned into a side street, dismounted and wheeled the moped into the front garden of a house a few doors along. She noted the number as she drove past, pulled into a space a short distance further on and switched off her engine.

'Right,' she muttered aloud, 'at least I know where you live. What now?' She adjusted her passenger door mirror to give a view of him bending over the moped, presumably securing it. Rather than turn and drive back while he was still outside and might possibly glance up and see her, she waited for him to go indoors, but to her surprise he came out and began walking along the pavement towards her. He had taken off his helmet; for a moment she thought he must have noticed her following him and was about to approach her, but he crossed the road several cars behind and continued along the other side.

About thirty yards further on he climbed into the front passenger seat of a black Mercedes parked by the kerb. He appeared to be having some kind of altercation with a man wearing dark glasses who sat behind the wheel. At one point the man turned his head sharply in a way that suggested he had heard something of particular and disturbing significance and held out a hand with an imperious gesture. Boris appeared to shrink back in his seat and then, as the outstretched hand became more insistent, took something from his pocket and handed it over. Moments later he got out of the car, which moved off and headed back to the main road. Sukey made a note of the registration number and at the same time got a good look at the driver as he passed; she judged him to be in his fifties, of distinguished appearance, with regular features, an olive complexion and black hair flecked with grey at the temples. He gave no sign of having noticed her as he drove by.

Meanwhile, Boris had started walking slowly back towards his house; this time he crossed the road ahead of Sukey. As he drew near she ducked and pretended to be searching for something on the floor, hoping he had not spotted her. To her relief his footsteps did not hesitate as he passed; she waited a few more seconds before straightening up, just in time to see him open his front door and disappear into the house.

Thirteen

When Sukey reached home there was a message from Jim on her telephone answering machine, confirming that he would be with her around eleven the following morning. As Fergus had predicted, he had called earlier in the week and suggested – a little diffidently, she thought – that they might 'do something together' on Saturday to celebrate his promotion. She had been happy to agree; the change of career and the move to a new location had inevitably had an effect on their relationship, which had become increasingly intimate over the past couple of years. It was true there had been areas of conflict, particularly over her tendency to do what Vicky had recently described as 'a little sleuthing on the side', but for the most part they had found contentment and fulfilment in one another's company. Lately she had found herself harking back with more than a little regret to the good times while putting the differences to the back of her mind, and she could not deny, even to herself, that she had been counting the days until Saturday. Just

153

the same, away from his influence she had found a sense of freedom that she would be very loath to forgo.

Before preparing her evening meal she wrote a report of her surveillance of Boris Gasspar. When it was finished she toyed with the idea of talking over with Jim her misgivings about the case against Stephen Lamont, but decided against it, partly because it might lead to an argument and she wanted nothing to spoil their time together. She put aside almost without a second thought the idea of showing him what she had written; he would simply advise her to show it to DS Rathbone, something she had already accepted it was her duty to do although she quailed at the prospect. She sensed that, although so far he had appeared fairly even-tempered, the sergeant was quite capable of giving a tongue-lashing to a presumptuous upstart of a newly qualified detective constable.

Despite her misgivings she slept well that night and when she awoke to bright sunshine she took it as an omen that the day was going to turn out well. When Jim arrived he made no attempt to kiss her – in fact, for the first half hour or so she was conscious of a slight restraint in his manner, as if he feared that any attempt at physical contact would meet with a rebuff. She made coffee and they drank it on her roof terrace, which gave a spectacular view across Bristol as well as a glimpse of the suspension bridge over the River Avon and had been a major factor in her decision to buy the flat. He asked questions about her neighbours and the local amenities, and admired her collection of terracotta containers planted with winter pansies and small shrubs. Little by little they began to relax and exchange news of recent events and activities, both at work and at leisure.

During a lull in the conversation he said, 'This chap Rathbone you're working with – how do you find him?'

On the surface it was a casual, almost a throwaway question, but there was an underlying hint of concern that gave Sukey a twinge of pleasure. Was he, she wondered, a tad jealous? She was careful to make her reply sound similarly off-hand. 'He's OK,' she said, 'although he treats me as if I'm still on probation – which I suppose in some way I am. He's well thought of in the department and he's had years of experience in the job, but he's very single-minded and he doesn't hesitate to shoot me down in flames if I have the cheek to suggest anything that doesn't fit in with his assessment of a case.'

Jim chuckled and said, 'Which I'm sure you have no hesitation in doing!'

'On the contrary, I only do it occasionally, when I feel really strongly about something.

Not that it gets me anywhere,' she admitted resignedly.

'So what case are you on at the moment?'

'The stabbing of an archaeologist called Doctor Whistler in a Bristol hotel.'

'Ah, yes, DCI Lord has a particular interest in that. The curator at the museum in Gloucester is a friend of his who had dealings with Whistler a couple of years ago. Nice old boy, according to Philip; he came to examine some Roman relics that turned up during excavations for a building site somewhere in the county. I'm told an arrest is imminent, by the way.'

Sukey looked at him in surprise. 'Who told you that?'

'DCI Richard Leach. He and I go back quite a long way, although our paths haven't crossed much for the past few years.'

She looked at him suspiciously. 'And was it solely interest in the Whistler case that prompted you to get in touch again?'

He looked slightly sheepish as he replied, 'Not entirely. I just wanted to know that someone was keeping an eye on you.' He turned to look at her and she read in his expression all that she had half-feared, half-hoped to see. He put a hand over one of hers and said softly, 'I still care for you, Sook. I care very much.'

'I know,' she said in a low voice. They sat in silence for a few moments with their hands clasped. Then something occurred to Sukey and she pulled her hand away. 'Just what else did you tell DCI Leach about me?' she demanded.

'That you have a sharp brain, a good eye for detail, and – ' he hesitated for a moment before adding mischievously – 'that you have a tendency to be a loose cannon.'

'Well, thanks a bunch,' she said, laughing in spite of herself. 'No doubt he's passed that gem to Greg Rathbone with a suggestion that he keeps me on a tight rein.'

'I don't think so. I did add that Chief Inspector Lord thought highly of you as a SOCO and that he gave strong support to your application to train for the CID.'

'Oh, well, that's all right then,' she said sarcastically. She glanced at her watch. 'It's getting on for lunchtime. I imagine you expect to be fed?'

'Naturally ... but don't provide too much food because this evening I'm taking you to Bristol's top floating restaurant.'

'That'll be great.' She led the way indoors while he followed with the coffee tray. 'Is there anything you'd like to do this afternoon?' she added while putting bowls of soup in the microwave and taking salad from the refrigerator.

'How about a walk over the Downs? Or maybe,' he added with a subtle change of tone, 'you have a better idea?'

His meaning was unmistakable and for a moment she felt her commonsense resolve to confine their relationship to an affectionate friendship beginning to waver, but she made a determined effort to keep it on course. 'A walk over the Downs would be lovely,' she said firmly.

'What would you like to drink?' he asked as they settled at their table. ' Much as I'd love to order a bottle of bubbly,' he added apologetically, 'I do have to drive back and I don't want to start my career as a DCI with a drink-drive charge.'

'Perish the thought,' she said, realizing as she spoke that his intention of going home that evening was not altogether welcome. 'A white wine spritzer has plenty of bubbles – how about that?'

'Good thinking. I'll have the same.' He gave the order and they sat back and took in their surroundings. Through the window of the converted barge they could see the reflection of streetlights dancing in the water of the Floating Harbour. 'This is nice, isn't it?'

'Very,' she agreed. 'I've walked along here quite a few times since I came to Bristol and thought how attractive this restaurant looked. Thank you,' she added as the waiter brought their drinks. She raised her glass. 'Here's to DCI Jim Castle, the scourge of

Gloucestershire villains.'

'Thank you.'

They clinked glasses and drank. Then she said, 'How come you know about this place?'

'Rick Leach recommended it. Now, what do you fancy to eat?' They studied the menu for a few minutes before settling on broccoli and Stilton soup followed by poached salmon in a lemon and tarragon sauce. 'It's remarkable, isn't it, how we so often make the same choice?' he said when they had given their order.

She shrugged and said, untruthfully, 'I hadn't thought about it.'

'In fact, we agree about a lot of things,' he went on. 'Wine, for example.' He was studying the varieties on offer as he spoke. 'What about a glass of Chilean Chardonnay? I don't think that would take me over the limit.'

He held out the wine list and as she reached for it her eyes fell on a couple who had just entered. She gave an involuntary start and hastily lowered her head to make a show of studying the list with close attention while the newcomers followed the waiter past their table. When she looked up she saw that Jim was eyeing the couple with a familiar look of concentration in his keen, greenish eyes.

'Do you know them?' he said in a low voice.

'The woman is PA to Professor Thorne,

who's in charge of the Department of Hellenic Studies at the university. I've only seen her once, when Greg Rathbone and I called to interview Thorne in connection with the Whistler killing. She did some photocopying for me – I don't know her name.'

'Do you know the man?'

She avoided his eye as she said, 'I've never met him. What's your interest?'

'I think someone should tell the lady to be a bit more careful in her choice of friends,' he replied.

'Are you saying he's some kind of villain?'

'His name is Oliver Maddox and we have reason to believe he's behind some very nasty goings on, including but not confined to people trafficking, but so far we've never been able to get any evidence against him.'

'What else?'

'Our information is that he'll take on anything for anyone prepared to pay for his services and he—' He broke off to give their order to the wine waiter; when the man had gone he leaned forward and fixed her with a penetrating look in his eyes. 'Sook, I have a feeling from the way you were so careful to avoid being spotted that you're keeping something from me.'

She sighed and nibbled at a bread roll before replying, 'Let's not talk about it now.'

'OK, I'll wait for your confession till we get back to your place.' His tone was light, but

160

she knew he meant business. 'Just tell me one thing: is it in connection with the Whistler case?'

She nodded. 'I'd more or less decided not to say anything to you because I know you'll give me an earful for being a "loose cannon", as you call it. I've written out a report for DS Rathbone and he'll probably hit the roof when he finds out what I've been up to, but I hope when he calms down he'll have the grace to admit I've hit on something worth investigating.'

Jim appeared to be about to say more, but at that moment a waiter brought their soup. True to his promise he did not refer to the subject again and the meal passed pleasantly enough as they chatted over a wide range of topics. He recounted episodes from current investigations, particularly those involving her former colleagues in the SOCOs team in Gloucester, and they chuckled together over her heavily embroidered accounts of her differences with Rathbone. The couple that had sparked their earlier exchanges were forgotten until suddenly a man's voice broke into their conversation.

'Chief Inspector Castle, how nice to see you!' Oliver Maddox had stopped beside their table, his companion at his side. In contrast to the fashionable but plain trouser suit she had worn in the office, she was wearing a midnight blue dress that might have come from the collection of a top designer and diamonds sparkled at her ears and throat. 'Allow me to congratulate you on your recent promotion,' Maddox went on, 'and good evening to you, Constable Reynolds.' He treated Sukey to a flash of white teeth.

Startled at the interruption, she hesitated for a second before recovering her wits and saying, 'I don't think I've had the pleasure.'

'But you have met this lady, I believe? She certainly remembers you.'

'Yes, of course.' Sukey nodded politely at his companion, who responded with a glacial half-smile.

'Hasn't the Chief Inspector told you that he and I are old friends?' Maddox went on, still addressing Sukey. His voice had a velvety undertone that reminded her of a self-satisfied cat; his smile persisted but his dark eyes under a strong brow were as hard as jet. She had the uncomfortable sensation that he was looking straight into her mind. 'His promotion is richly deserved, he's a superb detective,' he purred. 'Nothing escapes his eagle eye. I can't believe he didn't notice me pass your table.'

'Ms Reynolds and I have had plenty of other things to talk about,' Jim said pointedly, 'so if you will excuse us—'

'But, of course. I'm sure we have no wish to intrude. Until our next meeting, then.' He raised a hand in a polite salute and there was a hint of mockery in his smile as he moved with his companion towards the exit.

'I think it's time for us to go as well.' Jim signalled to the waiter and asked for the bill. He did not speak again until he had paid and they were back on the quay. Then he took her by the arm and said quietly, 'I'm afraid, Sook, you've strayed into some very murky waters. The minute we get back you're going to tell me all about it. And I do mean all,' he added in a tone that she knew only too well.

Back in her flat, she gave him a brief résumé of the enquiry into the murder of Doctor Edwin Whistler, the build-up of circumstantial evidence that had already convinced DS Rathbone and DCI Leach of Stephen Lamont's guilt and her own suspicion – pooh-poohed by both Rathbone and DS Douglas – that Boris Gasspar might have been in some way coerced into identifying him as the man who left the hotel by the staff entrance shortly before re-entering and enquiring for Whistler at the desk. 'The more I thought about it, I couldn't see Lamont as a killer and I was convinced that Gasspar was under some kind of pressure,' she said, 'so I decided to do a little … unpaid overtime, shall we call it? As a result of which, I wrote this.' She handed him the report. 'I'll make some coffee while you read it.'

When she brought the coffee he put her

report on the table and said, 'This man you saw with Gasspar – was it Maddox?'

'Definitely.'

'And you're sure he didn't see you?'

'I doubt if he could have recognized me from the distance between us while he was parked, and he didn't appear to glance in my direction as he drove away.'

'He'd already recognized me and he knew your name so the woman with him must have recognized you from the time you went to her office.' He sipped coffee for a moment before continuing, 'He obviously had no reason to conceal from her how he came to recognize me, which must have prompted her to tell him how she knew you.'

'You're thinking she may have some inkling of his background?' Sukey suggested.

He nodded. 'More than an inkling, I'd say. You said she's Thorne's PA; that would mean she had access to everything that was going on in his department, including Whistler's visit and the stuff he was carrying.'

'Only the epistle. Professor Thorne knew nothing about the other items.'

'So he says.'

'That's a point.'

'Tell me more about these other items.'

'I can't really add to what I've already told you. Doctor Makris has sent us a detailed description of the relics but he admits he's no idea of what they're worth – which of course is why they were sent to England. As to the so-called Pauline epistle, assuming it's genuine he says it would be priceless to biblical scholars but impossible to value in money terms.'

Jim thought for a moment before pulling out his mobile and punching buttons. 'Who are you calling?' she asked uneasily.

He silenced her with a gesture and began to speak in a brisk, urgent voice. 'Rick, sorry to disturb you on a Saturday evening, but something's cropped up and I think you should know about it right away. It's to do with Oliver Maddox ... that's right ... and Sukey, that is, DC Reynolds, has strayed across his path and come up with some very interesting information ... yes, I agree we have to give it top priority ... of course, I quite understand ... ten o'clock tomorrow at DC Reynolds' flat, then.' Before she could protest he dictated the address and ended the conversation. 'Sorry, he's got a houseful of relatives with kids so his place is out and this isn't the sort of thing you talk about over a beer in the local, so you have an unexpected guest for the night. At least, I'm assuming it was unexpected, but on the other hand—' With a sudden movement he took her by one hand, pulled her to her feet and into his arms. 'I've missed you and I want you like hell,' he said hoarsely, 'but if you don't feel the same, just say the word and I'll—'

165

She put her free hand behind his head and drew it down until their faces were almost touching. 'Tell me what the word is and I'll be sure not to say it,' she whispered, a fraction of a second before his mouth closed over hers.

Fourteen

'Cosy little pad you've found here, Sukey,' commented DCI Leach. His gaze took in every detail of her sitting room and the view across the city before homing in on her face and scrutinizing her with an appraising expression. 'I hope you're happy working here in Bristol.'

'Very happy, thank you, sir,' she replied.

'This is an informal meeting and I understand you and Jim are old friends, so let's skip the "sir" shall we? On the strict understanding that the arrangement ceases the moment I walk out of here,' he added. He spoke seriously, but she had a feeling that a smile lurked in the depths of his intensely blue eyes.

'Whatever you say.' Just in time she remembered not to add 'sir'. 'Please sit down; would you like some coffee?'

'No, thanks.' He glanced at his watch before settling into an armchair with his bony-wristed arms draped over the sides and his long legs stretched out in front of him. 'I'm due on the golf course in an hour, so let's get down to business straight away. I've had another chat with Jim this morning and he tells me you've written a report on your observation of Gasspar's movements on Friday so I'll run through that first.' She handed him the printed sheets and sat beside Jim on the couch facing him while he put on a pair of steel-framed glasses and began scanning the text. 'You seem pretty sure Maddox didn't see you,' he said when he had finished.

'As sure as I can be,' she said. 'He appeared to be looking straight ahead and I gave him only a very brief glance before he drew level with me. He's got a big car, the street where Boris lives is quite narrow and there were vehicles parked on either side, so he had to drive carefully.'

'But you managed to get his number without appearing to pay too much attention to him?'

'I'm long-sighted so I was able to read it as he pulled out.'

Leach nodded approvingly. 'Useful, that, when on surveillance – either official or unofficial,' he remarked, and this time a definite hint of a smile lit up his thin, slightly weather-beaten features. 'However, Maddox is as cunning as a fox, which is why he's managed to keep ahead of the game for so long. My guess is he spotted your car turning into the street behind Gasspar while he was waiting for him and watched to see where it went. You say you drove well past before parking?' Sukey nodded. 'Well, that's a standard ploy and I'll bet he made a note of the fact that you didn't get out of your car. He might also have seen you checking your rear view mirror from time to time, as I presume you did while you were watching for your target to go into the house?'

'Actually, no; my door mirror gave me a good view.'

'And you were careful to keep out of sight while Gasspar was on his way back?'

'Yes, and he walked straight past my car without hesitating so I'm sure he didn't know I was there.'

'Which means that if Maddox did spot you, which I think is more than likely, he had his own reasons for not sharing his observation with Gasspar. OK, now tell me what prompted this little excursion in the first place.'

'Boris was obviously ill at ease when we interviewed him the day of the attack on Whistler, but I accepted DS Rathbone's point about how coming from a former communist state would make him uncomfortable talking to the police,' she began, nervously at first but with increasing confidence, 'but it was when he came to Erika Henderson's office and found me there that he became noticeably agitated. When I showed him the three mock-ups the techies had given us and asked if he could identify Lamont he went to him without hesitation every time. He obviously wanted to get it over with and for me to leave as soon as possible.'

'So he had no trouble picking out Lamont?'

'None whatever.'

'Did you mention this to DS Rathbone?' Sukey shook her head and Leach gave another slightly enigmatic smile. 'You knew what his reaction would be so you thought you'd do a little further investigation on your own?'

'I gave Boris my card with my mobile number and told him to call me in confidence if there was anything worrying him. He was very reluctant to accept it, but I insisted and eventually he did, but he hasn't called. Ever since, I've been asking myself, supposing his passport and other papers are forged and he's been brought here illegally by someone who now has some kind of hold over him? Is that what's making him so jumpy and is that why he hasn't been in touch?'

'So, having followed him, presumably with the intention of finding out where he lives, what did you plan to do then?'

'To be honest, I didn't have a detailed plan,' Sukey confessed, feeling slightly foolish as once again she detected a glint of humour in Leach's expression. 'I ... I suppose I thought I might possibly get a sight of some of the people he mixed with, get a feel for his background away from the hotel, that sort of thing.'

'Something to convince Sergeant Rathbone that you had some grounds for your misgivings?' suggested Leach.

'Yes, I suppose so. When I saw him with Maddox it seemed I'd been right about him acting under pressure, but of course I had no idea then who Maddox was.'

'Well, it seems your bit of moonlighting may have done more than turn up a possible new lead in the Whistler murder,' said Leach. 'It would certainly be interesting to know what lies behind Friday's rendezvous. I see that while you were observing them in the car you thought you saw Gasspar handing something over to Maddox,' he went on, referring to her report.

'Yes, and from the impatient way Maddox held out his hand, he didn't seem willing to part with it.'

'Did you tell DS Rathbone about giving him your card?' She shook her head, expecting a reproof, but he simply continued, 'Greg told me of your misgivings, of course, and I admit I've been inclined to accept his assessment of them, especially in the light of the evidence piling up against Lamont. With Maddox coming on the scene we're likely to be into an entirely different ball game. If he's got a hold over Gasspar—' He broke off and gnawed reflectively at his upper lip for a minute or two before continuing. 'Let's begin with the assumption that Maddox wanted to get his hands on the stuff Whistler was carrying and that he knew about the arrangement with Lamont, almost certainly through his girlfriend in Thorne's office. He sends one of his operators to impersonate Lamont in the hope of getting Whistler to hand over the goodies voluntarily, Whistler smells a rat and refuses to co-operate so the guy knifes him and scarpers via the staff entrance, where Gasspar is conveniently waiting.'

'So you reckon Boris could have been primed with the story implicating Lamont?' said Jim.

Leach nodded. 'Of course, it's all conjecture at this stage, but it seems a possibility. He could even have been instrumental in getting the killer into the hotel, again through the staff entrance.'

There was a short silence during which both senior detectives appeared to be digesting this theory. Sukey opened her mouth to speak and then shut it again in a sudden rush of embarrassment. 'You've thought of something?' Leach said encouragingly. 'Don't be shy, let's have it.'

'I was only thinking that being implicated in a murder, plus the knowledge that if he didn't do as he was told might mean deportation or worse, is enough to make anyone jumpy under police questioning, however gentle.'

'I think we can agree on that,' said Leach. 'So what are you suggesting?'

'Assuming Maddox has got some hold over him,' she began hesitantly, 'it might be because he supplied him with false papers. Suppose we get our experts to carry out a thorough check; if it turns out he is an illegal might we perhaps do a little horse-trading – offer him protection if he's prepared to open up about his dealings with Maddox? Could we perhaps hint at an offer of a legitimate work permit as a bait?'

Jim looked doubtful. 'That sounds dodgy,' he said.

Leach nodded. 'I agree; we'd have to make a pretty strong case before going that far. It would need a decision at a high level.'

'In any case,' Jim went on, 'Maddox may have some other hold on Gasspar to ensure he keeps his mouth shut. We've never managed to get any of his underlings to grass on him either – they're all scared stiff of him. And wouldn't immigration have spotted any irregularities in his documents? They're pretty smart at weeding out the duds nowadays.'

'I've read recently that some forgeries are good enough to stand up to quite close scrutiny, especially when there's no particular reason to be suspicious,' said Sukey.

'And Maddox has got the connections and the wherewithal to make sure he gets the best,' said Leach. 'OK, we'll begin by asking Gasspar's employers for access to his records, saying it's part of a routine check and asking them to make sure he doesn't know about it. Now I must be off.' He unwound his rangy body from the armchair and stood up. 'I'll get Rathbone on to it first thing in the morning. Enjoy the rest of the weekend, folks.'

'I'll see you out,' said Jim before Sukey could speak. 'Maybe we could have that coffee now?' he added over his shoulder as the two of them left the room. She went to the kitchen and switched on the kettle; as she waited for it to boil her brain went suddenly into overdrive and when he returned she said, 'Jim, I've just had an uncomfortable thought.'

'What is it?'

'I'm positive Boris gave something to Maddox and my first guess was protection

173

money, but if DCI Leach is right about his role in the murder plan it would make more sense for Maddox to pay him.'

'True,' he agreed, 'and your next guess?'

She sensed that he too was troubled and her heart was thumping at the possible implications of what she had in mind. 'Do you think Maddox might have found out he had my card and made him hand it over?'

He took her by the arm. 'Come and sit down,' he said gently.

'The coffee's nearly ready,' she protested.

'It can wait.' He led her to the couch and pulled her down beside him. His expression was serious. 'I was one jump ahead of you, and so was Rick Leach,' he said. 'That's why I wanted a word with him in private, but now you've cottoned on by yourself we may as well talk about it.'

'So what do you think?'

'Either Boris told Maddox about the card, which seems unlikely from your observation of what went on between them, or the knowledge must have come from another person. Suppose Boris confided in someone he trusted, maybe showed them your card and asked for advice on what to do, and a third party overheard the conversation and reported it to Maddox. He's got spies everywhere.'

Sukey shuddered. 'You make him sound like a Mafia boss.'

'There are certain similarities,' Jim agreed dryly.

She closed her eyes and leaned against his shoulder. 'I'm scared,' she admitted. 'I've got visions of being knifed in a dark alley.'

Jim put an arm round her and gave her a comforting squeeze. 'Don't be daft, Maddox won't come after you. He's much too canny to set his dogs on a police officer. What worries us is that he may decide that there's a weak link in his organization that needs cutting out. In other words—'

'You mean he might have Boris killed?' Sukey faltered. She put a hand to her mouth. 'Because of what I did?'

'I wasn't thinking of Boris. Assuming Rick's theory is anywhere near the truth, Maddox needs him to support his story. I was thinking rather of the supposed confidant I mentioned a moment ago. Maddox might feel it advisable to have him eliminated. Or her,' he added as an afterthought.

'But it's not unusual, is it, to invite possible witnesses to make direct contact with an individual officer?' pleaded Sukey, horrified at the thought that she might unwittingly have precipitated another murderous attack.

'Of course not, and no one's blaming you.' He gave her a reassuring hug. 'In fact, Leach believes you've done a very useful bit of detective work and he'll be having a word with both you and DS Rathbone tomorrow about the next stage of the investigation. And meanwhile, I suggest you write up your version of our encounter yesterday evening with Maddox and the woman from Professor Thorne's office. I'll be making my own report to my Super first thing in the morning.'

The minute Sukey entered the CID office on Monday morning Vicky buttonholed her and told her to report immediately to DCI Leach. 'DS Rathbone is with him already and it's rumoured in the bazaar that something big is breaking,' she said, adding in a low voice, 'you wouldn't know anything about it, I suppose?'

'Why should I?' said Sukey defensively.

'You aren't the only one who gets hunches, you know.' Vicky cocked her head on one side and raised an enquiring eyebrow.

Sukey ignored the implied question and said, 'Well, I'd better not keep him waiting, had I?'

DCI Leach's office was on the third floor of the building and Sukey used the few minutes it took her to reach it to organize her thoughts as best she could. Leach was sitting at his desk with his back to the window with DS Rathbone opposite him. The sergeant was scanning a document that Sukey recognized as her initial report; when he had finished he handed it back to Leach before greeting her with a curt nod.

'Good morning Sukey, please sit down.' Leach waved her to the empty chair facing him. 'As you can see, I've put DS Rathbone in the picture regarding your observation of Boris Gasspar on Friday evening and I understand DCI Castle of Gloucestershire advised you to write a supplementary report. Have you done so?'

'Yes, sir, I have it here.' She handed over the single sheet; he scanned it briefly and passed it to Rathbone, who read it, grunted and gave it back.

'Right, you both know the situation so far. It seems we are now part of something far more wide-ranging than a straightforward murder enquiry. We have to tread carefully to make sure we don't foul up an ongoing investigation into which a lot of time and planning has been invested. For the time being I intend to limit our part to a detailed check on Gasspar's background – without alerting his suspicions, of course. I doubt if Maddox has got any other agents at the Mariners Hotel, but we must make sure it's done through someone we can trust. We'll want to know how he came to apply for the job, whether he produced references and if so whether they were followed up – you know the kind of thing. Greg, you've made contact with some of the admin staff there so I leave it to you to decide the best person to approach. Meanwhile, we await further instructions from higher up. That's all for now, thank you.'

As the door to Leach's office closed behind them and they began to walk toward the stairs, Rathbone said, 'I suppose you think you've been very clever?' There was an edge to his voice that she had not heard before.

'Not clever, Sarge, just lucky.'

'Let's hope your luck holds,' he said curtly, 'and from now on forget the undercover stuff and stick to carrying out orders.'

'Yes, Sarge,' she said meekly.

'About Gasspar, I don't think we'll waste time dealing with the hotel manager,' he went on. 'The prat will only panic if we show further interest in the man, thinking we suspect him of harbouring a terrorist or some such bollocks. His PA is probably our best bet – what's her name now?'

'Erika Henderson, Sarge.'

'Right. Go and see her, but impress on her that no one, but no one, not even her boss, is to know what you're after.' They had almost reached the CID office. 'Got that?' he almost growled.

'Yes Sarge.'

'Right. Get on with it.' He entered the room ahead of her without bothering to hold the door open behind him.

Fifteen

'Good morning, the Mariners Hotel.'

'Good morning. May I speak to Ms Henderson, please?'

'Who shall I say is calling?'

'This is the Department of Employment.'

'One moment please.'

Seconds later, a woman's voice said, 'Erika Henderson speaking. Is there a query about one of our employees?'

'This is DC Reynolds, and please don't greet me by name,' said Sukey quickly. 'I apologize for the deception. Are you alone in your office at the moment?'

'Yes, why?'

'I need to speak to you in the strictest confidence and it's important no one sees me with you. Can we meet away from the hotel, say during your lunch break?'

'This is official, I suppose?' said Erika cautiously.

'Absolutely. I realize this cloak and dagger stuff will seem unusual, but there's a very good reason. Just tell me where and when would suit you.'

'Well, as it's Monday I need to restock my fridge after the weekend so I was planning to go to the supermarket down the road,' said Erika after a pause. 'They have a coffee shop where you can get a sandwich or a salad. Shall we say twelve thirty?'

'I'll be there. And please, don't mention this to anyone. I'll explain when I see you.'

Sukey put the phone down and glanced at the clock. It was barely nine fifteen; she had the better part of three hours before the meeting. She became aware of DS Rathbone's steely glance across the table that separated their workstations.

'When and where?' he demanded, having evidently been listening to her end of the conversation. She told him and he said, 'OK, I've arranged to see Professor Thorne at eleven. You might as well come along.'

'Right, Sarge.'

A little over an hour later, as they went downstairs to the yard to pick up the car he had already booked, Rathbone said, 'I still think Thorne may have picked up some hint that Whistler had other stuff with him without even realizing it – possibly through a casual reference in conversation to the proposed visit to London.'

'You reckon his secretary might have done the same and told her boyfriend?' said Sukey.

'It's a long shot, but we might as well

180

check. I've asked him not to mention this meeting to her, by the way. You'd better leave the questioning to me this time,' he added as he settled into the passenger seat and clipped on his seat belt.

You're determined to take every possible opportunity of reminding me that I'm still a rookie, aren't you? Sukey thought to herself with a touch of resentment. At least he hadn't suggested accompanying her to the meeting with Erika Henderson. The short journey passed in silence; when they arrived he left her to park the car and went into the building without her. By the time she had found a space and followed him, he had announced their arrival to the blonde receptionist and the two of them were waiting in the hall. The woman's manner was no more welcoming than it had been on their previous visit as she conducted them to a small room on the ground floor, opened the door and said, 'Professor Thorne will join you in a moment,' in a tone that suggested a great favour was about to be bestowed on them.

Thorne himself, arriving a few moments later, greeted them affably and offered coffee, which Rathbone declined without reference to Sukey. 'Before I tell you the reason for requesting this meeting, sir,' he began, 'I must ask you once again to treat it as confidential.'

Thorne nodded. 'You made that very clear, Sergeant, which is why I instructed the receptionist to show you into this room, to avoid unwelcome interruptions.' As before, he was wearing a grey flannel suit with knife-sharp creases in the trousers, which he carefully hitched up at the knees as he sat down. 'Please tell me, are you anywhere near finding the perpetrator of this dreadful crime?'

'It so happens our enquiries have reached a critical stage,' Rathbone replied, 'but there are a number of questions still to be answered and it is possible you may be able to help us.'

Thorne spread his plump hands and said earnestly, 'I'll do anything I can to help bring the villain to justice.'

Rathbone gave a slightly dismissive nod as if to say this was no more than was to be expected. 'During a recent conversation,' he continued, 'you expressed your conviction that Professor Lamont is incapable of committing murder.'

'That is true, and I have not changed my opinion,' said Thorne, 'and before we go on, Sergeant, I should like to say that the poor chap has been considerably affected by your continued harassment. It has brought him to the verge of a breakdown and he is presently on indefinite sick leave. It has also caused distress to his sister, who as you know suffers from emotional problems.'

'It is never our intention to cause distress to innocent citizens, but in a case of murder we have to explore every possibility,' said Rathbone. 'That is why I am here, Professor; as I have already told you, we now know that in addition to the supposed Pauline letter, Whistler was also bringing with him several religious relics that could be worth a lot of money on the black market. I know I've asked you this question before, but I'm asking you once again: are you absolutely certain you had no idea Whistler was bringing any other items with him? We know there was no reference in the correspondence, but is it possible that some chance remark during a telephone conversation, something you hardly noticed at the time, might with hindsight have suggested there was more than just the letter?'

'I thought about it after you asked me the first time, and I can't recall anything significant,' said Thorne with another shake of his head. 'Unless—' He hesitated for a moment before adding, 'I seem to recall some mention of a trip to London that Whistler was planning before his return to Rhodes.'

'Can you remember who mentioned it?'

'I think ... yes, now I come to think of it, Lamont said something about Whistler having quite a tight schedule and he might have mentioned London.'

'Do you know the purpose of that visit?'

'I'm afraid not.'

'Did that conversation take place in your office?'

'Yes. As a matter of fact, Lamont had just taken a call from Doctor Whistler and it was when it was over that he mentioned London.'

'You were present during that call?'

'Yes, but Lamont's side of the conversation consisted merely of remarks such as, "I see" or "I understand" and something like "all right, I'll wait to hear from you". After he hung up he told me Whistler was having to alter his schedule to take in a visit to London, but he didn't go into any details.'

'You didn't think to ask?'

'Why should I? If it had been any concern of mine, he would have told me.'

'Can you remember what day this happened?'

'I'm afraid not. Several days before Whistler's visit, I imagine; I can't be more precise than that.'

'Was anyone else present?'

Thorne hesitated for a fraction of a second before saying, 'I suppose my secretary might have been with us. I can't be sure. Is it important?'

'That would be Ms Milligan?' Thorne nodded. Sukey, observing him closely, thought he appeared a little uneasy at the direction Rathbone's questioning had taken. 'How long has she been employed at the university?' the sergeant asked.

'I'm not exactly sure. Eighteen months, two years perhaps. I'd have to check.'

'Has she been your secretary for the whole of that time?'

'No, she worked in the registry for some months before she came to me. My previous secretary left, the post was advertised internally and she applied. The Registrar spoke highly of her and after an interview I appointed her.'

Rathbone cleared his throat and leaned forward in his chair. 'Please don't misunderstand what I'm about to ask you, Professor, but how well do you know Ms Milligan?'

'Well, really!' A dull flush crept into Thorne's pallid cheeks. 'Are you suggesting, Sergeant, that I have been having some kind of inappropriate relationship with a member of my staff?'

'Certainly not,' Rathbone assured him, 'and I apologize if I have given offence. What I am trying to establish is whether she has ever spoken to you about her private or perhaps I should say social life. She is a young and, I understand, an attractive young lady so I imagine she has a wide circle of friends.'

Still looking uncomfortable, Thorne fiddled with some brochures lying on a nearby table. 'Well, yes, I'm sure that's true,' he muttered.

'So has she mentioned anyone she has met recently? Someone in whom she showed, shall we say, a particular interest?'

'No, I can't say she has.'

'In that case, perhaps I should have a word with her.'

'I'm afraid she's not here at the moment. She has a dental appointment but she'll be in at two o'clock.'

'Then we'll come back at two.' Rathbone stood up and held out his hand. 'Thank you very much for your time, Professor – and in the meantime, may I remind you to say nothing about this conversation to her or anyone else.'

Thorne gave the required assurances and shook the proffered hand in evident relief that the interview was at an end. As they walked back to the car, Rathbone said, 'What did you make of that?'

'He did seem to get a bit hot under the collar when you asked how well he knew his secretary,' said Sukey, 'but I can't believe the delectable Ms Milligan would find Thorne particularly attractive when she can land someone like Maddox.'

'All the same, it certainly produced a reaction of sorts. Make sure you get back to the station after your meeting with Erika Henderson in time to pick me up no later than one thirty, ' he added as he settled into the passenger seat and clipped on his seat belt. 'I want to be there well before two so that he doesn't have a chance to talk to her before we do.'

'Right, Sarge.' Sukey was relieved to know that his mind was running on similar lines to her own. She would have hesitated to risk a snub by putting the idea forward herself. In the circumstances, she decided not to point out that Ms Milligan probably carried a mobile phone and there was nothing to stop him using it to warn her of the impending visit from the detectives.

'And a propos of your meeting with Erika Henderson,' Rathbone added, 'I hope I can rely on you to tell her as little as possible. And not a word about Maddox – understood?'

'Of course, Sarge.'

When Sukey reached the recently opened Spend and Save Supermarket, Erika Henderson was already unwrapping a sandwich at a table for two in a corner of the coffee shop. A bulging carrier bag lay on the empty seat. She nodded and smiled as Sukey approached. 'I hope this is all right,' she said, 'I sat here because it's reasonably tucked away.'

'It's absolutely fine,' Sukey assured her. 'I'll go and grab a sarnie and a coffee.'

'I can recommend the tuna mayo,' said Erika.

'Thanks, I'll try it.'

When Sukey returned with her tray Erika had finished her sandwich and was sipping her coffee. 'Just dump my stuff on the floor,' she said, indicating the bag of groceries, 'and tell me what this is all about. I've been burning with curiosity ever since you rang.'

Her eyes sparkled over the rim of her cup and Sukey saw her in a new light. At their earlier meetings, although she had been willing – indeed, anxious – to help the investigation and had more than once volunteered information, she had maintained a certain cool detachment. Today she was more like an excited teenager.

'Before I start,' Sukey said, 'I need your promise that you won't tell anyone about this meeting.'

Erika looked slightly hurt. 'You've already said that,' she said reproachfully. 'Of course I promise,'

'And it's important that nothing we say is overheard, so please remember to speak quietly.'

'Understood. Oh, do get on with it! I'm dying to know what it's about. And I only have half an hour,' she added with a glance at her watch.

'It won't take long,' said Sukey. 'In any case, I haven't got that long either. I take it you have access to all the hotel employees' records?'

Erika nodded. 'They're all on my computer.'

'How many other people have access?'

'Maurice Ashford, naturally. No one else; the database is protected.'

'What about application forms, references and so on?'

'They're kept in a locked filing cabinet.' Erika frowned. 'What's this leading up to?'

'We need to know more about Boris Gasspar,' said Sukey.

'Boris? Why?'

'We think he may know the whereabouts of someone we're anxious to speak to.'

Erika's eyes nearly popped out of her head. 'You mean a criminal?' she said in a squeaky whisper. 'Has this got anything to do with the murder of Doctor Whistler?'

'I'm afraid I can't answer that question,' said Sukey.

'Why can't you ask Boris yourselves?'

'I can't go into that either.'

'So, what do you want me to do?'

'First of all, tell me how he came to apply for the job?'

'We register staff vacancies at an agency specializing in hotel and catering staff. We needed a receptionist and they sent him.'

'Does he have a National Insurance number?'

'Of course. We wouldn't have taken him on without one.'

'Did he give any references?'

'Yes, from another hotel – somewhere in Croatia, I think it was. Or maybe Serbia, I'm not sure offhand. I remember their letter was in rather quaint English.' Erika gave a smile of amusement at the recollection.

'So he'd had some previous experience in the business?'

'Oh, yes, he knew his job. His previous employers spoke highly of him and we've found him a very satisfactory employee.' Her expression became concerned. 'I do hope he isn't in any kind of trouble. He does have an anxious look about him from time to time, but he always insists that he's OK.' Erika glanced at her watch again. 'Is that all you want to know? I really should be going.'

'We'd like to see his paperwork,' said Sukey. 'You probably won't want to part with the originals, but photocopies would be fine.'

'That's no problem. I can do it when Maurice is out of the office. How will I get them to you?'

'Call me when they're ready and I'll arrange to pick them up.'

'I take it you won't want to come to the hotel?'

'No; we could come back here if you like.'

'Why not?' Erika reached down to pick up her shopping. 'Is that all, then?'

'Just one other thing. You told DS Douglas

you heard Boris having what you described as "a furious row" in a foreign language on his mobile. I don't suppose you have any idea what language he was using?'

Erika shook her head. 'All I can say is that it definitely wasn't French or German, and I don't think it was Spanish or Italian either. I don't speak any of those languages but I've heard them all when I've been abroad on holidays.'

'Thanks. That could be helpful.'

'Is this person you're trying to find foreign then?'

'I don't know. In any case, there's nothing to suggest he was the person Boris was talking to.'

Erika gave a knowing look. 'All right, I won't ask any more questions.' She put a finger to her lips and whispered, 'This conversation never took place!' in a melodramatic undertone before heading for the exit.

Sixteen

When Sukey arrived back at the station after her interview with Erika Henderson it was a little after one fifteen. There was no sign of DS Rathbone by the entrance so she went up to the CID office, where she found Vicky standing by her desk with her jacket on and her bag over her shoulder, apparently on the point of going out.

'If you're looking for DS Rathbone, he's with DCI Leach, but he'll be back in a minute,' she told Sukey. 'He's just rung through to tell me to stand by to go with him to the Hellenic Studies Department at the uni to interview Professor Thorne's secretary.'

Sukey blinked in surprise. 'I went with him to see Thorne this morning,' she said, 'but the secretary was at the dentist so he arranged to go back this afternoon. I assumed I'd be going with him.'

Vicky shrugged. 'All I know is he told me you've got a car and I'm to collect the key from you.'

'Any idea why the change of plan?' asked

Sukey as she handed it over.

'Haven't a clue. Did anything come out of the interview with the prof?'

'Not a lot.' Sukey outlined the exchanges between Rathbone and Thorne and Vicky chuckled over her description of the latter's look of dismay when he thought he might be suspected of a liaison with his secretary. 'He looked really embarrassed, but I can't imagine she'd be interested in him. If he's there this afternoon you'll see what I mean.'

'Maybe he fantasises,' Vicky suggested.

'Could be. Anyway, she's coming back at two and Rathbone wants to make sure of getting in ahead of her, before she can speak to Thorne.'

Vicky raised an eyebrow. 'Why so?'

'He thinks there might be some sort of collusion between the two of them and as it happens the same thought occurred to me. On the face of it it's difficult to see how it could be relevant to the killing of Whistler – except, of course, that the secretary does have a very dodgy boyfriend and might have passed something on to him without realizing its significance.'

'Her boss is hardly likely to know about that, is he?'

'Who knows? He certainly didn't get it from us – at least, the Sarge never mentioned it this morning. Ah, here he comes.'

Rathbone strode into the room, yanked his

dark blue fleece jacket from the back of his chair, slung it over his shoulder and beckoned the two women over. 'DCI Leach has decided it's better if you don't come with me to interview the Milligan woman because she knows you've seen her in the company of Maddox,' he told Sukey as they obeyed the summons. 'We've no idea how much she knows about him; she may of course be completely in the dark about his dirty dealings, but with this big undercover operation going on we can't take any chances. There's to be absolutely no mention of him during this afternoon's meeting,' he said to Vicky. 'We want her to think the purpose is solely to clear up some loose ends about the Whistler case.'

Vicky nodded. 'Understood, Sarge.'

'It's just as well she wasn't there this morning, then,' Sukey commented. 'She could have got curious and wanted to know what we were doing there.'

'Right,' said Rathbone without looking in her direction. 'Got the car key, Vicky? Good, we'll be on our way.' Over his shoulder as they made for the door, he said, 'Sukey, while I'm out you can be writing up your meeting with Ashford's PA.'

'Will do, Sarge.'

During these brief exchanges, DS Bob Douglas had entered the office. The moment Rathbone and Vicky had left he strolled over to Sukey's desk. 'So you've been taken off the Whistler case?' he said.

'So it would seem. How did you know?'

'I was with the DCI while he was talking to Greg Rathbone. I'm more or less off it as well, now that we've shut down the incident room at the hotel – greatly to the manager's relief.'

'Have there been any other developments that I don't know about?'

'Not that I've heard of. Did you get any joy out of Ms Henderson this morning by the way?'

'She's going to let us have photocopies of Boris Gasspar's paperwork. He has a NI number and the hotel followed up a reference he gave them, so it looks as if he might be here legally after all. If that's the case, it rather puts the kybosh on my theory that he was blackmailed into giving false evidence against Stephen Lamont. Assuming the reference was genuine of course.'

Douglas chuckled. 'And you'd just love to find out it's phoney, wouldn't you? I know how you feel; it's great when one of your hunches pays off, especially when everyone else thinks you're barking up the wrong tree.'

Sukey gave him a grateful smile. The contrast between his sympathetic manner and Rathbone's thinly veiled contempt was heart-warming. 'Thanks for saying that. Tell me, do you still think Lamont is guilty?'

'To be honest, yes, but it's going to be difficult to build a case the CPS will allow to go to court. I admit that on the face of it Gasspar's link with Maddox does muddy the waters a bit, but it doesn't necessarily mean it has anything to do with the attack on Whistler. Lamont hasn't been able to produce a single witness to back up his story, whereas in addition to Gasspar more than one independent witness saw a man answering Lamont's description at a time he swears he wasn't there. They can't all have been got at by Maddox.'

'I suppose not,' Sukey admitted with a sigh. 'Well, I'd better get on and write up my report.'

When she had finished she printed off a copy, put it in DS Rathbone's in-tray and then went to the washroom. She was away for only a few minutes, but when she returned there was a general buzz of excitement in the office.

'What's going on?' she asked Anna, the civilian worker whom she had met at the incident room at the Mariners Hotel.

'Someone's reported seeing a body on the banks of the Avon, a mile or so downstream from the suspension bridge,' said Anna. 'The DCI has summoned DS Douglas so I guess he'll be assigned to the case.'

A few minutes later Douglas returned. Catching sight of Sukey, he came over to her and said, 'I guess Anna's put you in the picture. DCI Leach has put me on the case and as you're at a loose end this afternoon he suggests I take you along for the experience. I've booked a car.' He picked up his jacket and headed for the door. 'Come on, let's go.'

They left the city centre and headed along the Portway in the direction of Avonmouth. A mile or so beyond the famous Clifton Suspension Bridge the nearside lane had been closed causing a tailback of cars whose drivers, despite furious gestures from the police urging them to keep moving, persisted in slowing to a crawl while craning to see what was going on. Douglas got out of the car and walked ahead to speak to the officer directing the traffic; as Sukey at last drew level he signalled to her to pull in behind a long line of emergency vehicles, including two fire engines, an ambulance, several police cars, a police van and two smaller vans that Sukey recognized from her days working as a Scenes of Crime Officer. Ahead, the fire crews and a team of police frogmen were dragging various items of equipment from their vehicles and disappearing with them down the steep side of the Avon Gorge to the riverside path below.

A middle-aged couple standing on the footpath beside one of the police cars were talking to another officer, who made an excuse and broke off the conversation for a moment when he spotted DS Douglas. Evidently they were old friends, for he greeted him as "Bob" and Douglas addressed him as "Snoopy" before introducing Sukey by saying, 'Meet DC Sukey Reynolds. She's just finished her six months with Vicky Armstrong. Sukey, Sergeant Brown, Traffic Division.'

'Glad to know you, Sukey,' said the sergeant. 'I got that disrespectful nickname because my real one's Charlie,' he explained. 'You can just forget it – and that's an order,' he added.

'Yes, Sarge,' she said primly.

His manner, which had been only half serious, became grave as he said, 'You might find this a bit hard to take. A goner that's been in the water for any length of time isn't a pretty sight.'

'I know, I've seen one before,' said Sukey. 'During my five years as a SOCO,' she explained in response to his look of surprise. 'And that one had its head hacked off,' she added.

The sergeant pulled a face. 'That must have been seriously stomach churning,' he observed. 'Well, I'd better get back and finish talking to the Telfords.' He jerked his head in the direction of the man and woman who were still waiting a short distance away. 'They spotted the body while they were walking Monty along the riverside path.'

Hearing its name, the black and white cocker spaniel sitting patiently at their feet stood up and wagged its tail. 'They don't have a mobile,' he went on, 'so they came up here and managed to flag down a passing patrol car. I was taking some details when you arrived.'

While they were waiting for him to return, Sukey and Douglas went to the protective rail that ran along the edge of the gorge and peered down through a gap in the tangle of trees and bushes. The tide was low, reducing the river to a narrow channel and exposing a wide expanse of glistening mud the colour of milk chocolate. Gulls screeched and swooped overhead and a heron stood motionless at the water's edge a little way downstream from where they were standing, staring intently into the muddy depths and apparently unfazed by the activity on the opposite bank. They waited while the sergeant finished dealing with the couple, escorted them to their car and held up the traffic to enable them to pull out and drive away before walking back. He indicated a gap in the railing, where the last of the frogmen was just disappearing down a flight of steps.

'Down here and mind how you go,' he warned them. 'It's fairly steep, but there's a handrail of sorts. We haven't been able to get close enough to the body yet to establish any details, but it's near enough to the bank for us to see it's female,' he said as Sukey and DS Douglas cautiously followed him. 'There's a fire crew down there now, making a walkway over the mud. They've got to work fast because the tide's coming in. It's this way.' He set off along a grassy path in the direction of Sea Mills until, round a bend in the river, they saw a group of firemen laying a line of aluminium planks across the mud while teams of frogmen and SOCOs stood by, awaiting the opportunity to carry out their respective tasks. Two uniformed officers were shooing away a few curious would-be onlookers out on an afternoon stroll.

Sukey took a pair of miniature binoculars from the pocket of her denim jacket and focused them on the corpse, which lay behind a spit of mud that generations of rising and falling tides had sculpted into a shape like the head of some strange sea monster. The contours outlined by the clinging, mud-stained garments and the long hair wound like strands of seaweed over the face and throat confirmed that the victim was female and probably quite young.

'The headless body I mentioned just now had been in the water for some days and it looked pretty horrible,' she said, shuddering at the memory. 'It doesn't look to me as if this one's been in there all that long. What do you think?'

'I think you've got a point,' said Douglas,

who had been carrying out a similar assessment. 'Snoopy's right – they'll have to work
fast,' he added with a glance at his watch.
'According to my reckoning it was low tide
more than three hours ago and it's coming in
at quite a rate.'

They watched in silence while the firemen
laid the last plank in position. A man in
civilian clothes was the first to make his way
gingerly along the improvised walkway.
When he reached the motionless figure he
squatted down and took a stethoscope from
his pocket.

'That's Doctor Hanley, our forensic pathologist,' Douglas explained.

The examination was soon over. Hanley
returned to the bank and picked up the bag
he had left on the ground, spoke briefly to
Sergeant Brown and then walked over to
where Sukey and DS Douglas stood watching the proceedings.

'Afternoon, Sergeant,' he said. 'Young
woman, aged about sixteen at a rough guess.
I reckon she's been dead at least a couple of
days, but she hasn't been in the water as long
as that.'

'So it's not a drowning?' said Douglas.

The pathologist shook his head. 'Almost
certainly not. There appear to be some
injuries, but there's so much mud plastered
around I can't be sure whether they were
sustained before or after death. When you

get her to terra firma I'll have a closer look, but you'll have to wait till she's been cleaned up before I can do a detailed report.' He strolled over to a wooden bench beside the path and sat down.

Meanwhile a team of frogmen had made their way past the body and were examining the shallows prior to exploring the deeper water. Two SOCOs in white protective clothing who had followed close behind them began their examination, one taking photographs while the other squatted down to scoop up samples of mud and water and put them in sealed and labelled containers. The river was rising rapidly as the tide swept up from the Bristol Channel and by the time they had finished and Sukey and Douglas were able to make their own hasty examination in search of possible evidence it was lapping at the dead girl's feet. Minutes later they were forced to retreat to enable the firemen to bring her ashore.

'She's not much more than a child!' Sukey exclaimed. She felt a lump rising in her throat as she looked down at the slender form on the mortuary slab.

Doctor Hanley nodded. 'Sixteen at the most,' he said. 'Not exactly under-nourished, but not much fat on her either. Typical of kids of her age, of course – they all want to look like beanpoles so she's probably been watching her figure. To please the boyfriend, most likely,' he added. 'And from the state of her she's had quite a few.'

'Can you give us a better idea now of how long she's been dead?' asked Rathbone.

'As I said earlier, she was in the water for only a few hours, but she could have died a couple of days before that. I'll know more when I've examined the stomach contents.'

'Is that all you can tell us for now?' Rathbone asked.

'Yes – except that she's recently been subjected to a bit of rough treatment. Not serious stuff, probably some foreplay that got out of hand. See those bruises on the throat?' Hanley went on, pointing with a long, delicate finger at some livid marks below the girl's jaw. 'Whoever put those there might have intended to kill her, but I think it's more likely he accidentally squeezed a bit too hard in the heat of the moment.'

'You can't say which?' asked DS Douglas.

The doctor's grin transformed his thin, beaky features. 'No idea, mate,' he said cheerfully. 'It's your job to find out. All I can say for sure is that she didn't drown, she died of manual strangulation.'

Seventeen

It was after six o'clock by the time Sukey and DS Douglas got back to the station. They went straight up to DCI Leach's office.

'This is going to be a tough one,' Leach remarked when he had heard their account of the afternoon's events. 'I take it there was no ID on the body, Bob?'

'Not a thing, sir. We'll check the list of local mispers of course, but I'm pretty certain none of them answers to that girl's description.'

'Could she have been brought here from somewhere outside the area?' Sukey suggested.

Both men shook their heads. 'I doubt it,' said Leach. 'From what you two have told me, it's most likely that whoever did it had local knowledge.'

'I'd go along with that,' said Douglas. 'She was almost certainly dumped when the tide was full, or nearly full, probably by someone with a boat. We'll have to consult our river expert; he'll be able to give us some idea of where a body would have to enter the water to reach that particular spot before the tide was low enough to expose it.'

'It must have been there for quite a long time before the Telfords saw it,' Sukey remarked. 'It's surprising it wasn't spotted sooner.'

'Not really,' said Douglas. 'There's no river traffic when the water's low and more often than not you can walk the length of that footpath without meeting a soul. It's different at weekends, of course, but this was a Monday morning.'

'That's true,' she admitted, recalling that only a handful of people had turned up during the afternoon while the body was being retrieved. 'But what about the path on the opposite bank? I suppose most of the girl's body would have been concealed by that long spit of mud, but one of her legs was sticking out beyond the end of it. Anyone with reasonable eyesight could have seen it.'

Leach shook his head a second time, but he gave Sukey an encouraging smile. Her mind went back to the day he had called her for an interview after she had completed her probationary six months with Vicky. She remembered him saying that he wanted her to feel free to offer suggestions or make constructive comments as the occasion demanded. It was, she reflected wryly, an attitude that DS Rathbone had shown little inclination to adopt.

'Theoretically that's feasible,' he agreed, 'but in practice, anyone walking or cycling along there who happened to glance across would be more likely to assume it was a piece of rubbish someone had thrown overboard – if they noticed it at all. Cyclists tend to look ahead rather than around them. On balance, I'd say we were fortunate she didn't lie there until the tide covered her a second time. OK, you know what to do next, Bob. Keep me posted.'

'Yes, sir.'

On their way back to the main office, Douglas remarked, 'You've picked up quite a bit of local knowledge today, Sukey. It'll all come in handy some time or other.'

It had been an eventful day. On reaching home, over an hour later than usual, Sukey went into the kitchen and set one of the prepared meals she kept for such occasions to defrost in the microwave before taking a quick shower and changing into a sweatshirt and jeans. The light on her answering machine indicated that there were messages waiting; she poured out a glass of wine and sat down in an armchair with the phone at her elbow, but it rang before she had time to press the replay button. Jim was on the line.

'Thank goodness you're home!' he exclaimed as soon as she answered. 'I left a message and you didn't call back; I was getting worried.'

'Detectives don't always work regular hours,' she reminded him. 'There have been plenty of times when you didn't show and I imagined you being mown down by a thug with a shooter.'

'I know, I know!' he said. 'Scold me if you must, but you know me – one of the world's champion worriers.'

'All right, you're forgiven.'

'So what sort of a day have you had?'

'Eventful. To start with, I think you'll be interested to know I seem to be off the Whistler case.'

'Seem to be?'

'I was supposed to go with DS Rathbone to interview Professor Thorne's secretary – the one who was with Oliver Maddox in the restaurant the other night, but he took Vicky Armstrong instead. Your friend DCI Leach decided he didn't want her reporting back to her boyfriend that I was still involved in the Whistler investigation, just in case Maddox did spot me that afternoon and it was my card that he took from Boris.'

'It's probably a wise precaution,' said Jim.

'Actually, I wasn't all that sorry,' said Sukey. 'My exercise in unofficial surveillance hasn't made me flavour of the month with DS Rathbone and he's made no attempt to disguise the fact.'

'So what have you been doing today that made you work overtime?'

'Witnessing the body of a teenage girl being recovered from the river – or rather the riverbank. She was left exposed when the tide went out and getting her to dry land was quite a performance on account of the mud.'

'Suicide?' asked Jim.

'Definitely not. The pathologist reckons she could have been dead for a couple of days before she was put in the water. Come to think of it, she might be another victim of the Maddox mafia,' she added wickedly, picturing his change of expression as the thought registered.

'Good heavens, is that what—' He realized she was having him on. 'You just said that to wind me up,' he said reproachfully.

'Guilty – but you must admit I'm rather good at it.'

'You're rather good at other things as well,' he said with another, more subtle change of tone. 'When am I going to see you again?'

It had been a tiring as well as an eventful day. Without warning, she found herself engulfed by a mighty yawn. 'Gosh, I'm sorry,' she said. 'I hadn't realized how tired I am, and I haven't eaten yet either. Can we talk about it some other time? I'm simply not up to making plans this evening.'

'No problem,' he said softly. 'I'll call again soon. Take care.'

After he hung up she finished her wine and then checked her messages. She deleted the one from Jim and then listened to the next. It was from Fergus.

'Nothing special, just rang for a chat,' he said breezily. 'I'll try again later.'

The last message was from Priscilla Gadden. 'Sukey, I'm sorry to bother you, but I've had Hester Lamont here all day. She's found out somehow that you're in the police and involved in her brother's case, and she's desperate to talk to you. Can you possibly find a moment to call me back?'

'Not till I've had some food, I couldn't,' Sukey said aloud as she pressed the delete button.

She put her defrosted supermarket shepherd's pie into the oven, topped up her wine glass, put on a recording of Mozart piano sonatas and relaxed in her favourite armchair until the pie was ready. A little over an hour later, feeling somewhat revived, she sent a text message to Fergus on his mobile, promising to call him later, and then keyed in Priscilla's number. Tom Gadden answered.

'Sorry to call so late,' she began, 'but when I got home I found a message from Priscilla and it sounded urgent. Is she there, please?'

'She is, and so is the Lamont Limpet,' he said with a touch of impatience. 'If you can get this crazy female off my wife's back I'll be very much obliged. Wait a minute, I'll call her.'

When Priscilla came on the line she said, 'Oh, Sukey, it's so good of you to call. Could you possibly have a word with Hester? She's convinced now that Stephen is innocent and that she knows who killed Doctor Whistler.'

'Whatever's happened to make her change her mind? Has she found new evidence?'

'I've no idea. She won't tell me anything; she wants to speak to you.'

'I take it she's discussed this with her brother?'

'It seems she's tried to and he's told her to keep out of it.'

'That's probably good advice in view of her mental state,' said Sukey. 'Look, I honestly don't think I can help. There have been certain developments; I can't give you any details, but—'

'You don't mean the police are going to charge Stephen?' Priscilla interrupted in dismay.

'I'm not saying that, but if Hester has some important new evidence she should come to the station straight away and make a statement.'

'I've already advised her to do that, but she won't hear of it – at least, not without speaking to you first. She says you understand her problems; she keeps going on about how sympathetic you are and you should be a counsellor and so on. Tom's getting really hot under the collar and I'm at my wits' end

210

what to do with her.'

'I take it she's not in the room with you at the moment?'

'No, she's watching the television and Patsy's with her. Please, Sukey, will you at least listen to what she has to say?'

Sukey sighed. 'All right, put her on then.'

There was a brief pause before Priscilla said, 'I know this is asking an awful lot, but do you think you could possibly come here and talk to her? I think ... I know she'd talk more freely face to face. I wouldn't ask if you lived any distance away,' she hurried on, 'but as you're only just down the road ... or perhaps I could bring her down to your place?'

'Certainly not, and please, on no account tell her where I live,' said Sukey in alarm. 'I don't want her banging on my door at all hours and besides, it so happens I'm now working on a different case.'

'Oh dear!' Priscilla sounded distraught. 'What am I to tell her then?'

'All right, I'll pop round and see what I can do,' said Sukey resignedly.

'Would you? We'd be so grateful.'

'I'll wait for a bit and then come in the car. If I turn up within the next five minutes she'll twig that I live on your doorstep.'

'That would make sense,' Priscilla agreed. 'I'll make sure the gates are open for you.'

Hester Lamont looked even paler and more

211

fragile than Sukey remembered from their previous meeting. She was sitting with her head bowed and her hands clasped in her lap, but on hearing Priscilla say, 'Hester, here's Sukey come to see you', she raised her head and gave a wan smile.

'Thank you for coming,' she said simply.

'You want to tell me something?' Sukey said.

'Yes, but—' She gave a self-conscious glance at Patsy and her mother. 'If you wouldn't mind—?'

'We'll leave you to it,' said Patsy with evident relief.

As the door closed behind them, Hester clutched Sukey by the hand and said, 'I can't tell you how badly I feel at doubting Stephen. All this time he's been swearing he didn't kill that man, and I wouldn't believe him. I kept saying I understood why he did it and that I was really to blame, and he kept saying I'd got it all wrong and I didn't know what I was talking about and then I tried to cut myself again and he got really angry and said if I did it one more time he'd have me shut up for ever. And now I know he was telling the truth all along and I'll never forgive myself, never!' She burst into loud, wailing sobs that racked her thin frame for several minutes.

When at last she was calmer she drank some water that had been left on the table and said, 'I'm sorry, I didn't mean to break down like that.'

'It's natural; you've been under a lot of strain,' said Sukey. 'And now perhaps you can tell me why you're so sure your brother didn't kill Doctor Whistler.'

'It's very simple,' Hester said earnestly, her soft brown eyes fixed on Sukey's face. 'This morning I saw the man who did it.'

'You what?'

'The man who did it – I saw him,' Hester repeated.

'I don't understand,' Sukey said in bewilderment. 'Where did you see this man and how do you know he's the man who killed Whistler?'

'I was doing some shopping in Clifton Village and as I came out of the deli he was getting into a car parked just outside. He was the image of Stephen, except that his hair was shorter but Stephen does go to the barber sometimes ... and he was wearing jeans and Stephen hardly ever wears jeans ... but otherwise he, this man, was exactly like him ... and for a moment I was so sure it was him that I called out, "Stephen, whatever are you doing here?" because of course I thought he was in his study at home ... he's on indefinite leave while all this dreadful business is going on ... and he – this man I mean – looked a bit surprised and shut his car door and drove away in a great hurry.

And then I realized that it wasn't Stephen's car at all ... and all of a sudden it came to me. He must be the murderer and it's all been a, what do you call it, a case of mistaken identity.'

Eighteen

As she listened in astonishment while Hester poured out the string of breathless, disjointed sentences, Sukey found herself seriously doubting the woman's sanity. By the time she reached the climax of her story she was like someone who had seen a vision, hands clasped and eyes shining with expectation as she gazed at the one person she felt able to trust. Momentarily speechless after the verbal onslaught, it took Sukey several seconds to find a suitable response. Hester seemed to read her hesitation as rejection; the brightness slowly died from her expression and her hands fell limply into her lap. 'You think I'm crazy, don't you?' she muttered.

'No, of course not,' Sukey said quickly. 'It's just ... well, it's certainly a remarkable coincidence and I can understand why you've reacted in the way you have after seeing this man.'

Hope rekindled in the trusting brown eyes. 'Then you think I'm right?'

'There's no doubt that there have been cases of mistaken identity,' Sukey said carefully, 'and I do think this one is worth investigating, but all I can do is pass on what you've told me to the officer in charge of the investigation.'

'But don't you see, this changes everything!'

'It may well do, but it really isn't up to me to decide. What I suggest you do,' Sukey went on before Hester could start another protest, 'is write down very carefully everything you saw this morning, what time it happened, how the man was dressed, what kind of car he was driving and so on. I don't suppose you got the car number, by the way?'

Hester shook her head despondently. 'No, I'm afraid not,' she said. 'It was a big black car, I do remember that, and it had some sort of animal on the back shelf.'

'That's not a lot to go on, but it's something.' Sukey tried her best to sound encouraging. 'Is there anything else you remember about him? Was he wearing any jewellery – a signet ring, for example? Shut your eyes for a moment and try to picture him.'

Hester covered her entire face with her

hands, like a child playing hide and seek. 'I seem to recall something gold,' she said vaguely. 'A wristwatch, perhaps ... no, I remember now!' Her voice rose to a squeak of excitement; she lowered her hands and looked at Sukey in triumph. 'He wore an earring. How stupid of me not to think of it. I should have realized it couldn't possibly be Stephen.'

'Very good.' Sukey took a notebook from her pocket and scribbled a few lines. 'Would that be in his right or his left ear?'

'Right,' said Hester without hesitation. 'He came from my left and got straight into his car, so I didn't see the other side of his face at all.'

'Anything else? Any distinguishing marks like a scar or a tattoo, for example?'

'I didn't notice anything like that, I'm afraid.'

'Well, if you think of anything else, write it down with everything else you've told me and then call the police station and ask to speak to Detective Sergeant Rathbone. I'll tell him about this and if you don't feel up to coming down to the CID office he'll arrange to come and see you.'

'At home?' Hester looked aghast. 'But I don't want Stephen to know I've been talking to you ... he's always telling me not to meddle with things I don't understand.'

'Then I'm afraid you'll have to come to the

216

station.' Sukey stood up. 'I'm going home now and I think you should do the same or your brother will be worried about you.'

'It's all right; he knows where I am. Perhaps Tom and Priscilla would let me meet the detective here,' Hester said, sounding almost desperate. 'Then Stephen wouldn't know anything about this until it's all cleared up.'

Sukey felt a twinge of sadness. Clearly, Hester was still clinging to a pathetic belief in her theory. Aloud, she said, 'That's a good idea. Why don't you ask them?' Gently brushing aside the woman's earnest thanks, she made her escape.

As she returned to the hall, closing the door behind her, Priscilla appeared from another room. 'How is she now?' she asked anxiously.

'Calmer, but she's in a pretty volatile state of mind. She claims to have seen Stephen's doppelgänger in Clifton this morning and she's convinced that this man and not Stephen committed the murder.'

Priscilla's jaw dropped. 'How extraordinary! Do you think there could be anything in it?'

Sukey had been tired before she set out on this bizarre visit and the interview had taken more out of her emotionally than she realized. She put both hands to her temples in an effort to soothe away the weariness seeping into her brain. 'I honestly don't know,' she said. 'Coming from a more rational person I'd be inclined to take it seriously, but in Hester's case—'

'Yes, I know what you mean.' Priscilla cast an anxious glance over Sukey's shoulder and lowered her voice. 'What have you told her? Tom's insisting on taking her home the minute you've finished with her so that we can all get some rest.'

'That's all right,' said Sukey. 'That's what I advised her to do and I don't think she'll argue. I've also told her to write down what she's told me and then to ring the station and ask to speak to Detective Sergeant Rathbone. That seems to have satisfied her for the moment, but whether it'll be taken seriously is up to the SIO to decide. Senior Investigating Officer,' she explained in response to Priscilla's questioning look.

'I see. Well, thank you so much for coming.'

'No problem, but it's only fair to warn you that she may ask if she can meet the detectives here.'

Priscilla rolled her eyes in despair. 'Tom'll go ballistic!' she groaned.

'Her idea, not mine,' Sukey assured her. 'Anyway, one way or the other I'll keep you posted.'

As soon as she reported for duty the following morning Sukey managed to snatch a brief word with Vicky Armstrong. As she had anticipated, Vicky was sceptical.

'You don't reckon there's anything in it, do you?' she said.

'I don't think Hester was making it up – I mean, I'm sure she did see someone with a close resemblance to her brother and that must have put the idea about mistaken identity into her head. How much of what she told me is accurate and how much is embroidery is anyone's guess, but the fact is she's now beating her breast with guilt at having doubted him.'

Vicky shrugged. 'She's hardly a reliable witness, is she? I'll mention it to DS Rathbone, but I doubt if he'll act on it. Maybe you'd better put in a written report.'

'Yes, I'll do that when I've got a moment,' said Sukey. 'Just now I'm up to my eyes in the Avon river case. DS Douglas has just dumped the file of local mispers on my desk.'

'Lucky old you,' said Vicky cheerfully.

Sukey went to her desk and began work on the daunting task of checking reports of teenage girls missing from homes in Bristol and the surrounding areas. The most recent was dated over a week ago, which suggested that the unidentified girl whose body had been washed up on the muddy banks of the

Avon had either disappeared from home so recently that her absence had not yet been reported, or that she came from further afield and had for some unknown reason made her way to Bristol before meeting her violent end.

After a couple of hours of fruitless searching she felt in need of a break, so she pushed the file aside and wrote a brief account of her meeting with Hester Lamont the previous evening. After printing it off she put it in DS Rathbone's in-tray and went down to the canteen for a much needed cup of coffee. When she returned twenty minutes later she found him with her report in one hand and his phone in the other. As she entered he said, 'She's just walked in, sir. We'll come right away.' He cradled the instrument and glared at her.

'Just what do you imagine you're playing at?' he demanded.

'Playing, Sarge? I don't understand. All I did was—'

'Disobey orders,' he barked, brandishing the report under her nose and making no effort to keep his voice down. 'You were told you were off the Lamont case – or are you too thick to understand plain English? DCI Leach wants us both in his office about this load of garbage ... now!' He turned on his heel and headed for the door. Aware that heads were turning in her direction, Sukey felt her cheeks burn as she followed him out of the room. She braced herself for another verbal onslaught the minute the door closed behind them, but he marched along the corridor in silence, his face grim.

DCI Leach's expression as they entered his office was only marginally less unfriendly. He was seated at his desk and held out his hand for her report on her interview with Hester Lamont without inviting either of them to sit down. He scanned it briefly, put it on the desk in front of him and said, 'Perhaps you'd care to explain why you agreed to see this woman when you were expressly told you were to have nothing more to do with this case.'

It was hardly a fair statement as no such specific order had been given, but Sukey had the sense not to argue.

'I assure you, sir, that I had absolutely no intention of disobeying orders,' she said. 'I went to the Gaddens' house at the urgent request of Mrs Gadden because Hester Lamont had gone to see her in a state of agitation bordering on hysteria, begging to be put in touch with me because she had something important to say concerning her brother.'

'Why you?' said Leach.

'If you recall, sir, I met her once before at the Gaddens' house and I made a detailed report of the conversation.'

Leach pursed his lips and raised an eyebrow in Rathbone's direction. The sergeant cleared his throat and said, 'That's true, sir; the report is on the file. It's chiefly concerned with the unfortunate events in Ms Lamont's life that led to her mental breakdown. She was not aware at the time that she was speaking to a police officer.'

'But she knows now?' This time the eyebrow was directed at Sukey.

'Yes, sir, but I've no idea how she found out. When I spoke to Priscilla – Mrs Gadden – I told her she should advise Hester to get in touch with the CID office and tell them what was on her mind. She said she'd tried that but Hester flatly refused to confide in anyone but me because she said I'd been kind and sympathetic last time. The Gaddens were getting desperate, so in the end I agreed to listen to what she said. Everything that passed between us is contained in that report.'

Leach leaned on one elbow and fiddled with his glasses as he reread the single sheet of A4 paper. After a moment or two he looked up and met her eye. His expression was kindlier than when she and Rathbone first entered the office, although he did not smile. 'I can see that you acted with the best of intentions,' he said, 'but please remember in future that investigations can be put at risk through well-intentioned, but misguided, actions. Your proper course in this case would have been to decline the request and advise Mrs Gadden to contact us herself if Ms Lamont continued to refuse to do so. We could then have sent a trained counsellor to interview her. Is that understood?'

'Yes, sir,' said Sukey meekly.

'Good. Has there been any progress in finding an ID for the Avon River victim?'

'Not so far, sir.'

'Well, keep at it. That's all for now.' He handed the report back to Rathbone and said, 'You'd better follow this up, Greg. There may be nothing in it, but we can't risk a defence counsel getting hold of it ... assuming the Lamont case ever gets to court.'

'Right, sir.'

Sukey half expected some caustic comment as she and Rathbone made their way back to the CID office, but he had the grace to remain silent – possibly, she suspected, because his failure to refer to her earlier report had caused him a twinge of embarrassment.

Later, when she went down to the canteen for lunch, Vicky came and sat at her table demanding to know what had passed during the interview with Leach. 'The sarge was like a bear with a sore head for the rest of the morning,' she confided gleefully. 'We all felt for you when he started bawling you out so when he came back looking less than pleased with himself we wondered whether he'd been given a flea in his ear.'

'Not exactly, but I think he was disappointed I didn't get more severely reprimanded than I did.'

'Serve him right. He's a really good cop,' Vicky went on, 'but he's on a pretty short fuse at times. He ranted on for about five minutes about having to follow up what he called the ravings of a madwoman, but when he calmed down he told me to set up a meeting with me, Hester and the same FLO we sent last week when we took Lamont in. That should reassure her.'

'You will keep me posted, won't you?' said Sukey. 'I've still got a feeling about that case and in a way I wish I hadn't been taken off it, although – ' she glanced round and dropped her voice – 'I was never actually told as much in so many words, only that it was unwise for me to be at the interview with Thorne's secretary. What happened about that, by the way?'

'Not a lot. The woman was quite definite she'd heard nothing about Whistler planning to go to London and there seemed no reason to think she was lying.'

'I'll bet that pleased DS Rathbone,' said Sukey dryly. 'The last thing he wants is to come across anything that casts doubts on Lamont's guilt.'

Vicky nodded. 'That's true, but what he

wants more than anything is one solid piece of evidence that will justify charging Lamont.'

'Have the results of the DNA tests on his clothing come through yet?'

'Yes, and they're inconclusive, so we're a bit bogged down at the moment. We've checked the people Lamont and Thorne told us might have gone into their offices and possibly seen or heard something relevant, but we've had no luck there either. The next step is to renew our appeal for help from the public. That's going out on the news this evening.' Vicky pushed back her empty plate and stood up. 'Well, back to the grind. Any progress on the river victim, by the way?'

Sukey shook her head. 'I'm afraid not. Reports on finding the body got into the late editions yesterday and more details are in today's, but so far we've had no new report of a missing girl. A description has been circulated to the national media, but if we don't get a response soon we'll have to publish a picture.'

The response, when it came, was of a totally unexpected nature.

Nineteen

The following morning Sukey received a call from Erika Henderson to say that she had made photocopies of all the paperwork she had in her file concerning Boris Gasspar.

'Would you like me to put them in the post or would you rather I handed them over to you in person?' she asked and then added in a slightly lower tone, 'Actually, I would prefer to meet you if you can spare the time.'

'Any particular reason?' Sukey asked warily. The thought came immediately into her head that as she was no longer on the Whistler case she should, strictly speaking, refer this call to DS Rathbone and get his approval or otherwise to still attend the meeting.

Before she had a chance to explain her situation Erika said, 'Hold on a minute.' There was a pause, during which she could be heard in conversation with a man, presumably the hotel manager, who was in the room with her. After a few indistinguishable exchanges she said, her voice slightly raised as if he was about to leave, 'Right, Maurice,

I'll be with you right away.' Returning to the phone she said hurriedly, 'Sorry, I have to go now. Are you free at lunchtime today?'

'As far as I know, but—'

'If you're pushed for time, I could meet you somewhere closer to the police station than Spend and Save. There's a café called the Rendezvous near the centre that I use sometimes.'

'I know it,' Sukey said hesitantly. During the break in their conversation she had been trying to decide how best to respond to Erika's request. Whatever she had to say, it was clear that she had no intention of revealing it over the phone. She glanced round the office; there was no sign of either Rathbone or Vicky, no one to whom she could turn to for advice. This was ridiculous, she told herself; merely to collect something she had been told to ask for in the first place could hardly be construed as disobeying orders. In any case, Erika's reason for wanting to meet her might have nothing whatever to do with the Whistler case, and if it did she could simply explain the changed circumstances and refer her to DS Rathbone.

Having thus rationalized the situation she said, 'As things are at the moment I can make it. What time do you suggest?'

'Let's say twelve thirty?'

'All right, but if something crops up I may have to cancel. I'd better have your mobile number just in case.' She jotted it down and hung up just as DS Douglas appeared with a box file under one arm.

'Reports of missing girls from our friends in other parts of the country,' he announced as he dumped it on her desk. 'There should be enough in there to keep you out of mischief till lunchtime.'

'Thanks, Sarge,' she said. 'Where will you be if I come across anything interesting?'

'If that's a subtle way of asking what I'll be doing, the answer is I'll be at the morgue with the privileged few observing Doc Hanley dissecting the Lady in the Avon.'

Sukey grimaced. 'Rather you than me, Sarge, but why the delay?'

'Pressure of other work, so he says. I've seen quite a number of PMs in my time but I can't say I'm looking forward to it,' he added with some feeling.

As soon as he left she opened the file and began working through the reports. After a preliminary run through she weeded out those that were obviously irrelevant to the current enquiry and set them aside. Of the remainder, a considerable number were of girls whose families believed for one reason or another might have come to the South West. She was able to eliminate most of these fairly quickly, either because they were the wrong age or colouring or had distinguishing marks not found on the body of the

Avon victim and vice versa, but there were some that she put aside for more detailed investigation. She became so absorbed in the task that on glancing up for a moment she was surprised see that it was gone twelve o'clock. She returned the rejected reports to the box, put the rest into a folder and stowed them away in a drawer. She was on the point of leaving to keep her appointment with Erika Henderson when DS Douglas appeared.

'Thank goodness that's over,' he said, dropping into the chair next to hers.

Noticing that he was paler than usual, she said. 'Was it very gruesome?'

'No more than any other, but like I said it's never something I enjoy watching. As Doc Hanley has already told us, the cause of death was manual strangulation, but of course he had to stick to the rules and go through the complete procedure.' He took out a handkerchief and wiped his forehead. 'I was thinking of grabbing some lunch, but I'm not sure I can face food.'

'You ought to eat something,' she said sympathetically. 'Something light – soup and a salad, perhaps?'

'Maybe I could manage that. How about joining me? I promise not to put you off your nosh with a lot of gory details.'

'Actually, I'm supposed to be meeting someone for lunch. I could put it off till another time if you feel in the need of company,' she added, half hoping he would accept her offer and give her an excuse to cancel her meeting with Erika, but he gave a half-hearted smile and shook his head.

'No need for that, thanks all the same. There's sure to be someone in the canteen to chat to. How did you get on with the misper reports?'

'Nothing positive so far, but a few worth a closer look.'

'Good. We'll go over them together after lunch.'

When Sukey reached the Rendezvous café she found Erika already installed at a corner table. 'I've ordered an omelette,' she announced, holding up a menu. 'They do good ones here, particularly the mushroom.'

'Right, I'll take your advice.' Sukey went to the counter and gave her order.

'I said I wanted to see you, but I didn't explain why,' Erika said when she returned to the table. 'But before we go any further, have you found the person who killed Doctor Whistler? There was something on the news a few days ago about a man helping with enquiries and then nothing more. Am I right in thinking it was Professor Lamont?'

'I'm sorry, I can't answer any questions about that,' said Sukey. 'Apart from anything else, I'm not on the case any more, so if you don't mind I'd rather not talk about it.'

'Not on the case?' Erika appeared taken aback and Sukey sensed that she was disappointed. 'But why?'

'I can't tell you that either. Look, on second thoughts I don't think I'll stay for lunch. If you'll just give me the photocopies I'll get back to the station.'

'No, please, you've already ordered, you can't go now. At least listen to what I have to say. I do have a particular reason for asking about Professor Lamont.'

'I'd really rather you changed the subject. If what you have to say concerns the Whistler murder I suggest you call at the station and ask to see Sergeant Rathbone.'

Erika looked faintly embarrassed. 'I'd prefer to tell you first. I'm afraid he'd laugh at me or make me feel a fool by telling me I've been watching too many crime series on TV. I'm sure he's a good detective,' she hurried on, 'but to be honest, I didn't find him a very sympathetic character, if you know what I mean.'

Yes, I know exactly what you mean, Sukey agreed mentally. Aloud, she said, 'All right, you can tell me as long as you understand I can't comment or answer any questions.'

'Yes, I accept that, and I promise I'll come to the station and make a proper statement if you think I should.'

'So what is it then?'

Erika leaned forward and lowered her

voice. 'The other day, I saw—' she began and then broke off as a waiter brought their omelettes and cutlery.

'Saw what?' said Sukey a little impatiently when the waiter had left.

'Not a what, a who,' said Erika. 'His double. Professor Lamont's, I mean. No kidding!' she went on as Sukey's fork stopped in mid-air on the way to her mouth. 'It was uncanny. I went into an off-licence in Clifton Village and this man was there buying wine and I almost said, "Good morning, Professor Lamont" and then I realized it wasn't him at all. For one thing his hair was much shorter and he had a gold ring in one ear, which doesn't quite fit Lamont's image, but he was the same build and the facial likeness was so striking that I felt quite spooked for a moment. And then it occurred to me,' she went on, 'the man Boris Gasspar saw entering and leaving the hotel by the staff entrance, the one he's so sure was Professor Lamont, could easily have been this man. After all, he only saw him for a few seconds and he wouldn't have been paying particular attention – it was only when Professor Lamont came to the desk that he noticed the likeness. And if he wore a wig – this chap I saw in Clifton, that is – Boris could easily have been confused. I can see you think so as well,' she went on, as if encouraged by what she read in Sukey's expression.

After a few moments' stunned silence, during which she tried to get her chaotic thoughts into some kind of order, Sukey said, 'It could be a coincidence, but I think DS Rathbone should know about it. I suggest you have a word with him as soon as possible.'

'Do I have to? I thought if I told you and you thought it might be important, you could pass it on.'

'I'm sorry, you'll have to speak to him yourself. As I said, I'm not on the case any more, in fact I shall probably get my knuckles rapped for agreeing to talk to you.'

'How petty!' Erika said indignantly. 'I didn't know the police had such silly rules.'

'There are reasons,' said Sukey evasively.

'Well don't worry, I won't let anyone know I've been telling you all this.'

'But you will do as I suggest and go and see Sergeant Rathbone? I can promise you he'll take it seriously.' *He'll jolly well have to after what Hester told me*, Sukey thought with no little sense of satisfaction. 'You could ask for Detective Constable Vicky Armstrong if you'd prefer to talk to a woman,' she added.

'All right, I'll do that,' Erika said with evident relief. 'I'm so glad you think it could be important. There's one more thing. When this man left the shop I watched him through the window. His car was parked just outside and I made a note of the number as he pulled away. I wrote it on the back of this.' She held out one of her business cards. 'It was a black Mercedes with one of those ghastly nodding dogs on the parcel shelf,' she added.

'That was quick thinking,' said Sukey. She glanced at the number on the card before handing it back. 'Give that to Vicky Armstrong when you see her. Let's hope this man didn't notice the interest you were taking in him,' she added in a flash of unease.

Erika was quick to reassure her. 'I'm sure he didn't. He never so much as glanced in my direction and I memorized the number and wrote it down after he'd gone.' Her earlier hesitant manner had given way to the cool, professional efficiency Sukey had noticed at their first meeting. 'By the way,' she went on, diving into her handbag and taking out an A4 envelope. 'I almost forgot – the Gasspar papers! Sounds like something out of a Len Deighton mystery, doesn't it?' she said as she handed it over.

When Sukey arrived back in the CID office she found DS Rathbone at his desk. She handed him the envelope Erika had given her and said, 'These are the photocopies you wanted, Sarge, the ones relating to Boris Gasspar.'

'Thanks.' He glanced at the envelope, tossed it into his in tray and returned to a study of the file in front of him, then looked up and said sharply, 'How did you come by them? That didn't come through the post.'

'Erika Henderson gave them to me just now. We had lunch together,' she added with a hint of defiance.

'Are you two buddies or something?'

'Not exactly. She said she'd prefer to hand them over personally and as she was coming into town anyway I agreed to meet her. It seemed to make sense; things do go astray in the post from time to time.'

'Did she give any reason for wanting this personal meeting?' Rathbone snapped, his eyes narrow with suspicion.

'She didn't have time to explain over the phone. If she had, I'd have refused the request because what she had to say concerns the Whistler murder. I explained I was off it and she should tell you or Vicky if she had any new information. She promised to do that, but if you don't hear from her I think perhaps—'

She stopped as Rathbone's phone began ringing. He grabbed it and barked, 'Yes, what is it?' He listened for a moment and then said more gently, 'DC Armstrong's out. I'll see her – I'll be with her in a moment.' He put the phone down and stood up. 'She appears to have taken your advice,' he said. 'She's in reception.'

It was almost an hour before he reappeared and came over to Sukey's desk, where she and DS Douglas were working on the reports of missing girls that she had earlier set aside for further examination. She saw immediately that his attitude had undergone a noticeable change; instead of the previous mixture of mockery and irritation, it held a definite, albeit slightly grudging, hint of respect. 'I've just had a word with DCI Leach and he wants to see me right away,' he told her. 'It's possible he may want to speak to you as well, so stick around for a while.'

'Don't worry, Greg, I've got plenty for her to do here,' said DS Douglas, who was standing a few feet away. 'So what's going on?' he asked after Rathbone had left the room.

'Erika Henderson was very keen to tell me something that might or might not have a bearing on the Whistler murder,' she said, 'but as I'm off the case now I referred her to DS Rathbone.'

Douglas grinned. 'Very wise,' he said. 'You got carpeted for crashing in on operation Maddox, didn't you?'

'So you heard about that?'

'Of course. Greg wasn't best pleased with you, I gather.'

'You could say that, but it seems what he's just heard from Erika has made him feel more kindly towards me.'

Ten minutes later, they were both summoned to Leach's office. DS Rathbone was still there, standing with his back to the door. He swung round when Sukey and Douglas entered and all three waited for Leach to speak. He sat looking at them for a couple of seconds over the top of his glasses before saying, 'Well, Sukey, it seems circumstances are conspiring to bring you back on the Whistler case despite our efforts to keep you out of it.'

'Sir?' The monosyllabic response to this cryptic remark was all she could think of on the spur of the moment.

'DS Rathbone has just interviewed Erika Henderson from the Mariners Hotel and she has made the following statement. "On Saturday morning I was in the Clifton Wine Shop where I saw a man who so closely resembled Stephen Lamont that I almost greeted him by name",' he began, reading from a sheet of paper lying in an open folder on his desk. 'She goes on to give some details – you can read the statement for yourselves in a minute. The significance of this, of course, is that it gives some credence to a similar claim made by Hester Lamont – a claim both Sergeant Rathbone and I were disinclined at first to take seriously on account of the woman's volatile mental state. We did, however, manage to persuade her to make a formal statement and I have that here as well.' He picked up the second sheet, passed them both across the desk and waited

237

while Sukey and Douglas read through them. 'Any questions?' he asked as they handed them back.

'Yes, sir,' said Douglas. 'Do we know yet who the Merc belongs to?'

'Our information is that it's on contract hire to a company that owns a chain of launderettes, which we have reason to believe is part of the Oliver Maddox empire. It so happens the enquiry into the Maddox set-up is code-named Operation Dirty Linen,' he added without a trace of a smile.

'Is that a coincidence or do they suspect a link with money laundering?'

'Good question. They're being pretty tight-lipped about it – understandably so. Needless to say, I'll be consulting their SIO every step of the way, and no one here is to make the slightest move on their own initiative. Understood?' A chorus of 'Sirs' greeted the question, which the three took to be a sign of dismissal and began getting up to leave when Leach added, 'There's a couple of other things the three of you should know.' He referred to a file that lay open on his desk. 'About the body found in the river. Doc Hanley found traces of lorazepam in the dead girl's system. It's a drug commonly used by dentists to calm nervous patients and it was probably given to girls who objected to the demands of some of their customers to make them more compliant.'

'Charming,' muttered Rathbone.

'Quite.' Leach referred to the file again. 'Next, I have here a report from forensics on the clothing the girl was wearing. It was saturated and heavily stained with mud, but on examination it turned out that in the pocket of the skirt was a small scrap of paper. They managed to dry it out and found something written on it, fortunately in indelible ink and quite legible. It appears to be a mobile phone number. Does anyone here recognize it?' He read the number aloud and Sukey gave an involuntary gasp.

'It's my number, sir,' she said, 'but I didn't give it to that girl. I never saw her until the day her body was found. The only person I've given it to recently is Boris Gasspar.'

Twenty

'This is something we feared might happen from the moment Sukey reported seeing Gasspar in the company of Oliver Maddox,' said DCI Leach, 'and I'm sure you all realize what it means.'

'Obviously, Gasspar must know the girl we fished out of the river on Monday,' said DS Douglas.

'Not necessarily,' said Leach, 'although there has to be a connection. Sukey gave Gasspar her number on – ' he rifled through the reports in the folder before locating the one he was looking for – 'Monday of last week. He hasn't made any use of it, but we suspect Maddox somehow found out he had it and demanded he hand the card over, probably while Sukey had him under surveillance last Friday. But in the meantime, he must have confided the number either to the girl herself or – what I think is more likely – to a third party, who subsequently passed it on to her. And the reason she never used it is probably because one of Maddox's thugs silenced her before she had the chance.'

'Without realizing that the scrap of paper she'd written it on was in the pocket of the skirt she was wearing when he killed her,' Rathbone speculated.

'Exactly. And as we're reasonably sure she was killed a couple of days before being dumped in the river, that would mean they didn't waste any time.'

'Why do you suppose they waited all that time before dumping the body?' asked Douglas.

'We consulted our river expert on that. It seems there was an unusually high tide about eight hours before we found her. That's one more reason to believe the killers were local – they probably knew that and dropped her in the water at a crucial moment, calculating that it would be swept out to sea by the falling tide. If that had gone to plan it could have been weeks before it came ashore, maybe at Avonmouth or even further along the coast, but unfortunately for them it got caught up on a mudbank. Her long skirt would have been a factor as well – soaked with water it would have acted as a weight.'

'So what do we do now, sir? We can't pull Gasspar in and insist he tells us all he knows about Maddox, can we?'

'No, Bob, we can't. When I passed on the suggestion that we offer him immunity if he shopped Maddox I was strictly forbidden to do any such thing. I'll have to refer these latest developments to Superintendent Baird – he's the SIO at Operation Dirty Linen – and wait for his instructions. I will of course be sending him the paperwork concerning Gasspar's employment record that the hotel manager's PA got for us. I understand you've impressed on her that it's vital nothing gets out about this, Sukey?'

'I have, sir, and I believe we can rely on her discretion.'

'Let's hope you're right.' Leach glanced at his watch. 'Right, let's wind this up as quickly as possible and then I'll have this lot faxed to the Super with a request for a quick response. As we haven't been able to identify the dead girl, the press will soon be clamouring for a picture.'

'Could I ask, sir, if you have any theory about her connection with Gasspar, and, by extension, with Maddox?' said Douglas.

'From what Doc Hanley said in his report, she's had a pretty active sex life,' said Leach. 'That may have been of her own choosing, but in the light of what we now know, I believe it's more likely she was a victim of people traffickers. We know there are organized gangs bringing young women over from countries in Eastern Europe and the Balkans. They lure them here by promising them glamorous jobs in things like modelling that will bring them lots of money and once they're here they force them into prostitution. It's a filthy trade and it would be entirely in character for Maddox to be involved in it.'

'You think there may be a house on our patch where some of these girls are being held?' said Rathbone.

'It's a possibility. There are plenty of properties in multiple occupation in various parts of the city. Some of them we know are used by drug dealers and the two activities often go hand in hand. It wouldn't be difficult to keep half a dozen girls prisoner in such a house with guards to make sure they didn't escape.'

'Escapes do happen now and then, sir,' Sukey ventured. 'There was a case in Cheltenham last year, just before I left to start my CID training.'

Leach nodded. 'True. As I recall, a member of the public found a girl wandering the streets in a distressed state, became concerned and alerted the police. At the moment we haven't anything like that to go on.'

'So you think the dead girl might have been caught trying to escape?' said Douglas.

'Possibly, or she might have been overheard saying something to suggest that was what she was planning to do. We simply have no idea at the moment.'

'Presumably she wouldn't have access to a phone in the house so to make a call she'd have had to get out somehow,' said Rathbone. 'She'd then have the problem of finding a public call box if she was hoping to ring Sukey's number and she'd have needed money ... and there might have been a language problem.'

'That's true as well,' said Leach. 'If she did manage to get out of the house it would have made more sense to appeal to a member of the public. So far, no one's come forward to report anything of that nature. This is all speculation, of course; we may be completely wide of the mark, which is why I need to refer to the Super as soon as possible.'

'What about the two sightings of Lamont's double, sir?' asked Rathbone. 'Are we still thinking in terms of a link with Maddox and the Whistler killing?'

'That's a further complication,' admitted Leach, 'and again the short answer is we simply don't know. The fact that a key witness in the Whistler case has a connection with Maddox may be nothing more than a coincidence, but until we have more definite information we have to pursue it. I'd like to know more about the company that's leasing the car the doppelgänger was driving – I'll raise that one with the Super at the same time. There's one thing we can all do in the meantime and that is keep an eye open for this man. Any sightings of him or the car are to be reported to me immediately, but under no circumstances is he to be approached or made aware that he's under observation. It'll be up to the Dirty Linen team to mount their own surveillance in the hope they can establish a link to Maddox. Understood? Yes, Sukey?' he added, having evidently read in her expression that something had occurred to her. 'You have a question?'

'Well, sir,' she began hesitantly, 'it's obvious that Maddox is into some very lucrative scams big time. He probably rakes in millions one way and another. We know the items stolen from Doctor Whistler are valuable, but to a man like Maddox they'd only represent small change. As you say, we've no hard evidence as yet that he was involved in stealing them, but there is some reason to suspect that he was. I'm wondering why he'd bother – it seems a bit out of his league.'

'Good point,' said Leach. 'I'll mention it when I speak to Superintendent Baird. I can't off-hand think of a reason – unless of course he's a closet collector of antiquities. Do you have a theory of your own, Sukey?'

'Only that someone at the dig in Rhodes might have let him know that Whistler was carrying something else we haven't heard about, something even more valuable.'

'Or maybe he was just doing a friend a favour,' said Rathbone. His flippant tone made it clear that in his opinion the idea was not to be taken seriously.

Leach, however, did not smile. 'I'll include both suggestions in my report,' he said. 'Any more questions or comments?' There was a general shaking of heads. 'Right, that's it for now. I'll let all of you know as soon as I hear from him how he wants us to play this from now on; in the meantime we'd better carry on with the routine enquiries or the press will think we're sitting on our backsides while the villains get on with their villainy. And remember, every scrap of relevant information comes directly to me before any action is taken.'

Sukey, Rathbone and Douglas returned to

the CID office. Vicky was at her computer, writing up a statement she had just taken from a woman who had reported seeing a girl 'looking like what it says in the paper' entering a car with two men 'a few days ago'. According to the somewhat rambling account the witness gave over the phone, 'the men looked rather nasty bits of work and the girl didn't seem to want to go with them'. As the three approached she looked up and pulled a face.

'Any use?' said Rathbone

'Not a lot, Sarge,' said Vicky. 'This woman – a Mrs Purdie – can't even be sure what day it was except that it was "towards the end of last week". From her description of all three people involved they might have been members of the same family, possibly Asian. The men were young and could have been the girl's brothers, but as Mrs P so charmingly put it, "of course they all look the same".'

'Bit of a racist, eh? What about the car?'

'Again, pretty vague. She says it was black but she couldn't describe it except that it was "big and shiny and new-looking".'

'No nodding dog in the rear window I suppose?'

'She didn't mention it but I have a feeling that if I'd asked her about it, she'd have "suddenly remembered" there was one.'

Rathbone grimaced. 'As you say, not a lot

of use.'

'There is one thing she did seem sure of, for what it's worth. This incident took place in Mellor Street, which isn't far from the street where Sukey spotted our star witness from the Mariners Hotel.'

DCI Leach summoned the team again on Friday morning to inform them that Superintendent Baird had given permission to release an artist's impression of the dead girl to the press. 'That's the good news, such as it is,' he told them. 'The bad news is that Inspector Comino of the Greek police has been in touch with him, demanding to know what we've been doing for the past fortnight and why hasn't he been kept informed. Which is a bit rich, considering that no one here had heard of him until yesterday, but it seems he and Doctor Makris of the Ministry of Culture have been comparing notes. If we don't come up with something positive during the next forty-eight hours he's threatening to come here to take charge of the investigation personally.'

'Bloody cheek!' said Rathbone.

'I can understand his vexation,' said Leach. 'There have been reports lately of a serious rise in the theft of art treasures from Greek museums and archaeological sites and they feel their heritage is being stolen from them. They've formed a special division of the police, known as the Art Squad, to try and stamp it out. Just the same, we don't want him coming here and raising a dust. If Maddox is involved in the trade and Comino latches on to him it could seriously jeopardize Operation Dirty Linen. Let's hope the picture will bring about the breakthrough we need.'

By chance the picture was not published until the first edition the following day, being elbowed out by extensive reports, full of salacious details, of a scandal involving a star of a local football team and the young and sexy blonde winner of a recent television game show. And it was this chance that provided yet another tenuous link in the chain.

For several weeks Sukey had been considering replacing some of the furniture she had brought with her from her former home in Gloucester. She had once casually mentioned this to Major Matthews during one of his neighbourly enquiries as to how she was settling in and if she needed any information about local services etc. He had recommended a large furniture retailer, and it was on the Saturday morning, the day after Inspector Comino had issued his ultimatum, that she decided to take his advice. It so happened that the store was in the same part of Bristol as the house she had observed Boris enter just over a week ago, but no such thought was in her mind as she wandered through the various departments, making notes of prices and picking up catalogues, occasionally taking a rest in one of a seemingly limitless range of armchairs on offer. Bewildered by the choice, wishing that either Jim or Fergus was with her, she resisted the blandishments of a helpful sales assistant and retreated to the store's café for a restorative cup of coffee before setting off for home. On the way back to the car she stopped at a small general store to pick up a few groceries; as she entered she pulled up short in front of a stand piled with copies of the morning edition of the local paper. The front page bore a banner headline reading 'Do you know who she is?' and below it was a drawing of the girl whose body she had watched being recovered from the banks of the River Avon.

Taking care not to show any particular reaction, she put a copy in her basket before moving towards the first aisle with her shopping list in her hand. Moments later she heard someone behind her give what sounded like a cry of despair. Turning, she saw a young man staring fixedly at the pile of newspapers with an expression of mingled horror and fear on his face. He clapped a hand over his mouth and then crossed himself while mumbling something incomprehensible under his breath before picking up a copy with a hand that shook so violently that he had difficulty in getting hold of it. His head was half-turned towards her and as she saw him in profile she noticed that he bore a strong resemblance to Boris Gasspar. His brother perhaps, or his cousin?

Sukey's training and instinct told her that it would be unwise for him to see her there. She retreated behind the nearest row of shelves and stood for several seconds examining rows of different brands of tea and coffee while keeping an eye open in case he should suddenly appear in search of whatever he had entered the shop to buy. She was not, however, surprised when through the window she saw him run out of the shop clutching the newspaper in one hand. Perhaps that was all he came in for anyway or possibly the shock of seeing the drawing had driven everything else from his mind. She was in no doubt that he had recognized the girl, but did he know who she was, where she had been living, where she had come from and by what means? Was she, in fact, a victim of people traffickers and if so, were they controlled by Maddox? The questions flooded into her mind with the speed of the rising waters that less than a week ago had flowed up the Avon, swept up the frail, lifeless victim and carried her away, only to abandon her on its muddy shores barely a mile downstream.

Twenty-One

There was a shout and a sudden commotion as a teenager in jeans and T-shirt rushed out of the shop, stopped for a moment looking this way and that and then gave another shout before racing off along the street. A customer was heard to remark, above a round of tutting, 'Chap went off without paying for his paper,' which everyone agreed was undoubtedly the case. A short while later the pursuer returned in triumph, this time at a more leisurely pace and jingling some coins in his cupped hand, which earned him a round of spontaneous applause.

'Nice work, Wayne,' said the woman on the till as he handed her the money.

'He were just going into the caff up the road,' he explained. 'Paid up right away, no worries. "Very sorry, forgot," he says. Didn't have the right money but didn't bother about his change either. In a right state, he were.'

'Did you see his face when he picked up the *Mercury?*' said a woman who was unloading her shopping at the checkout, speak-

ing to no one in particular. 'Looked petri-
fied, he did – you'd have thought he'd seen a
ghost.'

'Maybe he knows who the dead girl is,' said
the woman behind her in the queue. She
held up a copy of the newspaper and waved
it around. 'She do look a bit foreign, don't
she, and I thought he did too. Were it in
Marco's you saw him, Wayne?' she asked the
lad, who had returned to his task of stacking
shelves with tins of soup.

'Thassright, the caff on the corner,' he
replied.

'Ah, that explains it. You do see a lot of
foreigners in there,' she said knowingly.

The first woman, evidently anxious not to
be left out of the conversation, said, 'I went
in for a cup of coffee once and while I was
there a whole crowd of them came in, jab-
bering away in their funny language. That
was the last time I went in...'

'Marco's Italian,' someone pointed out and
received a scornful sniff in reply.

'I buy my sandwiches from Marco and I
often see foreign workers in there,' said the
woman on the till as she rang up the first
woman's purchases. 'He says they like to sit
and chat to their mates – treat it like a sort of
club, they do and he doesn't seem to mind.
They come in here sometimes for their bits
of grocery ... always very polite, never any
trouble. That's five pounds and seventy-five

pence, please.'

'Never any trouble till now, you mean,' said the woman as she rummaged in her purse with skinny fingers. 'You'd better keep an eye on them from now on – especially that one,' she added with a jerk of her head in the general direction of the door. 'Me, I don't trust people what can't even talk English proper,' she announced to all and sundry as she handed over the money and departed.

Sukey had edged closer to the till to catch the conversation. As one by one the women left she moved away, picked up the items on her list, paid for them and left the shop. Outside, she walked a few paces along the street in the direction Wayne had taken in his pursuit of the fleeing customer; a short distance ahead she saw an advertising board on the pavement bearing the words 'Café Marco' in brightly coloured letters with a list of specialities on offer scrawled below in chalk. Bearing in mind DCI Leach's instructions, she resisted her natural inclination to investigate further; instead, she set off for the car park with the intention of calling the CID office in the hope of being able to contact either Rathbone or Douglas and report what she had seen. To reach it she would have to walk along the side street past Marco's; she figured that if the young man was indeed related to Boris they might both be in there, so rather than risk being spotted she crossed over the road and continued walking for a couple more minutes before crossing back again. Her intention was to approach the corner from the opposite direction and so avoid passing in front of the café; she had almost reached it when a black Mercedes turned ahead of her and pulled up outside.

Her heart thumping with excitement, Sukey stopped short and held her breath. What happened next registered on her brain like a series of snapshots viewed in quick succession: the registration number of the car: the nodding dog on the parcel shelf: the tall man with a gold stud in his right ear who stepped out and without bothering to lock the door headed for Marco's: and finally, but no less striking, his uncanny resemblance to Stephen Lamont.

By chance, she was outside a bank where a small queue had formed at an automatic cash dispenser. It offered an ideal vantage point for keeping watch and she took out her card and joined the line while keeping a sharp lookout in case the man reappeared. Something in his bearing and the purposeful way he strode round the corner and pushed open Marco's door told her that he was not there for refreshment. Whatever his errand, her instinct told her it would not take long and she kept her eyes glued to the door of the café as the queue shuffled forward. She took out her mobile and was about to key in the office number when a woman behind her said plaintively, 'Do you want to use this machine or not?' Still keeping an eye open for her target, she hurriedly inserted her card and entered her PIN.

She was just withdrawing her money as the man emerged. She hastily stuffed card, money and receipt in her shoulder bag with one hand while juggling the mobile with the other and still watching him to see what he would do next. He made straight for his car, which she had already noted was illegally parked on double yellow lines; as he opened the driver's door a traffic warden, who had evidently been waiting out of sight round the corner, crossed the road and approached him with a pad of forms in one hand and a pen in the other. Another bit of luck, she thought to herself as she pressed the 'ring' button and waited for a reply. Wouldn't it be great if, like so many motorists issued with parking tickets, the man were to argue and become aggressive, tear up the ticket and throw it in the warden's face, do anything to delay his departure. But instead of writing out a ticket, tearing it off and giving it to the driver, the warden pulled a loose sheet from the bottom of the pad and handed it over. It was too far away for her to see but on reflection she would have been prepared to bet that there was nothing written on it. In return, he received something that might have been a small brown envelope and walked quickly away.

It had all happened so discreetly and the switch was made so quickly that for a moment she wondered if her eyes had deceived her. Then she heard someone say, 'I've seen that happen before.' It was the woman who had been behind her in the queue for the cash machine. 'Don't know who the driver is, but I reckon that warden's on to a nice little earner. Now if you or I had parked there—'

'You're saying he takes handouts to let people get away with parking on double yellow lines?' said Sukey, affecting shocked astonishment.

The woman shrugged. 'Never seen him do it with anyone else, but I've noticed that one before. Maybe he belongs to the Mafia or something.' Tittering at what she evidently considered a witticism, she went on her way while the driver of the Mercedes started his engine and drove off with the dog nodding benignly through the rear window.

'CID, Rathbone speaking,' said an impatient voice in her ear. 'Is anyone there?'

'Yes, Sarge, it's me, Sukey.'

'What is it?'

'I've been doing some shopping in Gloucester Road and I was on my way back to my car when I saw—' As concisely as possible she outlined the chain of events that had

256

prompted her to make the call.

'Is the guy who bought the paper still in the café?' he asked.

'As far as I know. I haven't seen him come out, but—'

'You're sure he didn't see you watching him?'

'He never looked my way, but in any case he was so shocked when he saw the girl's picture that I doubt if he'd have noticed anything.'

'Good. I'll call the DCI immediately – he'll probably want to speak to you so you'd better stand by.'

'Do you want me to stay here and keep watch?'

'Better not, in case Gasspar's in there as well. Whether or not your man's related to him, this could be the breakthrough we've all been waiting for. Get back to your car and wait there till I call you.' There was a click as Rathbone ended the call. Feeling slightly deflated, Sukey followed his instructions. She had just settled into her car when her mobile rang. A man's voice with a strong foreign accent said, 'Ees thees the perleese laydee?' The words sounded muffled, as if he had a hand over the mouthpiece.

Sukey experienced another surge of adrenalin as she replied, 'Detective Constable Reynolds speaking. Who's calling, please?'

'My name not matter.' He pronounced

each word carefully with a pause after each one. 'Please, I weesh speak you.'

'Yes?'

'Ees very important.'

'All right, I'm listening.'

'Not speak on phone. Must see.'

'All right. Come to the police station in—'

'No, no.' He was beginning to sound agitated. 'We meet somewhere.'

'Where are you?'

'Not matter. You say where I see you.'

Throughout the conversation Sukey's brain had been working furiously. She could not be sure, but it seemed more than likely that her anonymous caller had obtained her number from Boris Gasspar and might even be the young man who had rushed out of the grocery store and into Marco's in apparent distress. On the one hand she had been given strict instructions to sit tight and await further orders; on the other, it was essential to keep this contact going. She had to play for time.

'Please listen carefully,' she said, speaking slowly and distinctly. 'Do you know the Gloucester Road?'

'Yes, I know eet.'

'There's a turning off it leading to a car park and there's a café called Marco's on the corner. Do you know it?'

'No. no. Not meet in Marco's.' She could hear his agitation increasing.

'That's all right, I just want to be sure you know where the car park is.'

'Yes, yes, I know car park.'

'Can you be there in half an hour?' That should give her time to contact Rathbone again and either get clearance for her to meet the man herself or send someone else. 'I or another officer will meet you.'

'No, no other!' he insisted. 'I weesh see you, I speak only weeth you ... please, very important.'

'All right. I'll be there in half an hour, OK?'

'OK,' he said – a little reluctantly, she thought, as if he was not entirely happy with the arrangement.

She ended the call and immediately rang the office again. An unfamiliar voice told her that DS Rathbone was speaking on another line and she left a message asking him to call her back urgently. She took out her notebook and scribbled a note of the incident and then sat and waited for Rathbone's call, but the minutes ticked by and still there was no word from him. She had been waiting, fuming with impatience, for over fifteen minutes when to her dismay she saw the man who resembled Boris approaching. Much too early, of course, but fortunately she had parked some distance from the entrance and was able to watch him unobserved. He stood on the pavement looking first left and then right along the street, from time to time glancing at his watch and taking a few steps in each direction in turn. Whenever an approaching car signalled its intention to enter the car park he stepped eagerly forward, peering at the driver and then retreating as if satisfied that it was not the one he was seeking.

'Maybe I should have told him what car to look out for,' Sukey muttered and then remembered that in all probability Leach, instructed by Superintendent Baird, would insist on sending someone else anyway.

Five minutes to go and still no call from Rathbone. Then another car approached; this time it slowed down and drew level with the man. The registration number was unfamiliar and Sukey knew immediately that it was not a pool car; this was not the police. Something was wrong; as the man stepped eagerly forward she opened her mouth to call out a warning but her shout was drowned in a roar of gunfire before the car sped away.

As Sukey leapt out of her car and began to run towards the figure lying face down on the ground, her mobile rang. Her hand shook almost uncontrollably as, still running, she pressed the reply button. 'Sorry it took me so long to get back to you,' Rathbone was saying, but for a moment she was unable to respond because of the tightness in her throat. 'Are you there?' he demanded. 'What's going on? I can hear screams. For God's sake Sukey, are you all right?' At first he sounded impatient; when she still did not reply, a note of concern crept into his voice. In some strange way it helped her to find her own. 'Yes, I'm OK, but—' She had to break off and swallow hard to stop herself from gagging. She could hear agitated voices, a child was screaming. Pull yourself together woman, you've got a job to do, she told herself fiercely. She reached the victim, saw the pool of blood forming round him, crouched low to feel for a pulse and spoke again into the phone. 'Sarge, there's been a drive-by shooting outside the Stone Street car park. Young Caucasian male, the one I told you about. Still alive but pulse feeble. I need back up and an ambulance,' she said, and this time her voice was firm and clear.

Twenty-Two

'My God!', 'What happened?', 'Is he dead?', 'Shouldn't someone call an ambulance?'

Questions whirled through the air from all sides as the half-dozen or so people who had heard the shots tore across the car park in

Sukey's wake towards the spot where the man lay on the ground. They stood in a circle round her, pressing forward, craning their necks, pointing, speaking to one another in hushed whispers. One woman made the sign of the cross, her lips silently moving. The air seemed to vibrate, as if the echoes from the gunfire were still audible.

'Keep your distance everyone!' she called, waving them back, 'and please put that down at once, sir!' she added, seeing a man stoop to pick something off the ground. He glared at her, his expression truculent.

'Who d'you think you are to give orders?' he demanded.

'I'm an off-duty police officer,' she informed him crisply. 'This is a crime scene and no one is to touch anything.' Shock would no doubt kick in when the crisis was past, but for the moment she felt icily calm. She stood up to face him; he was head and shoulders taller than she was and well-built, with a shaven head, two days' growth of stubble on his chin and a flabby mound of flesh that rose like a pallid molehill above the top of his jeans. He took a step towards her, but she stood her ground. 'Kindly put down whatever it is you have just picked up,' she repeated.

'It's only a spent bullet,' he said with a sneer, holding out his hand. 'See?'

'It's evidence,' she retorted.

'And how do I know you're a copper anyway? Where's your ID?'

'For God's sake, do as the lady says, Bill.' A heavily made-up blonde with enormous gold hoops swinging from her ears jabbed him in the back. 'She looks as if she knows what she's doing.' Reluctantly, he dropped the bullet on the ground, but remained where he was, resisting the woman's efforts to pull him away. The other onlookers drew back, their expressions varying between shock and morbid curiosity. Two women held handkerchiefs over their mouths; another was comforting the crying child; the men stood gazing as if mesmerized at the figure on the ground. One of the bullets must have torn through the victim's shoulder, leaving a gash and an ugly red stain on the back of his shirt. Sukey watched with mounting alarm as the edge of the pool of blood crept outwards on the tarmac.

'You can't just leave him lying there bleeding to death,' protested the man addressed as Bill. 'My name's Hassell,' he went on, 'I've got a first aid kit in my car and I could—'

Sukey shook her head. 'Thank you for the offer, Mr Hassell, but it's better not to touch him in case we do further damage. An ambulance should be here any minute; the paramedics will know what to do.' She looked past him at the rest of the onlookers and said, 'I've called for more police and I'd be obliged if those of you who actually saw what happened or feel they can give useful information would wait by their cars until they arrive.'

In response, the crowd withdrew a short distance, stopped and turned round, plainly reluctant to move out of sight of the action. Sukey bent down and once more laid a finger on the victim's neck, relieved to find the feeble pulse still there, praying for help to arrive quickly.

Meanwhile, more shoppers returning to their cars stopped to stare; to her surprise, Hassell took over the task of shooing them away saying, 'Keep back everyone; this lady's a police officer and she's in charge. An ambulance and more officers are coming and they won't want you lot getting in their way.'

Even as he spoke, the sirens began to sound and the crowd hastily retreated still further. The ambulance arrived first, sweeping round the corner with its blue light flashing. It pulled up and a couple of paramedics leaped out and bent over the victim. When they touched him he let out a faint groan and a sigh of relief drifted like a trail of smoke among the onlookers.

'D'you reckon he'll be OK?' Bill called out, but the paramedics either did not hear, or they ignored the question. He repeated it to Sukey, who responded with a helpless gesture.

'It's hard to tell; all I can say is the pulse is weak but it seems to be holding up.' As she spoke, the ambulance crew attached a drip to the semi-conscious man's arm and eased him on to a stretcher. In a matter of seconds they had him in the ambulance; the doors closed and it raced away, siren blaring, blue light flashing, leaving behind a bright scarlet stain on the tarmac.

Moments later the police arrived and took charge.

'Here Sukey, get this down you,' said Rathbone.

Her hands were shaking and the hot tea almost spilled over as she lifted it to her lips. Her teeth chattered on the edge of the mug, but its warmth was comforting to her chilled fingers and the hot liquid gradually sent a restorative glow through her body. He waited until she had drunk the last drop and handed the empty mug back to him. He put it down on the desk and said, 'Better now?'

'Much better, thank you, Sarge.'

'Feel well enough to talk?'

'Sure.'

'First of all, you haven't told me why you wanted to speak to me so urgently. Did you anticipate the shooting?'

'Sarge, if I'd had the remotest suspicion that anything like that was going to happen

I'd have moved heaven and earth to get armed back-up without delay.'

'Then what?'

'After I spoke to you I went back to my car as instructed. I'd just got there when my mobile rang and a man with a strong foreign accent wanted to know if I was "the police lady".' Shakily at first, but with increasing confidence, she described the events of the next half hour. As she spoke she seemed to see the sickening act of violence she had recently witnessed being re-enacted in her mind's eye like the re-run of a film: the approaching car that wasn't a police car slowing down to draw level with the man waiting by the roadside: her futile attempt at a warning: the noise of the gunfire: the man's arms flung in the air and his body spun round by the impact of the bullets before crashing to the ground: the screech of rubber as the hit squad's car sped away. She ended by saying simply, 'I took charge until uniformed arrived and an inspector told me that CID were on their way. I went back to my car and waited for you.'

She had no idea how long she had waited; it might have been five minutes or twenty-five. She had only a vague recollection of Rathbone pulling up beside her in a pool car, ordering her into the passenger seat and driving her back to the station. He hadn't spoken a word during the journey except to

266

say that someone would bring her back later to pick up her own car. Now that she had told her story she waited passively for further instructions.

Rathbone had been writing rapidly while she was speaking. He thought for a moment and then said, 'OK, the first thing we have to do is establish where that call came from. Give me your mobile and I'll have it checked.' Without a word she handed it over. 'Stay here; I'll be right back.'

She sat back and closed her eyes, feeling utterly spent. When Rathbone returned, his voice seemed to come at her out of a void. 'I've spoken to DCI Leach; he wants to see you and he's on his way here. I don't suppose you've had any lunch?' She shook her head. Food was the last thing she had been thinking of, but all of a sudden she realized she was empty. 'There isn't time to go to the canteen, but I've brought you an energy bar to keep you going,' he said gruffly and slapped it on the desk in front of her. 'When you've eaten that we'll go up and wait for him in his office. Oh, and I've called in Libby Mayhew, one of our FSOs; she's a trained counsellor.'

'I don't need counselling,' Sukey protested.

'You're still in shock and you might need help in recalling details,' Rathbone said firmly. 'This is big, Sukey; you're a key witness in a major investigation and Operation Dirty Linen needs every scrap of help you can give.' With that somewhat ominous remark he waited while she obediently ate the energy bar and then escorted her out of the room and upstairs to Leach's office.

Libby Mayhew was already there; a few minutes later Leach walked in and sat down behind his desk. 'I've spoken to Superintendent Baird and he's coming as well,' he said. 'While we're waiting, we might as well get a few details of the actual attack on record. Exactly what time, and where, did it take place, Sukey?'

Her stomach gave a lurch as she reached for her notebook, realizing that she had no recollection of writing anything in it about the shooting. Yet surely she must have done; it would have been a mechanical response once she had, under the uniformed inspector's instruction, withdrawn from the scene. And there it was: Date: place: time: observations: action taken. She was dumbfounded to realize she had even recorded the make and number of the car. It must have registered automatically the moment she realized it was not one of the police vehicles.

She had just finished going through her notes when Superintendent Baird arrived. He made a somewhat comical contrast to the tall, gangling Leach, being short and stocky with a mop of sandy hair, a freckled face and steady grey eyes. He was wearing an Argyll patterned pullover, corduroy trousers and golfing shoes. 'I hope we can get through this quickly, I'm supposed to be teeing off at two o'clock,' he observed as he sat down. 'I suppose there's no news of the victim?' he added, almost as an afterthought.

'Not yet, sir. We have two armed officers at the hospital and they're in constant contact.'

'Good. All right Leach, let's have the complete picture.'

'May I suggest we let DC Reynolds give it herself, sir? I'm sure you'll find her a very competent witness. She has recorded the basic details in her notebook and I've jotted them down here.' Leach pushed a pad towards Baird who picked it up and ran his eyes over the top page. 'As yet she's had no opportunity to make a full written report.'

Baird turned to Sukey and despite his brusque manner his expression was not unfriendly. 'Now Reynolds,' he said, 'I understand from DCI Leach that he decided to take you off the Whistler case, but that you subsequently became involved in it on the insistence of certain witnesses. Before we deal with this morning's incident, perhaps you could explain exactly how this came about.'

For the moment Sukey was nonplussed. Then she said slowly, 'Well, sir, it started when Hester Lamont refused to speak to anyone but me about what seemed to all of us a very implausible theory of mistaken identity that she believed could help her brother. Then Erika Henderson called to say the paperwork we had requested about Boris Gasspar was ready and during the conversation she indicated she had something to tell me about the murder of Doctor Whistler. I told her I was no longer on the case and advised her to speak to DS Rathbone, but she seemed reluctant to do that and insisted on telling it to me first.'

'What reason did she give for that? Come on, speak up,' he added impatiently as she hesitated in embarrassment.

'She thought I was more likely to take her seriously than ... well, than any of the male officers, sir.'

Baird raised an eyebrow, but all he said was, 'Go on.'

'I agreed to meet her; she gave me the paperwork and told me she too had seen a Lamont lookalike in the same place as Hester. I assured her it would be taken seriously and advised her very strongly to come in and make a formal statement without delay. I immediately reported the conversation to DS Rathbone and while we were speaking Ms Henderson came to reception and he went down and took her statement.'

'Which is here on the file,' Baird remarked. 'So as far as you were concerned, that was to be the end of your involvement in the case?'

'Yes, sir.'

'And then along comes yet another looka-like, this time to a key witness in the Whistler murder. Right, now give a detailed, step by step account of the events that led up to the shooting today.'

For the second time within an hour, beginning with the reaction to the newspaper picture of the dead girl on the part of a man who resembled Boris Gasspar and ending with the same man being gunned down before her eyes outside the car park less than an hour later, Sukey described what had happened. From time to time Baird interrupted with a question; as the interview went on, weariness began to take its toll and she began repeating herself and stumbling over her words. It was then that Libby Mayhew intervened, gently but firmly reminding Baird that she was still in shock, demanding strong coffee and insisting that she be allowed some respite before continuing.

When at last Baird appeared satisfied he sat back and said, 'This man who resembles Lamont whom you saw pay Marco's a short visit and subsequently pass a discreet back-hander to the traffic warden – do you have any theory about the reason for him being there?'

'Well sir, from what the passer-by let drop it appears it wasn't the first time. I gather a

271

lot of Marco's customers are immigrant workers and it did cross my mind that this man might be running some kind of protection racket. I've had the feeling for some time that there's someone with a hold over Gasspar that makes him particularly reluctant to talk to me and I've been wondering whether there's something dodgy about his papers that's made him afraid to come forward.'

'We've asked the Home Office to double-check his references, sir,' Leach interposed.

'Good.' Baird turned back to Sukey. 'So you think maybe he asked this man, who you think may be a relative, to contact you on his behalf? It's a bit unlikely, isn't it?'

'Either that, or Boris showed him my card and asked for his advice. Maybe they talked it over and Boris decided not to follow it up, but when this other man recognized the picture of the dead girl he decided to act on his own initiative.'

'And what about the dead girl herself? How do you account for your number being found in her pocket?'

'I can only suppose one of them gave it to her, sir. Maybe she was in some kind of trouble and they suggested I might be able to help.'

'It's pretty obvious she was in trouble,' commented Baird dryly. 'I see from the file you have a theory about that, Leach. People traffickers, girls forced into prostitution, that sort of thing?'

'We know it happens, sir, and according to the pathologist this girl had been sexually active and roughly handled.'

'Assuming someone is running a racket of this kind on our patch, is there any reason to suspect Marco?'

'None that I know of, sir.'

'Rathbone?'

'My first thought was drugs, sir, but I've checked with the Drugs Squad and they've no reason to suppose Marco's a dealer, or that any dealers frequent his place.'

Baird frowned. 'So what takes Lamont Mark Two round there on some sort of regular basis, I wonder?'

There was a silence, interrupted by the telephone on Leach's desk. He picked it up, gave his name, wrote on his pad, grunted 'Thank you' and put it down. 'We may have an answer to your question, sir,' he said. 'The victim of the shooting made his call to Sukey's mobile from the payphone at Marco's café.'

Twenty-Three

There was a protracted silence as everyone digested this new development. Baird looked at his watch, shrugged, took out his mobile and keyed in a number. 'Dave? Something's come up and I'm not going to be able to make it. Many apologies.' He put the phone away, frowned and rested his chin on his left hand while doodling on his pad with the right. The others waited in silence; when Rathbone's mobile rang, heads swivelled in his direction and it seemed to Sukey as if there was a collective holding of breath as he put it to his ear.

'Yes, Murray. Uh-huh ... uh-huh ... so far so good ... well, don't relax for a second, we're dealing with a pretty ruthless bunch ... if you want reinforcements let me know ... and not a word to the press, OK? Do we have an ID, by the way?' There was a pause in the conversation, during which Sukey noticed Rathbone's expression change. Then he said, 'OK, thanks. Keep me posted. Cheers.' He snapped off the phone and said, 'Sergeant Murray, sir, in charge of the armed unit at the hospital where they've taken the victim of the shooting.' He was addressing Baird, but the others leaned forward simultaneously as if afraid to miss a word. 'First indications are that by some miracle no vital organ has been damaged. There's been considerable loss of blood, of course, and he's in intensive care while they assess the need for surgery. No idea at this stage as to when he'll be fit to be interviewed. And by the way, the name on a bank card found in his pocket is Mr J. Gasspar.'

'I thought he looked like Boris!' Sukey blurted out and immediately felt her colour rising at her failure to observe protocol. 'Sir,' she added apologetically.

Baird appeared not to notice the gaffe. 'A brother, or possibly a cousin,' he commented, 'and alive, praise the Lord!' He spoke with a fervour that took her by surprise and at the same time made her unexpectedly warm to him. 'It looks as if it was a rush job and their top marksman wasn't available,' he went on. 'Which is fortunate for us, but I wouldn't like to be the chap who carried out the attack if it turns out their intended victim is able to give us vital information. He's to be guarded round the clock like royalty, tell Murray,' he added, speaking directly to Rathbone.

'He understands that, sir.'

'I take it there's no news of the getaway car?'

'Reported stolen from outside a house in Portishead a week ago, sir. From a street round the corner from police headquarters,' the sergeant added with a certain grim relish. The news from the hospital had brought about an immediate lessening of tension and even Baird smiled at this gem.

'Implying we can't keep an eye on our own backyard, eh?' he remarked, one eyebrow lifted. 'The press boys'll go to town on that one if it comes out. Right,' he continued, turning serious again. 'We need to find out a bit more about Marco and his café. Was it just an unlucky chance that one of Maddox's mob overheard this chap making his call to DC Reynolds? Or is there a link between Marco and Maddox via the Lamont looka-like who keeps bobbing up like a jack-in-the-box? I'm inclined to the latter possibility. The payphone in Marco's could easily be monitored in some way. Is Marco under orders to keep his eyes and ears open and alert a member of the mob if one of his customers says or does something of interest to Mister Big? His name hasn't cropped up in our investigations before, but I think we need to know a bit more about him. I'll get one of my team on to that. As for you, Reynolds – ' he turned his gaze on Sukey and she was conscious of the sharp intelligence and the strength of will reflected in the keen grey eyes – 'since the victim of the shooting was so emphatic that he wouldn't speak to anyone but you, I have no option other than to keep you on the case, especially as we now have a link with the Avon river victim. You'd better go and see him as soon as he's fit to be interviewed. And good work getting the car number,' he added.

'Thank you, sir.' The after effects of shock were forgotten; she was gratified by the compliment, but her pleasure was far outweighed by the excitement of being part of a major operation. She found herself praying that she would prove a worthy member of the team.

'And it'll be interesting to see if the other Gasspar shows any reaction either to the shooting or the picture of the girl. I understand you have a reliable contact at the hotel where he works?'

'Yes, sir, the manager's PA. She's very intelligent and has shown a great interest in our enquiries into the Whistler murder. I've naturally refused to answer her questions, but I believe I can rely on her co-operation – and her discretion.'

'Right. Check if she's on duty over the weekend and if not get in touch with her first thing on Monday and find out if she's noticed any change in Boris's behaviour since that picture appeared in the *Mercury*.'

'If she isn't on duty, should I perhaps ask for her home number?'

'Better not. It's unlikely anyone would give

it without wanting to know who's calling, and that could lead to someone starting a rumour that something's afoot.'

'Very good, sir.'

'You're in touch with the men at the hospital, Rathbone,' Baird continued. 'I'll leave it to you to keep DCI Leach informed and he'll decide when to send DC Reynolds along to interview the victim. And naturally, I expect to be kept up to date with every development, however small.'

'Sir.'

'And one other thing. You mentioned, Leach, that DC Reynolds had drawn attention to the fact that the proceeds of the Whistler robbery were unlikely to count for much on Maddox's annual balance sheet compared with his more usual sources of revenue.'

Leach looked startled for a moment and then said, 'She did say something to that effect, sir.'

'And I further understand,' Baird's gaze swung in Sukey's direction, 'that one explanation you offered, Reynolds, was that this robbery might, so to speak, represent the tip of the iceberg – in other words, that there may be even more valuable items to be, shall we say, acquired?'

Sukey nodded. 'It seemed a possibility, sir.'

'And now we have the Greek police taking an interest in this case,' Baird went on thoughtfully. 'Perhaps we should take another look at the set-up between Maddox and his lady friend at the university. I don't see a mention of this being raised in any of the interviews with Professor Lamont?' This time his gaze homed in on Rathbone, who stirred a little uneasily.

'That's true, sir,' he admitted, 'but it's only fair to point out that neither the name Maddox, nor the man's reputation, means anything to Lamont.'

'So far as we are aware,' Baird pointed out. 'And there's also the matter of the telephone call that Whistler made to Lamont some time before he was due to come to England. Thorne claimed to have no idea what it was about, other than that there was mention of a trip to London, but I don't see any reference to Lamont's version. Why is that?'

'Lamont hasn't been interviewed since we learned of the conversation, sir.' said Rathbone. 'He'd already admitted knowing about the various items Whistler was bringing with him, so—'

'So you'd better go and see him again and find out exactly how and when he came by the information, what was said during that call and whether there were any further calls either way, apart from the one he made to check that Whistler had reached the hotel safely.' Baird's tone was brusque and Sukey avoided looking in Rathbone's direction. 'And take DC Reynolds with you,' the Superintendent went on. 'On second thoughts, you'd better get him to the station. The sister might be around if you went to the house and we don't want to cause another bout of hysteria.'

'Very good, sir.'

'Right.' Baird closed his file and stood up. 'Thank you everyone. That's all for now.'

Back in the CID office, Rathbone said, 'You'd better go and have a bite to eat before you leave, Sukey.' His tone was almost subdued and she felt a wave of sympathy for him. 'When you come back I'll arrange for someone to take you to pick up your car,' he added.

'Thanks, Sarge, but before I go I'd like to get my full report on the file.'

'Good thinking. Let me know when you're ready and,' he hesitated briefly before continuing, 'first thing Monday we'll fix an appointment to see Lamont.'

It was long after five o'clock when she reached home. It wasn't until she had parked and locked her car that she realized there were several items on her list that, with part of her mind speculating about the incident in the shop, she had forgotten to buy. Unable to face the drive to the nearest supermarket, she walked down the road to pick them up from a corner shop a short distance away.

Because of its original use for the storage

of hay and in all probability as living quarters for stable hands, the ground floor of her flat consisted of nothing but a narrow hallway from which a short staircase with a half-landing led to the two upper floors. On the first was a bedroom with a small bathroom, which Fergus occupied during his visits and flippantly referred to as the guest suite, together with a capacious storage area containing the central heating boiler. Sukey's own living quarters were on the floor above. As she closed the front door behind her she suddenly became aware that she was physically as well as mentally exhausted and for the first time since moving in she felt a pang of regret at the unconventional layout, which at the time had seemed, by its very individuality, to be particularly attractive.

Wearily, she plodded up the two flights of stairs and dumped her shopping on the kitchen table. When she had put it away and taken a quick shower she poured out a generous measure of wine and, glass in hand, stepped out on to the roof terrace – another feature that had convinced her that this was exactly the kind of place where she would feel comfortable. It was a fine, mild evening and the setting sun bathed the city in a warm golden light. From her vantage point she could pick out the Cabot tower on Brandon Hill and beyond, on the far side of the Floating Harbour, she caught a glimpse of the flags fluttering from the masts of Brunel's great iron ship, the SS Great Britain, proudly restored to something like her former glory. In another direction altogether and well out of her line of vision lay the area that had been the setting for the scene of hideous violence she had witnessed earlier. The memory of those few nightmarish moments would no doubt haunt her for days to come, yet for the moment, far from a sense of horror, she experienced a feeling of elation. She knew she had responded well to an unexpected and terrifying challenge; she had received a compliment from the Senior Investigating Officer; even Rathbone, recently so openly hostile, had shown her not only respect but consideration. Drawn in by circumstances, she was now part of a team carrying out a major operation.

That the victim of the shooting had survived without life-threatening injury was little short of a miracle and for the sake of the investigation as well as for his own she found herself praying that he would soon be well enough to be questioned. Meanwhile, she looked forward to a chat with Erika who, she had no doubt, would be delighted to give support. Her spirits renewed, she finished her drink and went indoors to see about dinner. She had just put some potatoes on to boil and was about to prepare a salad to go with her ready-cooked chicken joint when her phone rang. Jim was on the line.

'Sukey? Are you all right?'

'Of course I'm all right. Why shouldn't I be?'

'You must be a bit shaken after that drive-by shooting this morning. I heard it on the news and—'

'The media haven't got hold of my name?' she asked in a sudden panic.

'Relax, I heard it from Rick Leach. He says you kept your head and did a sterling job in managing the scene until uniformed arrived. You even got a bouquet from Superintendent Baird, no less.'

'Hardly a bouquet, more a gentle pat on the back,' she said modestly.

'Well anyway, I'm proud of you. I'm concerned for your safety as well,' he added, his tone more serious. 'I understand you're back on Operation Dirty Linen. You will be careful, won't you, Sook? It's not exactly a tea-party.'

'You think I don't realize that?'

'I'm sure you do, but I can't help worrying about you. By the way, if Fergus rings and asks if you know anything about the incident, I suggest you say as little as possible and above all keep stumm about your part in it. He might be tempted to boast to his mates about his Mum's heroism and as you probably know there's a news blackout until further notice.'

'So I understand. Gus is in London this weekend at a friend's wedding so he may not even have heard about it and I've certainly no intention of mentioning it.'

'That's good. That's really all I wanted to say for now. I'll keep in touch and ... I still care, you know,' he added almost diffidently.

'I know,' she said.

She went back to the kitchen. By the time her meal had been cooked and eaten and the used crockery and cutlery stacked in the dishwasher it was almost nine o'clock. She read for a while and then switched on the TV news at ten and found herself watching an item about the Stone Street drive-by shooting. She hastily switched off and went to bed.

She lay awake for a while, her brain hyperactive after the excitement of the day. As she waited for sleep to come her thoughts turned to the scene in Baird's office and the thinly disguised reprimand he had handed out to DS Rathbone. There was no doubt he had been guilty of more than one lapse in his conduct of the Whistler enquiry. It was not what one would expect from a man of his experience. Vicky had more than once remarked that he was "a really good cop" ... but? Did she too have reservations? Was there a reason for these apparent oversights?

Twenty-Four

Sukey had mentally earmarked Sunday morning for a visit to the fitness club she had joined shortly after moving to Bristol. After the stress and excitement of the previous day she was looking forward to a session in the gym followed by a refreshing swim in the pool and – as the weather was exceptionally mild for the time of year – lunch in the poolside bar. It might still be possible, but first she had to call the Mariners Hotel to find out whether Erika Henderson was on duty. She had just finished her breakfast and was reaching for the phone when her mobile rang. Erika herself was calling.

'Sukey? I'm glad I caught you. That man who was shot in Stone Street yesterday morning – do you know anything about him?'

'Erika! I'm glad you called; as a matter of fact I was going to call you.'

'What about?'

'I'd rather not talk about it on the phone. Are you on duty today?'

'Yes, till five o'clock.'

285

'What about your boss?'

'Maurice? It's his day off; I'm here on my own.'

'Then I'll come and see you this morning, if that's all right. Around ten o'clock?'

'Yes, that'll be fine.'

'And by the way,' Sukey added, 'I don't want to come in through reception. If I call your mobile number from the car park, will you let me in by the staff entrance?'

There was a moment's hesitation before Erika replied, 'All right, if that's what you want.' From her tone it was obvious that she was burning with curiosity, but she made no further comment other than, 'See you later,' before hanging up.

As usual on a Sunday morning, the roads were relatively quiet and Sukey reached the hotel shortly before ten. There was plenty of space in the car park and she found a slot close to the staff entrance. As she switched off her engine and keyed in Erika's number she noticed Boris's Vespa parked under some trees. Evidently the fact that the victim of the shooting was one of his relatives had not kept him away from his job. She recalled how agitated he had become at the possibility of losing it when he had begged her and Rathbone not to tell the hotel manager that he had left his post for an unauthorized cigarette, implying that his family depended on his support.

She waited until Erika appeared and opened the door before getting out of the car and
hurrying into the building. Neither spoke
until they were closeted in Erika's office and
the door firmly shut. She gestured to Sukey
to sit down and said, 'You're being very
mysterious. Why were you going to call me?'

'First of all, tell me why you're interested
in the Stone Street shooting.'

Erika poured two cups of coffee from a jug
on her desk and gave one to Sukey before
sitting down beside her. 'It's Boris,' she said.
'A member of staff happened to be in reception when the late edition of the *Mercury* was
delivered yesterday. Boris was just leaving
and he picked up a copy; of course the story
of the shooting was on the front page and
Debbie told me that he looked devastated –
no, terrified was the word she used – when
he saw it. She said he let out something that
sounded like a sob and crossed himself
before rushing away from the desk without
speaking to anyone. A few minutes later they
saw him roaring out of the car park on his
motor scooter like a bat out of hell. He'd
finished his shift anyway and by the time I
heard about it he'd long gone, so I had no
chance to speak to him. He's in this morning
as usual, but he looks absolutely terrible and
all he says when asked if there's anything
wrong is that he's got a bad headache.'

'Has anyone mentioned the shooting to

him, do you know?'

'I don't think so. He's never been one to chat to the other staff and I get the impression they don't like to ask him. He's carrying out his duties as usual, but his mind is obviously elsewhere. I thought of asking him to my office to see if I could get him to confide in me, but on second thoughts I decided it would be better to speak to you first. I know you said you weren't on the Whistler case any more, but I didn't think there'd be any harm in asking your advice. Anyway, I didn't have Sergeant Rathbone's number,' she added defensively.

'You did exactly the right thing,' said Sukey.

'Well, that's a relief,' said Erika with one of her characteristic giggles. 'Does that mean if I notice anything else I can speak to you and not Sergeant Rathbone? Not that he wasn't quite nice to me when I called at the police station, by the way.'

'Oh, DS Rathbone's OK, but he's got a lot on his plate at the moment.' Sukey was vaguely surprised at finding herself defending her unpredictable colleague. 'But in any case,' she added, 'things have moved on and I'm back on the case.'

Erika's eyes lit up. 'How do you mean, moved on? Are you close to making an arrest?'

'So far as I know, they haven't moved on

that far,' Sukey replied. 'Information is only given out on a need to know basis and as I'm the most junior member of the team I only see my part of the picture.'

'You haven't told me yet why you were going to call me,' Erika reminded her.

'As it happens, you've already told me what I wanted to know.'

'You mean if Boris had seen the report of the shooting?'

'That, and whether he'd shown any particular reaction.'

'So you already suspected that he knew the victim?' said Erika shrewdly.

'From what you've just told me there doesn't seem to be any doubt of it.'

'Gosh!' Erika put a hand to her mouth. 'Do you know who he is? Is he going to be all right?'

'I'm sorry, I can't tell you anything except that we believe the men who carried out the shooting are members of a gang that's the object of a pretty big undercover operation. I can't stress too strongly how important it is that you don't let anyone know I've been here asking these questions.'

'I won't say a word to anyone,' Erika promised, 'but isn't there anything else I can do?'

'Just keep your eyes and ears open, and let me know at once if you see or hear anything significant, but don't give any details over the phone. I'll arrange to see you somewhere away from the hotel.'

Back in her flat, Sukey wrote an account of the meeting and sent a text message to Rathbone reading simply, 'Have seen EH – interesting,' before going to the gym as planned. After a workout and a swim she ate a leisurely lunch and then, feeling relaxed and refreshed, she drove home and spent the afternoon reading. Later, she tuned in to the local news channel; the Stone Street shooting was, naturally, still the main item, but apart from giving the registration number of the car used by the gunmen and repeating their appeal for witnesses, the police had released no information about either the identity of the wounded man or his medical condition, except that he was 'fighting for his life' and that armed police were at his bedside.

An hour later, just as she was sitting down to her evening meal, her landline phone rang. The caller was DCI Leach. 'Rathbone reported your text,' he said, 'I'd like to hear more, but from now on we're to use the phone as little as possible. Is it all right if I call round?'

The request took Sukey by surprise. 'You mean now, sir?' she said.

'Unless it's seriously inconvenient.' His tone gave nothing away but it wasn't difficult to guess what lay behind the remark.

'It's no problem,' she assured him. 'I'm just

having a bite to eat, but—'

'Shall we say in half an hour?'

'Yes, sir, that'll be fine.'

When Leach arrived he sat down without waiting to be asked, declined Sukey's offer of coffee and said, 'The ban on phones applies to emails as well for the moment. We're pretty sure these villains have access to all the latest technology, which accounts for the way they've managed to keep a jump ahead of us so far. They almost certainly know your mobile number so you're being issued with a new one, but for the time being it's for use only in emergencies. Right, let's have your report.'

'It's here, I've done a printout.' She handed him the single sheet. 'And no, I haven't emailed it to the incident room,' she added before he had a chance to ask.

'Good.' He scanned the report and handed it back. 'You'll be interested to know that a man in a state of some distress was at the hospital yesterday evening, pleading for information about the victim of the shooting. He refused to give a name; needless to say he was firmly turned away, but from the description it was almost certainly Boris Gasspar and it's pretty obvious that J. Gasspar is a member of his family. The question is, assuming the shooting was a response to J's attempts to contact you, what does he know that Maddox and his mob are so anxious for him not to pass on to the police? More worrying still, if Boris shares that information, is his life in danger?'

'Probably not, sir. If, as now seems likely, Doctor Whistler was killed by this Stephen Lamont lookalike, his evidence will still be important to whoever's been master-minding this crime. But if he's here illegally and terrified of being exposed and deported, that could be an equally strong motive for him continuing to toe the line.'

'Well, we've had the report on his papers and they all seem to be in order, so Maddox must have some other hold on him. It's vital we find out what it is.'

'My guess is that he confided in J and showed him my card. Maybe he asked for advice; maybe J advised him to contact me and ask for help, but for some reason we don't know about he was too scared. J made a note of the number and at some point decided to act on his own initiative. After what's happened to him, Boris will be even less willing to talk to us.'

Leach nodded. 'So far that seems pretty straightforward, but there's the additional complication of your number turning up in the pocket of the dead girl. Did J give it to her, and what sort of trouble was she in that he believed you should know about? Had Maddox's mob forced her into prostitution and had she somehow managed to escape from wherever she was being held?'

'If that's the case, sir, then J must know where that is, otherwise how could he have been in contact with her?'

Leach nodded. 'Good point. Let's hope J will soon be well enough to be interviewed. I'll bring Mr Baird up to speed with the latest developments; meanwhile, I understand from DS Rathbone that he's planning an early meeting with Professor Lamont. I think you should be there – I'll mention it to Rathbone.'

'Very good, sir.'

Leach got up to go. At the door, he said, 'I think you're turning out to be a very useful member of the team, Sukey.' She opened her mouth to thank him, but he forestalled her by saying, 'So long as you continue to control your tendency to be a loose cannon.'

When Stephen Lamont arrived at the station on Monday morning Sukey was shocked at the change in his appearance. He seemed to have aged by ten years; he had lost weight and his eyes had a haunted expression.

He slumped into the chair that Rathbone indicated and said, in a voice that had none of its former resonance, 'How much longer is this going to go on, Sergeant? I've heard nothing from you or your superior officers since the last time I was here. I'm living in limbo; I can't work, I can't concentrate.' He ran nervous fingers through his mop of grey hair. 'My sister is suffering as well, although I have to say she's being very supportive – more than I deserve. Poor Hester, I've been very hard on her in the past, but I'm beginning to understand something of what she's gone through, even though in her case I have no idea of the cause.'

'I appreciate that you're in a very difficult situation, sir,' said Rathbone, and Sukey was struck by the gentleness of his tone. 'We too have been having our problems and there have been some recent developments that have thrown a completely new light on the murder of Doctor Whistler.'

Lamont sat bolt upright. 'You've found new evidence? Evidence to support my account of what happened that day?'

'Without revealing any details, sir, I think I can say that certain facts have come to light that have made us reconsider our assessment of the case. We believe you may have information that could help us – I'm not suggesting you have deliberately withheld anything,' Rathbone added hastily, seeing Lamont about to protest, 'but it is possible that you either said, or heard another person say, something that did not strike you as significant at the time.'

'What sort of information?'

'I want you to cast your mind back to the time when you and Doctor Whistler were making arrangements for his visit. At some point in your discussions, he informed you that in addition to the document in which you had a particular interest, he had also been entrusted with certain other items and told to take them to London for examination by a Greek expert who is currently in this country for medical treatment. He described several of those items and indicated they were of considerable monetary value.'

Lamont nodded. 'That is correct.'

'I take it this was during a telephone conversation?'

'Yes.'

'Can you recall anything else he said about this additional errand?'

Lamont gave a wry smile. 'I certainly can. He wasn't happy about it because having to go to London meant he'd have to cut short the time he'd been planning to spend in Bristol. I'd promised to show him some places of interest in the city.'

'Where did this conversation take place?'

'In Professor Thorne's office.'

'Is that where you normally take your calls?'

'No, I have my own office, but if neither I nor my secretary is there they get switched to Archie's PA.'

'Which is what happened on this occasion?'

Lamont made a vague gesture. 'I suppose

it must have. I don't remember exactly.'

'I take it Professor Thorne was present?'

Lamont frowned. 'Yes, of course; I was there to consult him on another matter. After the call ended I said something like "Whistler's got to go to London and he's very put out about it". It was only a throw-away remark because I was feeling a bit irritated – Whistler was making a great fuss about having to alter his arrangements. Archie didn't make any comment – I'm not even sure he heard.'

'We know he heard the reference to London.' Lamont raised an eyebrow but Rathbone did not offer any explanation. 'Now, Professor Lamont,' he went on, 'please think very carefully before you answer my next question. Did your end of the conversation include any reference to those additional items that Doctor Whistler was bringing with him? By that I mean, anything which could have suggested they were particularly valuable?'

Slowly, Lamont shook his head. 'Almost certainly not. To be frank, I wasn't really interested in them and as his change of plan did not affect me in any way I saw no reason to prolong the discussion.'

'Did you at any time tell anyone else about these additional items?'

'I believe I mentioned them to my sister, but only in a general sense – that is, I didn't go into details. She may have mentioned them to one of her friends – I could ask her if you like.'

Sukey half expected Rathbone to say they already had that information from her report on her first meeting with Hester, but all he said was, 'That would be helpful.'

'How is Hester?' asked Sukey. It was the first time she had spoken since the interview began and Lamont looked at her in surprise, as if he had forgotten her presence.

'As a matter of fact she has been a great deal better lately, thank you,' he replied.

'That's good news anyway,' said Rathbone. 'Well, thank you Professor Lamont. If you should think of anything else, please let us know at once.'

'Of course.'

Lamont got up and went through the door that Rathbone held open for him. A few paces along the corridor he stopped short and turned round. 'I don't suppose it's important, but Lottie Milligan was in her office throughout my conversation with Whistler.'

'Was her door open while you were speaking?' asked Rathbone.

'Not that I remember, but I do recall something I only half noticed at the time. The usual procedure when putting a call through is for her to say, "I have so-and-so on the line for you". As soon as I say, "Put them through" she waits for a moment to make sure the connection is there and then puts her own telephone down. You can hear the click.'

Rathbone gave him a keen look. 'And?'

'I can't swear to it, of course, but on that occasion I don't remember hearing the click.'

Twenty-Five

The minute Rathbone and Sukey returned to the CID office after their interview with Lamont they informed DCI Leach of the possible new lead. Leach ordered an immediate written report; meanwhile he would pass the information to Superintendent Baird who would no doubt want to question them in person. In less than an hour they were summoned to Leach's office.

Baird was already there, accompanied by a young man neither Sukey nor Rathbone had met before. Baird introduced him as DC Haskins, a member of the team Operation Dirty Linen. 'Before we consider this latest development, he's going to bring you up to date,' he explained. 'Right, Haskins, go ahead.'

Reading from a prepared statement, Haskins began, 'Since receiving DC Reynolds' account of her observation in Mold Street ten days ago of a meeting between Boris Gasspar and a man answering to the description of our target, we have maintained a surveillance operation on the house Gasspar was seen to enter. We observed several young men coming and going and established that some of them were regular visitors to a café called Marco's in Gloucester Road.

'I went in there one day when I knew two of them were present, ordered a coffee and sat down at the next table. They were speaking in heavily accented English, indicating that it wasn't their native language but that they were using it as a *lingua franca*. After a minute or two one of them, who appeared to be having difficulty in finding an English word, said something in Polish that I immediately understood.' He looked across at Rathbone and Sukey as if half expecting some kind of reaction from them; receiving none, he continued with his narrative.

'It so happens that my wife's family comes from Warsaw and because her father is elderly and has no English I have made some effort to learn Polish. I struck up a conversation with these two men; the Polish one was called Stefan and he was delighted to have the chance to speak to someone in his own language. I helped him with one or two problems with his English and the three of us went on to have a pleasant conversation for a few minutes. Stefan introduced his friend as Jozsef and said he was from Albania. After a little while they got up to leave, saying they had to go back to work. Out of what I intended to come across as a polite interest I asked them what jobs they had and they answered quite openly; Stefan said he was an electrician and Jozsef described himself as a general handyman.'

Baird glanced round the room. 'Any questions so far?' As everyone shook their heads he said, 'Good. Continue, Haskins.'

'I left it for a couple of days before going back. On Thursday they were there at lunch-time; I spotted them as I walked to the counter to give my order and nodded and smiled at them. I noticed they didn't look exactly overjoyed to see me; in fact, they got up very hastily before I could join them and went out, leaving their drinks unfinished on the table. I came to the conclusion that they'd been warned off talking to me.'

'Did you remark on this to anyone else in the café at the time?' asked Leach when Haskins' recital came to an end.

'Yes, to Marco.'

'What did he say?'

'Nothing much. He grinned and shrugged and said something about foreigners being a bit odd. Which coming from him was a bit of a joke, seeing as his family's Italian, but he's lived here since he was a child and considers himself a true Bristolian.'

'Thank you, Haskins,' said Baird. 'That puts you two in the picture,' he added to Sukey and Rathbone. 'We have three reasons to suspect a link between Marco's and Maddox.' He began counting on his fingers. 'One, the call to DC Reynolds was made from his café and half an hour later the man we believe made the call was the victim of a drive-by shooting as he waited for Reynolds: two, customers are discouraged from fraternizing with the locals: three, the Lamont lookalike appears to be a regular caller there. Any conclusions to be drawn from that?'

'Regarding the regular visit from the phoney Lamont,' said Rathbone, 'it doesn't sound like a protection racket, more a case of handing over payment for services rendered, like passing on useful bits of information.'

Baird nodded. 'That appears the more likely. One thing is clear; Maddox knows we're snapping at his heels and no doubt he's doing his best to plug every possible avenue of enquiry open to us. We've reason to believe he has some kind of hold over Boris Gasspar because of his reluctance to talk to Reynolds and now we have two more men reacting in the same way. Let's assume for the moment that Jozsef is the J. Gasspar who finished up full of lead in the ITU. If so, how did he come by Reynolds' mobile number? Did Boris give it to him because he was too frightened to use it himself? Or did he merely show it to him and J decided to act on his own initiative? How did it find its way into the pocket of the Lady in the Avon?' He fixed a steely gaze on Sukey and she felt goose bumps rising in response. 'Any ideas, Reynolds?'

'Well, sir,' said Sukey, a little hesitantly because of the four pairs of eyes fastened on her, 'if we assume the girl had been forced into prostitution, which seems likely in view of the fact that she'd been drugged, she must have been kept in a house being run as a brothel, presumably by the Maddox mob. It would have to be a secure house, but it's possible some of the women made attempts from time to time to break out.'

'True,' said Baird. 'In that case she was probably one of them, which is why they drugged her. Go on.'

'Maddox seems to have a hold over both Stefan and Jozsef. Maybe the women did some damage and Jozsef was told to fix it. Perhaps the girl, thinking he was an outsider and not a member of the mob, begged him for help and he felt sorry for her and gave her my number.'

Baird's glance swept round the room. 'Has anyone got anything to add to that?'

'One point, sir,' said Rathbone. 'Surely, if they were being held against their will, the girls would have to be under constant guard by people Maddox felt he could rely on. Why couldn't one of them be a resident handy-man?'

'Reynolds?'

'Perhaps an extra pair of hands was need-ed, sir – or maybe the guards were women.'

'That's a point. I suppose there's no reason why they shouldn't be. Maybe Maddox recruits them from ex-prison guards who've been sacked for brutality – it would be right in character. All the indications about him so far suggest that we're dealing with a control freak who enjoys tormenting his victims.' Baird turned back to Haskins. 'I believe you've been able to find out where Jozsef and Stefan work?'

'Yes, sir, they both have regular jobs with small, reputable businesses and their papers are in order. I've been able to establish that Jozsef didn't report for work this morning by ringing the company and speaking with a Polish accent, but it didn't seem to have occurred to the woman who answered the phone that he might have been the victim of the shooting.'

'The news blackout is still in force and the media are co-operating,' said Baird. 'I take it there's been no report of suspicious activity in or near the hospital, Rathbone?'

'No, sir, just Boris turning up every so often begging for news and being told to go away.'

'Poor devil.' For a moment the professional mask slipped, revealing the human being behind it. 'Now let's have your report on this morning's interview with Lamont.'

'Right, sir.' Rathbone read out the statement he and Sukey had prepared together. Everyone listened intently and when Rathbone had finished he handed it to Baird, who put it beside the open file on his desk and sat for a few moments tapping his pen against his top teeth.

'In the light of her known association with Maddox,' he said after several moments' contemplation, 'we've been keeping an eye on the Milligan woman. She's been seen out and about with him a few times since Reynolds and DCI Castle of the Gloucestershire force observed them in the floating restaurant just over two weeks ago, but we've observed no suspicious behaviour on her part. It now appears feasible that it was from her that he came to hear about the goodies Whistler was bringing with him. He must know enough about Greek antiquities to recognize that they were valuable enough to interest him.'

'They must be worth more than a couple of grand to rate the attention of a hit man,' observed Leach. 'I don't suppose the putative Pauline epistle has enough monetary value to interest Maddox, but he could probably find a customer for it.'

Baird nodded. 'Some unscrupulous collector who wouldn't be too concerned about where it came from,' he agreed. 'Of course, it's by no means certain that there was any intention to kill Whistler. Even if he'd been conned into handing over the items, believing that he was giving them to the right person, he would no doubt have done as Gasspar did – identify Lamont as the thief when he realized what had happened. Which brings us to another question: how did Maddox manage to find someone with such a strong resemblance to Lamont? Whatever the explanation, it's just the sort of situation that would appeal to him. Another of his less endearing qualities is his warped sense of humour,' he added grimly.

'Excuse me, sir,' said Sukey hesitantly, 'it might have been Ms Milligan who gave him the idea. Maddox might have introduced her to the hit man at some time. She would almost certainly have commented on the likeness; she could even have shown Maddox a copy of a prospectus with photographs of the senior members of the faculty.'

'Good point, Reynolds,' said Baird. 'Another thing we know about Maddox is that he has a fascination for women, so she'd probably do anything he asked of her. Right,

Haskins, we continue to keep Milligan under observation. Report to me if she so much as sneezes without good reason. Otherwise, carry on as before. Rathbone, maintain the guard over J. Gasspar and you, Reynolds, stand by to interview him the minute the medics give permission. Thank you everyone, that's all for now.'

Following its publication in the British press, the artist's impression of the girl found in the river had been circulated through Interpol and very quickly identified as their youngest daughter by an impoverished farming family in Albania. It seemed the girl had gone willingly to England, with her parents' consent, with a man who had promised her a chance to train as a model. Nothing had been heard from her since; the distraught parents had been brought over to make a formal identification and the following day during the lunchtime news bulletin they had made an impassioned plea through an interpreter for help in bringing her killer to justice.

This prompted several calls from the public who confirmed an earlier report of a girl seen getting into a car with two men in their twenties. Neither answered to the description of Lamont's double and the consensus was that the men were coaxing rather than forcing the girl into the car, but that she appeared 'rather reluctant to go with them' and 'once actually tried to walk away but one of them caught her by the arm and stopped her', as another witness described it. Another said the men were 'a bit foreign looking'.

'Still not much to go on,' DCI Leach observed to the team after studying the reports, 'but it's interesting that she didn't seem to be putting up much of a struggle. In any case, we can't be a hundred per cent certain that this was the girl we fished out of the Avon.'

'If it was, they might have cooked up some story to make her go quietly,' Sukey suggested. 'Maybe they even led her to believe she'd be allowed to go home – anything rather than cause a scene that could prompt a member of the public to call the police.

'Or one of them could have stuck a needle in her with a shot of the drug that was found during the PM,' said Rathbone.

'Or it might just have been a family matter,' said Leach. 'Without something a bit more specific, it doesn't help much, I'm afraid.'

It was not until the following Monday that a message came from the hospital that the injured man had recovered sufficiently to be questioned for a short period. It had already been decided that Sukey should be the first to see him and she was given detailed instructions before setting off for the hospital. As she drove into the huge sprawling site, everything appeared normal. The patient was still in a private room in the Intensive Therapy Unit, but she had been told to use a car park some distance from the one that visitors to the unit would normally use.

She found a vacant space and made for the nearest entrance. Two uniformed police were on guard; they did not appear to be armed, but she had no doubt that armed backup was on immediate call. As she approached, a man was in conversation with the officers; he appeared to be pleading for admission and was being firmly repulsed. As, looking somewhat forlorn, he turned away she realized it was Boris Gasspar. Their eyes met; he appeared first startled, then alarmed. He broke into a run and as if by magic two armed officers appeared and wrestled him to the ground. Sukey hurried over as they were about to handcuff him.

'It's OK, I know him and he's not dangerous,' she assured them, showing her ID. They allowed him to get to his feet, still holding him by the arms. 'Boris, please tell me,' she said, 'the man who was shot – do you know him?'

He nodded, nervously licking his lips. 'He's my cousin,' he said, his voice barely a whisper.

'Then I can give you good news. He's

recovering. He will live.'

He gave a great sigh, bowed his head and murmured something with closed eyes. When he opened them again they were overflowing with tears. 'Thank you. Thank you very much. I see him now?' he begged.

'I'm afraid not, but I promise we'll let you know how he's getting on.'

'Thank you,' he said again. 'I go now?'

'What do you think?' asked one of the officers, who were still holding him by both arms.

Sukey thought quickly. She could see no reason why they should hold him, but felt unable to take the responsibility of saying he could go. 'I suggest you take him back to your car and call CID,' she said. 'Ask for DS Rathbone, mention my name and tell him I've identified your detainee as Boris Gasspar. I have to go now.' Leaving them to it, she went back to the entrance where the two officers on guard had been keeping a close eye on developments.

'You know that guy?' one of them asked as she showed her ID and gave the reason for her visit.

'Yes, and we're pretty sure he's related to the shooting victim,' she said. 'All he wanted was to know how he was doing; I don't think he'll give you any more trouble.'

'At least it broke the boredom,' said the other with a grin. 'Here comes another medic, by the looks of him. They keep popping in and out, mostly for a fag. There's no smoking in the hospital.'

Glancing over her shoulder, Sukey saw a young man in a white coat with a stethoscope round his neck and his identity card hanging on a cord. He paused to stub out a cigarette in a disposal unit fixed to the wall before approaching the entrance. She saw the two officers intercept him; they made him wait while they checked his ID against what looked like a register before admitting him. Having some idea of the length of Maddox's reach, Sukey realized that she had been feeling a little apprehensive and it was a relief to know that tight security was still being maintained.

Ahead of her was a long corridor with signs and arrows indicating various departments and further corridors leading off on either side. For the moment there was no one about and the way ahead of her seemed to stretch into infinity. She walked on for a short distance, her footsteps echoing on the bare floor, before realizing that she should have taken a turning to the right. She stopped short, swung round and cannoned into a man in a white coat who had been following her, a man whom she recognized as the one who had entered the building behind her. She hastily apologized; he mumbled something incomprehensible and for a split second she detected what appeared to be a flicker of recognition in his eyes. Then he too turned, hurried back and headed along the corridor she had missed.

Twenty-Six

Sukey's heart was pounding as she tried to decide what to do. The officers guarding the entrance had allowed him in so presumably they were satisfied that he was a bona fide member of the medical team. But supposing the badge he wore was phoney or had been stolen? His sharp, sallow features were sufficiently striking to make her certain she had never set eyes on him before, yet the more she thought about it, the more convinced she felt that he had recognized her but for some reason wanted to conceal the fact. Why? She recalled one occasion in a super-market when, thinking a complete stranger was a friend, she had called out a greeting before realizing her mistake. Her embar-rassed apology had been accepted with a smile, but this man's attitude had been entirely different. Some sixth sense told her he should be challenged and if necessary asked to provide further proof of his identity.

He had turned into the corridor she now realized she should have taken, but by the time she had gathered her wits and hurried after him he was nowhere to be seen. The sign they had both passed by indicated that it led to the Intensive Therapy Unit. Surely, she reasoned, if he genuinely was one of the hospital staff, he would have known the way. And the ITU would certainly be his destination if he was an impostor who had tricked his way into the hospital with the intention of silencing forever the victim of the Stone Street shooting. There was no doubt now in her mind; she must alert the armed officers guarding the patient of a possible threat before heading there herself.

She took out her mobile and keyed in the contact number she had been given in case of an emergency. She heard a man's voice say, 'Sergeant Murray', but before she had a chance to speak a hand was clamped over her mouth and an arm like an iron band encircled her chest, threatening to squeeze the breath from her body. She felt herself being dragged backwards through a door that had opened silently behind her; the mobile fell from her grasp and struck her foot; instinctively she kicked out at it in the desperate hope that it would be picked up by someone who, on hearing an urgent voice on the line, would realize that something was seriously amiss and have the sense to raise the alarm.

Sukey had some training in self-defence. She was wearing shoes with hard soles; raising her right knee she dragged her heel as hard as she could downwards against her assailant's shinbone. She heard him give a gasp of pain; the pressure round her ribs eased a fraction and the hand round her mouth relaxed just enough to enable her to bite hard into his thumb. He uttered a curse; his grip relaxed a little more and she gave a backward jab with both elbows, hoping to wind him, but he was ready for it and all she encountered, before a blow to the head knocked her out, was hard, unyielding muscle.

When she came round she was on the floor and the man was bending over her, winding her body mummy-fashion in a sheet. There was a gag in her mouth and already her arms were pinned to her sides, but her legs were still free. She aimed a kick at his groin, but he grabbed her ankles and bound her legs together. Looking round she saw shelves piled high with bed linen and towels and realized that they were in a laundry store. The man grabbed another sheet, laid it on the floor, rolled her over on it several times and tied the ends firmly behind her back. 'Not ideal, but the best I could do in the circumstances,' he said with a sneer before slipping quietly out of the room and locking the door behind him.

Her head was throbbing painfully. He had left her lying face down, but she managed to roll over on to her back. After a few seconds she became aware of the sound of running feet and confused voices. Surely, she thought in a surge of hope, this meant that the armed guard who had answered her call had become suspicious and raised the alarm. If so, they would all be on red alert, but they would have no idea of the nature of the threat or from what direction it was likely to come. Somehow, she must attract attention so that she could tell them who to look out for. She could neither call out nor stand up, but she could at least bend her knees and dig her heels into the tiled floor. By using them as a lever she managed to pull her body towards the door.

Fortunately the room was little more than a cupboard and the distance was not great; nevertheless a lifetime seemed to pass before she was able to start pounding on the door with her feet. At last she heard a shout of, 'Someone's locked in here!' There was a scraping sound as a key turned in the lock and the door began to open. She managed to roll out of the way and ended up lying face down again, panting with exhaustion. Hands rolled her none too gently on to her back; someone in dark blue trousers was standing over her and she looked up to find herself staring into the muzzle of a gun.

They were taking no chances. Another man appeared and removed the gag before yanking her to her feet and starting to un-wind the sheets that imprisoned her while the first one barked, 'Who are you?' She gave her name and rank and began to explain how she came to be there, but not until her hands were free and she was able to produce her ID did they accept that she was genuine and not a diversionary tactic on the part of the enemy. Meanwhile, more precious seconds had ticked away.

'We must get to the ITU before the man who attacked me gets to Gasspar,' she almost sobbed.

'This way,' said one of her rescuers and the two broke into a run as he spoke, with Sukey struggling to keep up. 'Don't panic,' he said over his shoulder, 'only the medics are allowed near him.'

'He is a medic – at least, he's posing as one,' she panted as they raced along. 'He must have faked an ID ... the guard let him into the building a minute or so behind me ... I got suspicious when he didn't seem sure which way he was going.'

Without slackening speed the leader spoke into his radio to relay the information. Then he shouted, 'Take him out ... now!'

'What is it?' Sukey gasped.

'He's in there with Gasspar,' he said grimly. 'Leave us to deal with this.'

They charged on ahead, brushing aside everyone in their path while Sukey, still suffering the effects of the blow to her head, stumbled dazedly after them. When she reached the ITU she heard shouts and the sound of a scuffle coming from one of the private rooms. Outside stood a young nurse; her eyes were wide with terror, the knuckles of one hand were crammed against her mouth and tears were pouring down her face. Sukey went over to her. 'How long was he in there with Gasspar before the police went in?' she asked.

'Only a few seconds,' the nurse whimpered. 'I was a bit doubtful because I hadn't seen him before, but it isn't always the same doctor treating him ... and he showed his pass ... he said Jozsef needed some medication ... the police guards were a bit jumpy as well and they checked the name against the list of doctors and it was there so they said it was all right to let him in ... and then all of a sudden they rushed in after him with their guns and ... oh, please God, let Jozsef be safe!'

'Amen to that,' Sukey said fervently. As she spoke, the door was flung open and four burly officers in body armour emerged, half dragging, half carrying the phoney doctor, who was handcuffed but still struggling

316

violently, kicking out at his captors and screaming abuse.

'I don't understand, but I doubt it's the kind of language a gentleman would use before ladies,' remarked one of the four as he threw a blanket over the man's head before he was hustled out of the room. 'There's a syringe on the floor under the bed, but we got to him before he had a chance to use it,' he informed Sukey, almost as an after-thought. 'I'm sure you know what to do with it. And Nurse, it'd be as well to check on your patient. He's had quite a fright.'

The nurse was obviously still badly shaken but she nodded and went into the patient's room while Sukey waited outside, uncertain for the moment what her next move should be. Then she had an idea; when the nurse came out she said, 'I need to go in and retrieve the syringe. Can you give me a pair of surgical gloves and some sort of sterile container?'

'Yes, of course, but if you don't mind I'll come in with you. Jozsef's a bit nervous and if someone he doesn't recognize were to go in now I think he'd get upset.'

'I'll bet he would – and so would I after a scare like that,' Sukey agreed. 'I'm DC Reynolds and I was supposed to interview him today – that's why I'm here. We believe he can help us with our enquiries into some very serious crimes. Do you think he's well

317

enough or should I come back tomorrow?'

The nurse hesitated. 'I knew you were coming, of course,' she said after a moment, 'but after what's happened I don't feel I have the authority to let you see Jozsef without permission from a doctor. And on second thoughts, I think it would be better if I collected the syringe for you. I'll be careful how I handle it; I watch police programmes on the telly so I know all about fingerprints and things,' she added, and for the first time her tense expression relaxed and she gave a conspiratorial smile.

'I suppose it'll be all right,' Sukey replied. She had almost forgotten her own frightening experience, but now the excitement was over the memory of the struggle began to filter back into her mind. As the nurse vanished once more into Jozsef's room she became aware that her head was throbbing more violently and her legs were turning to jelly. The room began to spin around her; she grabbed at a convenient chair, sat down and closed her eyes.

When Sukey came round she was lying on a bed with a nurse on one side and DC Vicky Armstrong on the other. She stared at them in bewilderment, tried to sit up and was gently pushed back on to the pillow by the nurse. 'Just lie still while I check your blood pressure,' she said.

318

'I don't understand,' said Sukey while the nurse fitted a cuff round her arm and switched on the monitor. 'What happened? What am I doing here?'

'You had a nasty blow to the head and suffered mild concussion, but somehow you managed to keep going and raise the alarm,' explained Vicky.

'Yes, I remember now.' Sukey's thoughts were beginning to clear. 'They arrested the man who attacked me and tried to kill Jozsef. After it was over I wanted to talk to him but the nurse wouldn't let me without a doctor's say-so. I sat down to wait and—'

'And passed out,' said Vicky.

'How long for?' Sukey looked out of the window. 'It's getting dark. What time is it?'

'Just after six. You started to come round after a few minutes but the doctor who checked you over wanted to keep you under observation for a couple of hours, so they gave you a sedative and you've had a nice long sleep. How's the head?'

'Still a bit sore, but I'll live. What about the blood pressure?' she asked as the nurse removed the cuff from her arm.

'It's fine, and so's your pulse.'

'Does that mean I can go?'

'As soon as you're ready.' The nurse packed her monitor away and left the room.

Sukey threw off the blanket that had been covering her and stood up. 'I can't go without seeing Jozsef. Has he been given the all clear?'

'Sukey, I'm sorry to disappoint you,' said Vicky, 'but as you were temporarily *hors de combat* Greg Rathbone said I'd better see him and get his statement ASAP.'

'But he said I was the only person he'd speak to,' Sukey protested.

Vicky gave an apologetic grin. 'If you remember, he only asked to talk to the police lady – he had no idea what you looked like and so—'

'You pretended to be me,' said Sukey indignantly.

'No, I just said I was a police officer and waved my ID under his nose and he was perfectly happy to talk to me. The good news is that he's spilled a whole canful of beans and we know now why Boris has been so cagey. I'll tell you about it on the way. Just a minute.' She broke off to take a call on her mobile. 'Yes, Sarge, she's been discharged from the hospital and I'm taking her home ... what? ... Gosh, there's never a dull moment in this job is there? Hold on, Sarge, I'll ask her.' She put a hand over the phone and turned to Sukey. 'Operation Dirty Linen's under way, and DCI Leach would like us all back at the station to interview Thorne's secretary who's just turned up in a state of the jitters saying she wants to make a statement. Do you feel up to it or would you like

320

me to take you home first?'

'Are you kidding?' Sukey's voice rose to an excited squeak. 'I wouldn't miss this for the world.'

Vicky spoke once more into the phone. 'She's fine Sarge; we're on our way.'

Twenty-Seven

Despite Sukey's protests that she was perfectly fit to drive, Vicky insisted that she hand over the keys to the pool car in which she had driven to the hospital.

'Greg Rathbone's orders,' she said as they clipped on their seat belts. 'He's come over all solicitous for you. I wonder why? Is there anything you'd like to tell Auntie Vicky?' she added with a mischievous twinkle in her eyes.

'Don't be daft,' said Sukey, laughing in spite of herself. 'He's probably trying to make up for being so hard on me earlier. You've known him for some time – is he always on a short fuse or just naturally subject to mood swings?'

'Funny you should ask that.' Vicky switched on the ignition and drove slowly towards the exit from the car park. 'We've all noticed lately that he's been more inclined than usual to be tetchy ... and we've had to cover up for him more than once when he's missed something quite important.'

'Yes, I've noticed that,' said Sukey. 'Have you any idea what's behind it?'

'Strictly *entre nous*, Bob Douglas confided the other day that he's having matrimonial problems. It's not surprising; being married to a copper can't be easy.'

Sukey nodded. 'Jim's marriage went pear-shaped after a couple of years,' she said.

Vicky gave her a sideways glance. 'Do I take it he's not anxious to repeat the experience?'

'We've never discussed it.'

Vicky nodded. 'It's the best way. It's the same with Chris and me. Ours is a strictly NLTC relationship – no long-term commitment on either side. It's worked well for three years so far. Anyway, that's enough of that. Want to hear what Jozsef had to say?'

'I thought you'd never get around to it.'

'It was all they needed to trigger Operation Dirty Linen. You were dead right; Maddox had a hold over Boris, big time.'

'What kind of hold?'

'Outwardly, he's the owner of a legitimate international employment agency with branches in several Eastern European and Balkan countries. He fixes up guys like Boris and Jozsef with jobs in this and other EU countries where they earn wages several times greater than they can get at home. He even finds them places to live – in houses owned by one of his own companies. That's another of his sidelines.'

'I suppose it means he can keep an eye on them?' suggested Sukey.

'Possibly – I hadn't thought of that. Anyway, that's his public face; his private one is rather different. In return for helping them to raise their and their families' standard of living, he requires them from time to time to carry out certain services on his behalf – such as repairing damage in a bordello with no questions asked.'

'Or reporting any of his protégés who make calls to police officers?'

Vicky nodded. 'Exactly. It's almost certain that either Marco or one of the regulars in his café overheard Jozsef's phone call to you and grassed him up to one of the Maddox mob, who promptly summoned a hit squad.'

'We figured it had to be something like that, didn't we?' said Sukey. 'Presumably Boris is so scared of getting similar treatment that he's prepared to give false evidence against Stephen Lamont?'

Vicky was silent for a moment, staring at the road ahead. At length she said, 'It's even nastier than that. The Whistler job was a bit more complicated than fixing a window some poor girl had smashed in an effort to escape a life of enforced prostitution, so Maddox had to figure out a different method of getting him to co-operate. After all, a dead Boris couldn't have given evidence against Lamont.'

'That's true. So what did he do?' Sukey prompted, as Vicky still seemed reluctant to continue.

'I warn you, it's pretty horrid. A few days before the Whistler murder he took Boris to a local house he was running as a brothel and forced him to witness some of the nastier things the clients do to the girls there. Boris has a sister back in Albania and he was told that if he didn't do exactly what Maddox wanted she'd be abducted and taken to a similar establishment where she'd get the same treatment.'

'The man's a monster!' said Sukey in horror.

'A monster, a psychopath, a megalomaniac, you name it,' said Vicky grimly. 'Plus he gets a sadistic kick out of seeing people squirm. He thinks he's invincible as well – he moves quite freely among his minions without any apparent fear of betrayal. You saw that for yourself the day he picked up Boris in his car.'

'Poor Boris, it's no wonder he wouldn't talk to me,' Sukey said sadly. 'So what made Jozsef risk blowing the whistle?'

'It seems it happened much as we figured

– Boris has been really unhappy about the prospect of committing perjury and he asked his cousin's advice and showed him your card. Jozsef advised him to use it to shop Maddox and ask for police protection for himself and his family in Albania, but he didn't dare for fear of what would happen if Maddox's mob got to them first. He wouldn't part with the card either, but Jozsef happens to be good at memorizing numbers so when he was on his own he wrote yours down.'

'And later gave it to the girl who ended up in the Avon?'

'So it seems, although by the time he reached this point in the story he was getting tired and the details are a bit vague.'

'I'm not surprised. His English is pretty shaky and telling you all this must have been quite a struggle.'

'It wasn't as difficult as I expected. He understands a lot, but he needs help in finding the right words to express himself. Anyway, you were right when you suggested he was sent to a house that Maddox was using as a brothel to carry out some repairs, but exactly how he came to give the girl the number isn't very clear as yet. Seeing her picture in the paper was enough to make him decide to contact us, come hell or high water.'

They had reached the station. Vicky parked

the car and they got out. 'Right,' she said as they made their way up to the CID offices, 'let's hear what Ms Milligan has got for us.'

They were directed to an interview room where Lottie Milligan was already seated at a table opposite DCI Leach and DS Rathbone. Sukey's impression of her at their two previous meetings was of an extremely attractive, self-possessed woman who could no doubt be charming when she chose but who had treated her on the first occasion with thinly disguised hostility and on the second – on that memorable evening in the restaurant when she was escorted by Oliver Maddox – in a distinctly condescending manner. Today, the change in her was so remarkable that Sukey had to look at her a second time to make sure she was the same person. She sat huddled in her chair with her head sunk between her shoulders; her skin under the make-up had a greyish tinge, the hair that had fallen in flattering waves on either side of her face now clung limply to her temples and her mouth drooped at the corners, giving her a hangdog expression. Most striking of all was the deadness in her eyes, which stared out through her fashionable glasses like pale blue marbles. It was as if her whole personality had changed along with her appearance.

Leach told Sukey and Vicky to sit in the chairs placed on either side of her, introduced them and then said, 'Ms Milligan, will you please confirm that you are here of your own free will?'

She nodded and whispered, 'Yes, that's right.'

'We note that you wish to make a statement and we will be recording this interview, but you are free to leave at any time. Do you understand?'

She nodded again; Rathbone switched on the tape recorder and said, 'Right, Ms Milligan, please begin.'

'It won't take long,' she said, in a voice as dead as her expressionless eyes. 'Oliver Maddox is a corrupt and heartless monster who deserves to be put away for life. He's responsible for the deaths of Doctor Whistler and the girl you found in the river ... many others as well for all I know. He deals in drugs, he's into money laundering – that's where he makes most of his money. He runs brothels, he deals in stolen art treasures ... you name it. He owns all kinds of dodgy enterprises ... I can give you details ... and for a while he owned me.' Her voice cracked and she stared down at her hands, which were restlessly fiddling with the handbag that lay in her lap. 'I'm sorry,' she whispered brokenly, 'I'll be all right in a moment.'

'Just take your time,' said Leach.

'I didn't care what he did,' she said after a moment, 'I was completely under his spell.

I'd have done anything for him. It was my idea to get Sonny Bright to pretend to be Stephen Lamont and steal those things from Doctor Whistler, because of the resemblance. Oliver thought it was a huge joke and he enjoyed forcing that poor man at the hotel to tell lies for him. I was horrified when it ended in murder, but he just shrugged it off. All he was interested in was getting his hands on the things Doctor Whistler had brought with him.'

'Have you any idea what he did with them?' asked Leach.

She shook her head. 'I'm afraid not. If you search his house you might find something about them on his computer.'

'What happened next?' prompted Rathbone.

'Nothing. That is, things went on as before. We did something most nights – meals in expensive restaurants, theatres and concerts, sometimes just the two of us, sometimes with his friends ... and he came to my flat every night and we made love. I know I should have put an end to it, but I couldn't ... even then, I was afraid of him although at the same time it was all so exciting ... he seemed so all-powerful, like a Mafia boss in a movie.' She gave a sad little laugh that failed to conceal the anguish in her eyes. 'He doesn't make many mistakes; that's why he's got away with his crimes for so long ... but he got careless yesterday evening.'

Another wave of emotion threatened to engulf her, but she fought it back bravely. 'We were going to the theatre,' she went on. 'I arrived a bit early; his housekeeper was just going back into the house after putting out the garbage so I didn't have to ring the bell. She said, "Mr Maddox is in his study – he's on the phone, but I'm sure he won't be long." His study leads off the hall and I heard him talking and for some reason I went and listened outside the door. He was saying something about tickets so I guessed he was planning a trip. Whoever was on the other end must have asked if he was taking me with him because he said, "Take Lottie? You must be joking. She's outlived her usefulness – I don't want to be lumbered with her where I'm going".' She raised her head and stared round at the detectives with a look of incredulity on her face. 'He was going to dump me!' she wailed. 'I couldn't believe it ... the number of times he swore he loved me! How could I have been such a fool?' This time a combination of shock, misery and humiliation got the better of her and she broke into uncontrollable weeping.

Leach switched off the tape and he and Rathbone waited while Sukey and Vicky did their best to comfort the stricken woman. When she was calmer, Leach gave her a glass of water and said, 'Ms Milligan, would you like to take a break before continuing?'

She shook her head. 'No,' she said in a hoarse whisper. 'Please, I'd rather go on.'

'Good.' He signalled to Rathbone, who restarted the tape. 'Before we go any further, do you have any idea when Maddox was planning to leave, or where he intended to go?'

'None at all, I'm afraid.'

'Did you tell him what you'd overheard?'

'No, I didn't dare. I sat down and when he came out of his study he looked at me and said, "Lottie, you look ghastly. Are you all right?" I told him I had a migraine and I didn't really feel well enough to go to the theatre, so he took me home. After he left I got frightened; I thought, maybe he only pretended to believe me about the migraine, maybe he's guessed I overheard what he was saying and thought I might be planning to shop him for cheating on me. I know what he can do, how he can get to people, he's got so much power it's unbelievable. I didn't feel safe any more so I packed a bag and spent the night at a hotel. I still don't feel safe, I'm afraid to go home, the only thing I could think of was to come here and tell you everything. I want him punished for all the evil things he's done.' In a sudden, dramatic change of mood, she leapt to her feet and glared wildly at the four police officers. 'Why are you still sitting there?' she screamed. 'Go out and arrest him! I want him put away for the rest of his life!'

'Please, Ms Milligan, sit down,' said Leach calmly. 'You have nothing to fear from Oliver Maddox any more. He and a number of his associates were arrested a few hours ago.'

Twenty-Eight

The following day an explosion of sensational headlines in the local and national press announced that the police, in a co-ordinated series of raids in and around the city, had rounded up a significant number of people of both sexes and were holding them at various police stations on suspicion of being involved in drug dealing and money laundering. At the same time a number of women who had been forced into prostitution had been released from a house in Mold Street.

Superintendent Baird, while delighted at the success of Operation Dirty Linen, was concerned that as few details as possible of the people detained, and particularly of Oliver Maddox and his lieutenant Sonny Bright, should reach the press.

'The last thing we want is trial by media,'

he warned the team. 'Nothing would please this lot better than to give a bunch of dodgy lawyers an excuse to plead that they couldn't expect a fair trial.' At the subsequent press conference he made it clear that further arrests were likely and that much work still remained to be done before any of the detainees could be charged. To everyone's relief, after the initial flurry of excitement, the newspaper editors and radio and TV presenters switched their attention to the next headline-grabbing story.

'Superintendent Baird has asked me to thank you all for your contribution to the success of Operation Dirty Linen,' DCI Leach informed Detective Sergeants Rathbone and Douglas and Detective Constables Reynolds and Armstrong when, some days later, he summoned them to a meeting in his office. 'As I'm sure you all realize there are still hours of detective work ahead and a hundred and one loose ends to tie up. A few of them have already been satisfactorily dealt with and I'm sure you'll be pleased to know we've recovered the stuff that Sonny Bright stole from Whistler.'

'That's great news, sir,' said Rathbone.

'It's certainly good news from our point of view, and Inspector Comino of the Greek police is naturally delighted – although there may be a bit of a problem there. He wants to come and pick up the things right away but

we need them as evidence, so there'll probably have to be a bit of top-level diplomacy.
That's for someone else to sort out, thank
goodness.'

'What about the Pauline epistle, sir?' asked
Douglas.

'I understand Comino is happy for Professor Lamont to be allowed to study it as planned, on the understanding that it is returned
to Greece once he has finished with it.'

'One thing has puzzled me from the beginning, sir,' said Sukey. 'When I went to talk to
the paramedics who took Doctor Whistler to
hospital they said he had been trying to say
something that sounded like, "Not Greek".
Have we any idea what he meant?'

Leach gave a wry smile. 'Oh yes, as a matter of fact we have. Sonny Bright answered
that question at a very early stage. It seems
he's been nursing a grudge against Maddox
for some time – he claims he's not been getting his fair cut of the spoils – so he's being
very co-operative, no doubt in the hope that
it will be to his advantage when he comes to
trial. He says that when he went to Whistler's
room, pretending to be Lamont, all went
well until the moment when Whistler handed over a small holdall containing the things.
He said something completely incomprehensible to Sonny; presumably he was speaking Greek and expecting a response in the
same language, which of course the genuine

Lamont would have given. Sonny merely looked blank, whereupon Whistler realized he was an impostor and tried to snatch the holdall back. They tussled and Sonny pulled the knife on him; he swears he was only trying to frighten him and didn't intend to kill him, but the old boy very foolishly struggled and the knife went in by accident.'

'I wonder if the jury will buy that?' commented Douglas.

Leach shrugged. 'That remains to be seen.'

'What about Marco, sir?' asked Sukey.

'He was pulled in during the first sweep and questioned in some detail about the people who use his café, but we're pretty sure he's clean and he's been released without charge.'

'And Boris and Jozsef?' added Vicky. 'Are their families all right? Jozsef said Boris was absolutely terrified for his sister.'

'They're all fine,' said Leach. 'As a matter of fact, the boys have both gone home on a short visit, just to reassure themselves. Their employers have been very understanding, I'm pleased to say.' He glanced round at the group. 'Any more questions?'

All four shook their heads. 'Right, back to work all of you. There are still plenty of villains out there.'